He Will Obey

An Anthology of Female Domination Stories

edited by Jay Willowbay

Silver Pigtail Commemorative Edition

2020

He Will Obey

Copyright © 2020. All rights reserved.

This Silver Pigtail Commemorative Edition Copyright © 2021.

Cover created by Irish Ink Publishing

Contents

Jared's First Session

by Luna Lavender

Jared's forehead glistened in the 12:50pm sunlight as sweat dripped from his scalp. *Gulp.* He struggled to swallow as his throat felt like it was getting tighter with every step he took toward the door of the mansion. He didn't know what to expect. This was his first session, after all.

He looked up at the gigantic house he was walking toward, taking note of the modern, minimalistic design.

I could only dream of living in a place as nice as this. Jared thought to himself.

When he got to the front gate, he noticed that it was propped open with a brick, and taped to the front was a piece of paper containing a cursive inscription:

"Jared, come through the gate and close it behind you. Ring the doorbell and I'll let you in. – Goddess Luna"

As he walked towards the door, Jared looked over at the open garage and saw a lavender colored Lamborghini parked facing out with a vanity plate that reads "GODDESS".

Fitting Jared thought.

Parked right next to that he saw a cream-colored BMW SUV.

That must be her everyday car.

When Jared got to the door, his hand froze just as he was about to ring the doorbell. Perspiration was forming on his scalp and running down his forehead.

Am I ready? Jared thought to himself

Before he could come to his own decision, she was already opening the door.

"Jared?" the woman at the door asked.

He looked up at her face and couldn't help but freeze. *She's way more beautiful than in her pictures online. God, those eyes...* Jared took in her beauty.

"You're Jared, right?" she asked again.

"Y-y-y-yes. That's me," Jared stuttered as he came back to consciousness.

She just smirked and said, "Come on in," with a wave of her hand.

As Jared followed this new mysterious woman into her house, he realized this wasn't the usual type of house he was used to. Normally they looked a certain way: The living room set up with a couch facing the TV and maybe a coffee table in the middle, dining room with a large table and chairs to sit at with family, etc. But this house didn't look anything like that.

In what seemed like it was supposed to be the living room, instead of a couch, there was a long massage table and no TV. The dining room table held dozens of stacks of cash, in differing bills. Mostly stacks of 100s, but he could see some that were 50s and 20s, as well. What seemed to be two bodyguards were standing next to the woman counting the money at the table, eyeing Jared as he walked past wondering why he was staring at the mountain of cash.

As she led him through the unusual house, he couldn't help but notice all the artwork on the walls. It was mostly exquisite oil paintings of women in the nude. Not really pornography, though. No, they were more like depictions of Goddesses from Greek mythology. Beautiful, voluptuous, powerful Goddesses worthy of being worshipped.

When they got to the base of the staircase, she told him to take off his shoes. He complied, of course, and followed her up the stairs.

This was when when he really started to pay attention to her. She was shorter than him, about 5' 4", and was wearing a black business casual dress that came to the middle of her thigh. He tried not to stare, but her ass was so round and just right there in front of his face as they walked up the stairs, he couldn't help it. He wanted to touch it so badly, but knew that would be disrespectful of him, so resisted his urge, with great difficulty.

When they got to the top of the stairs, Luna looked back at Jared and with a smirk she asked, "Are you ready?"

Am I Ready? Jared thought to himself.

"I'm... nervous," he replied.

"You should be," she said immediately, still smirking, eyes holding Jared's stare.

That just made Jared's heart beat even faster, and made him feel more nervous, but in the best way possible.

"I'm ready," Jared declared.

Luna giggled and told Jared to follow her with nothing but her eyes. He complied, of course, and followed her through the first door on the left.

This room looked like it was meant to be the master bedroom, but like the rest of the house downstairs, the way it was furnished was odd. On one side of the room, there was a big, comfortable, dark purple chair that could be reclined as much or as little as you want. Next to that, was a black office chair.

On the other side of the room was a bed made with dark purple satin covers and big, fluffy white pillows. With its back facing the floor-to-ceiling window was a cream-colored couch with a glass coffee table in front of it. The window had a sheer curtain pulled so no one could see inside, but the sunlight could still light up the room. There were two lamps on either side of the couch, but neither were turned on since the sunlight made the room bright enough at this time of day.

Luna sat down on the couch and patted the cushion next to her for Jared to sit down. He walked over and sat down carefully, heart still pounding, and face feeling flushed.

What happens now? Jared wondered eagerly.

"So, Jared, are you excited for our session today?" Luna inquired.

"Extremely nervous, but also excited," Jared replied.

"Great, I'm glad to hear that. Before we get started there are some ground rules I need you to adhere by during our session, okay?

1. Only respond to me when I ask you a question or tell you to talk.

2. Only refer to me as Goddess or Goddess Luna.

3. Do exactly as I say, when I say to do it.

4. Only cum when I say to.

Do you think you can handle those?"

Jared loved being told what to do, so he just replied, "Yes, Goddess, I can follow those rules."

"Good. Now, what tribute have you brought for me today?" Goddess Luna asked, although she knew full well what it was.

Jared put his hand in his back pocket of his pants and pulled out his wallet. He opened it up and pulled out a small stack of $20 bills. He handed it over to Goddess Luna and watched as she licked her thumb and counted out loud:

"20, 40, 60, 80, 100. 20, 40, 60, 80, 200." She paused.

"200?" she asked with a disgusted look. "Was that what we agreed on Jared?" She burned holes in him with the fire in her eyes.

"No, Miss-Goddess Luna, it wasn't. We agreed on $400, but I need to give the rest of it to you via credit card. Can I do that Goddess?" Jared responded, fear and excitement in his voice.

She sighed, looked around the room, then back at Jared.

She finally responded, "No, you may not. We agreed on $400 in cash. Either hand over the other 200 right now, or leave."

Jared didn't think this was possible, but he got more excited with every second she continued focusing on his eyes. He felt like he was being enveloped in her energy and piercing his soul with her sharp blue eyes. He couldn't help but sigh with pleasure as she took control.

"Are you even listening, Jared? I need the other 200 right now. I'm serious." Goddess Luna said as she was becoming more and more impatient.

"I'm sorry Goddess, I have it right here Goddess. I'm sorry for being difficult, Goddess. Will you forgive me?" Jared reached in his other back pocket and handed her another wad of 20s.

Luna licked her thumb and started counting again.

"20, 40, 60, 80, 300. 20, 40, 60, 80, 400. 20, 40, 60, 80, 500. That's more like it." Luna grinned as she looked at the cash. Then, she took a purple envelope off the glass coffee table, stuffed the cash inside, then walked over to the door they came through, and opened it just enough to stick her hand through. Another person must have taken the envelope on the other side of the door because when her hand slipped back in the room it was empty.

When she turned back around, the first words out of her mouth were, "Get on the floor where you belong, slave."

Jared's heart skipped a beat with the sharpness of her tone. He hadn't seen this side of his Goddess yet, but knew he had to do everything she told him to. He dropped to the floor and asked, "How do you prefer me to be on the floor, Goddess?"

"Just get on all fours and wait for me to tell you your next instruction."

Jared did as he was told and got on all fours. Goddess Luna walked over to him and just paced in front of him for a minute. She seemed to be doing some type of silent meditation before she started.

While Jared was on his hands and knees, he got a chance to see his new psychological seductress's sexy calves and shiny, black peep toe high heels that protected her gorgeous feet. Her calves were perfectly smooth and toned and her toenails were painted a light purple to match the rest of her house.

Just as Jared was marveling at the sight of her toes, Goddess Luna snapped her fingers and Jared looked up immediately.

"While you're down there, kiss my feet," Goddess said as she pointed one of her feet in his face.

Jared was grateful for the opportunity, so he obeyed. He took as much time as she allowed to kiss each foot, which was only about ten seconds each, but he enjoyed every second of it.

"Now, stand up," Goddess Luna instructed.

Jared did as he was told and got on his feet.

"Go sit in that chair right over there," Goddess Luna said as she pointed toward the purple chair that Jared noticed when he first walked in.

"Yes, Goddess," Jared replied as he bowed his head. Then, he walked over to the chair and sat down. He leaned back, and realized the chair was extremely comfortable.

Goddess Luna followed him after grabbing a pen and the spiral bound notebook off the coffee table and sat down on the office chair next to him. She talked to him as she opened her notebook to the right page.

"What do you think of that chair? Isn't it comfortable?" she asked to keep his mind occupied as she sifted through the notebook.

"Yes, Goddess. It's extremely comfortable," Jared responded, eager for what was about to happen.

Goddess Luna found the page she was looking for, and just responded, "Good, because you're going to be there a while."

"Now, I want you to close your eyes," Luna directed.

Jared closed his eyes and followed every order his new Goddess gave him.

"Take a deep breath in through your nose, and out through your mouth. Just in through your nose, and out through your mouth."

Jared started breathing deeply.

"Just keep taking deep breaths. In through your nose, and out through your mouth. And with each breath you take, you feel more and more relaxed."

Jared started feeling very tired and relaxed.

"It may seem like I'm repeating myself, but that's all a part of the induction. And each time I repeat myself you feel more and more relaxed."

"Just keep taking deep breaths."

"In through your nose."

"Out through your mouth."

Jared felt as if he was sinking into the chair, while simultaneously floating above it. The feeling was both exhilarating and peaceful at the same time.

After a few minutes of Jared taking deep breaths, Goddess Luna instructed, "You may bring your breathing back to normal now."

Jared's breathing became a little faster and shallower.

"Now that you are nice and relaxed, I'm going to count down from 10 to 1. With each number I count down you will feel even more relaxed. When I get to 1, you will be in the state of hypnosis and under my complete control. You will do everything I say. You won't be able to resist. Do you understand, Jared?"

"Yes Goddess," were the only words that could leave his lips. He felt as if he was already under her control.

Goddess Luna started counting down, taking a few seconds between each number.

"10… 9… Feeling more and more relaxed with each descending number."

"8… 7… Getting closer to the state of hypnosis."

"6… 5… 4… 3. Deeper and deeper relaxation. 2… Almost there… 1."

When Goddess Luna got to 1, Jared's body went completely limp. She noticed his eyelids were fluttering and his breathing was shallow. He had completely submitted to her exactly as she intended.

"You are now in the state of hypnosis and you are under my complete control. Ultimate submission. No thinking, just obeying my every command. Now, raise your right arm above your head."

Jared's arm slowly lifted above his head. His hand was still limp.

Goddess Luna jotted something down in her notebook.

"Good. Now, place your right hand on top of your head."

Jared's hand immediately fell to land on his head.

Luna wrote something else.

"Good. You may put your arm back down now," Goddess Luna instructed.

Jared's arm dropped to his side.

"Now, since you and I both know I have complete control over your entire body, I'm going to make you cum without even touching you, or having you touch yourself. A totally hands-free orgasm. Sounds nice, right? I bet your cock is starting to tingle already just from me talking about it. But I'm not going to let you cum yet. Oh no. I want to play with you first."

Even though Jared couldn't think straight, his heart started beating faster and his cock did start to tingle. He was ready for whatever she wanted to do with him.

"I want you to tell me your most embarrassing sex story. Tell me right now," Goddess Luna demanded.

After a few seconds Jared responded, "When I was in my Junior year in college, I was about to have sex with my girlfriend for the first time. I was so excited to have sex with her, I ended up cumming immediately after shoving my cock inside her. She wasn't even completely naked, and I couldn't even last 3 seconds. She broke up with me a day later. When I asked if it was because I came so quickly, she said it wasn't because of that, but I knew it must've been the reason."

Goddess Luna giggled and recorded his story in her notebook as she said, "Thank you for telling me that great story. How embarrassing." She giggled again.

"At least I know you won't be able to cum before I say so today. You know how I know that? Because your entire body is mine. I own you. I'm in control of *everything* your body does, *not you*."

"Now, tell me something you don't want anyone to find out about. I bet I know what it is," she said with a smirk, pen in the writing position.

After a moment Jared responded, "You, Goddess. I don't want anyone to find out about you and that I'm here with you."

"I thought so. You'd probably do anything to prevent people you know from finding out, wouldn't you?"

"Yes, Goddess. Anything," Jared responded, body still limp and eyelids still fluttering.

Goddess Luna wrote in her notebook again.

"That's good to know. Tell me, who finding out that you're here with me would make you most embarrassed?"

"If my friends found out, I would die. They would mock me forever," Jared responded honestly.

"Friends…" Luna murmured as she jotted the word down.

"You better keep doing exactly I say, then," she said sharply.

"Now stand up and take off your shirt."

Jared got on his feet, unbuttoned his long sleeve shirt, and slipped his arms out of the sleeves. Goddess Luna took his shirt and hung it up on a hook on the wall next to her.

"Now repeat these words after me: Goddess Luna owns me."

"Goddess Luna owns me," Jared repeated.

"Goddess Luna controls me."

"Goddess Luna controls me," Jared repeated again.

"Goddess Luna owns my body and my wallet."

"Goddess Luna owns my body and my wallet," Jared repeated with a smile.

"One more: I make financial sacrifices for Goddess Luna because it brings me joy to serve her with my wallet," Goddess Luna suggested.

"I make financial sacrifices for Goddess Luna because it brings me joy to serve her with my wallet."

"Good. Now I'm going to write something on your chest with my pen and when you see it tonight in the mirror before you take a shower, you will immediately send me a money transfer of $500 with a memo that says 'Thank you Goddess.'"

Goddess Luna stood up, set her notebook down on her chair, and walked in front of him. She carefully placed her hand on his chest as she wrote six characters.

As she carefully wrote on his bare chest, she teasingly said, "You won't know what I'm writing until you look in the mirror tonight. Are you scared?"

"No, Goddess. I know whatever you do is best. You own my body," Jared responded.

"That's right," she said as she finished the last letter and put the pen on her cap.

"So, what are you going to do immediately after you see what I wrote?" Luna asked.

"I will immediately send you a $500 money transfer with a memo that says 'Thank you Goddess,'" Jared responded.

"Good boy, Jared. Here's your shirt. Put it back on so I don't have to see your torso anymore," she said as she handed him back his shirt.

"Yes Goddess."

Jared slipped his arms back in his shirt and buttoned it up, still standing, eyelids still fluttering.

"Carefully sit back down in the chair behind you," Luna instructed.

Jared backed up and when he felt the fabric of the chair against the back of his legs he sat down.

"Now, I bet you're ready to cum aren't you?"

"Yes Goddess, I want to cum so bad," Jared responded desperately.

"I know you do. I can see your cock bulging through your pants. Now I'm going to count down from 10 to 1. When I tell you

'Cum now' you will cum instantly. Not before. Only when I tell you those exact words. Do you understand me?"

"Yes, Goddess. I understand," Jared responded, still with desperation in his voice.

"Good. Okay, I'm going to count down starting now."

Goddess Luna started counting down slowly, teasing Jared with each pause in between.

"10... 9... your cock is tingling and wants a release so bad."

Jared's cock kept getting harder, it started to hurt a bit under his pants. He tried to adjust it, so it was more comfortable, but when he touched himself Goddess Luna snapped at him.

"Did I fucking tell you to touch yourself?"

"No Goddess. I'm sorry Goddess. It's just that my cock is so hard. It hurts, Goddess. May I please adjust it?" Jared pleaded.

"You may adjust yourself. Next time ask before you touch yourself unless I specifically tell you to. Do you understand me?" Goddess Luna growled.

As Jared adjusted his cock he responded, "Yes, Goddess I understand. Thank you Goddess. I'm sorry Goddess. I will ask you from now on."

"You better. Are you done?" she asked, annoyed.

"Yes, Goddess, I'm done."

"8… 7… 6… 5… halfway to 1. Will I let you cum today? I'm not sure."

"4… 3…"

She paused for longer this time. Jared's cock was bulging and twitching with every second that passed.

"2…"

Jared felt like 30 minutes had passed since she'd said the last number. His cock was so desperate to cum. He knew he was going to burst as soon as she said the words.

"Our time is up. I'm going to count up from 1 to 10. When I get to 10 you will be out of hypnosis, but all my suggestions will stay with you," Goddess Luna declared.

"1… 2… 3… with each ascending number you feel more awake. 4… 5… 6… you can start to feel your fingers and toes now. 7… 8… feeling more awake now. 9… 10. You are now fully awake and out of hypnosis. You can open your eyes when you're ready."

Jared opened his eyes and looked at Goddess Luna.

"When are we going to start?" Jared asked confused, realizing the light in the room was different now.

Goddess Luna just giggled and said, "You did fairly good Jared. I'm looking forward to our next session. When you go down the stairs there should be a bottle of water waiting for you next to your shoes. Make sure you drink that on your drive back home, okay?"

"It's over? I don't remember anything. Is that normal?" Jared asked, confused.

"Yes, that's completely normal for some people. It will start coming back to you after you sleep tonight," Goddess Luna reassured him.

"Okay, thank you Goddess. May I leave now?"

"Yes, you may. Have a good night," she said with a wink.

Jared stood up and walked out of the room. He made his way down the stairs and saw the water bottle she was talking about right there next to his shoes. As he was putting his shoes on one of the guards he saw when he first got there walked up to him.

"I'm going to escort you out, Jared," the guard told him.

"Okay," Jared responded as he stood up, water bottle in hand.

He followed the guard through the oddly decorated house as they made their way to the front door.

The guard opened the door for him, and Jared walked out.

When he got to the gate, he looked back to wave only to see a closed door.

Strange place Jared thought to himself.

*

He got in his car and started the drive home, drinking the bottle of water as Goddess Luna had instructed him. It was now 3:16pm. He couldn't believe he was there for 2 hours. He still couldn't remember anything that happened but had a feeling there was something he had to do that night.

When he got home, he heated up some left-over pasta that was in the fridge and watched reruns of *Supernatural* on TV.

After a few hours he started feeling tired, so decided to get ready for bed. He went into the bathroom and started getting undressed, first taking off his shoes and socks, then his pants and underwear. Last was his button-up shirt that he didn't even remember taking off during the session.

He was looking at himself in the mirror as he undid each button, starting from the bottom. As he undid the third one from the top, he saw a little bit of the pen markings on his chest. As he undid the last two, he was able to read what it said, and read it aloud:

"Cum Now"

His cock got hard immediately, and he came the most he ever had in his 45 years on Earth. His cum got all over the mirror and in the sink in front of him. After his cock was done twitching, he took his phone out of his pants pocket and opened up the PayPal app.

Without thinking, he searched for Goddess Luna and typed in $500. In the payment memo he wrote 'Thank you Goddess' and tapped send.

God, that's hot Jared thought to himself.

She must have programmed me to do that.

After sending the money, he got a paper towel and some Windex to clean up the mirror, took a shower and went to bed for the night, to dream of his Goddess.

About the Author:

Goddess Luna lives in sunny Southern California, and is a qualified hypnotist who has turned this talent to findom. She has been writing for over a decade, but not put anything forward to publication until now. See more about her at www.slaveforluna.com.

Sadistic Wet Dreams

by Duchess Cashmere

One night I woke up in a pool of sweat. It dripped down the crevice of my eyelid. Hell, I thought something was crawling on me, I was scared as shit! Threw back the covers, jumped outta bed ... I looked down at my PJs and I was soaking wet. The bed covers and everything was wet. What the hell was I dreaming about?

Perhaps I was making love on a blanket in a field of jasmine and honeysuckle. Maybe I was getting head while overlooking the ocean atop a ferris wheel. It could be that I was being brought to orgasm on the main stage at the Exxotica conference.

There's no telling the debaucherous dreams that dwell in the mind of Duchess Cashmere. Any manner of delicious scenario could have produced such a downpour as this…

Unfortunately, none of that is the case. The Duchess is a lady of a particular age, and ladies like me have hot flashes.

After I showered, I went out to get some breakfast because I was starving. I made my way to the local spot on the beachfront, called Biscuits. The place was packed which was odd in the wee hours of Friday morning. All the people dressed in night club white with neon accessories. How strange? Glowing bracelets, green fishnet body stockings, gentlemen tagged with electric blue bandanas, ladies wearing yellow foam crowns and pink furry go-go boots. They were all quite a sight to behold. People watching is one of my favorite things. So I posted up in the cut just to look at them interact with each other. I noticed they were all very loving and affectionate with each other. Just touching and rubbing and kissing.

One man in particular was not so discreetly fingering the lady in pink under the table. She caught me looking at them, and I could not look away. She whispered to him and he looked at me too. I pulled hard on my cig and watched them deliberately, I sat up straight and focused in on the show; all three of us connected by the sexual æther. When he raised his hand up from her vulva, she licked the juices off and then they tongue kissed viciously.

I tell you ... I ... was ... shook! She whispered something to him, and he called the waiter over to their table. With a quick turn their server was approaching my table. My heart dropped down in my stomach, my mind was racing, and I was mentally preparing for *conflict.*

"Excuse me ma'am, but that couple over there would like to buy you a cocktail, they said anything you desire," the waiter said with a slick smile on his face. *Well I'll be damned*, I thought to myself, hell I might have said it out loud. I ordered a peach margarita on the rocks, and when it drink arrived, I gave them a salute, and lil Miss Pinky began to saunter her sexy ass in my direction; I thanked her for the drink.

She replied, "It's the least I could, you just gave me an orgasm."

"Umm, I think your man did that." I shot back quickly.

"No ma'am, that was you Majesty," she almost whispered.

Majesty ... I was so confused. Before I could question her, the crowd in neon let out a cheer as the serving staff started bringing out food.

"See you next time Majesty" she said gleefully, did a lil twirl and she dropped a business card on the table and skipped away. The Business card read:

Pinky & the Brain ... sls.com, KIK app, and kaside.com ... huh I'd never seen anything like that before. *Well I'll be damned they are swingers.*

The server brought my food, and I spent the next few minutes tumbling down the information vortex. I had seen swingers on TV before, but I'd never thought I would come across them in my hometown.

From my research I found out quickly that they were part of a Glow Party put on by an out of town swingers group. *Well well, this is very interesting indeed.* I hit them up on the KIK app and began to converse with both of them from across the restaurant. I felt like a special agent sitting there carrying on this whole secret operation.

Pinky & the Brain, a multicultural non-monogamous submissive bisexual couple …. wow that was a mouthful. Luckily for them I knew what all of that meant already. I have been a student of all things sexy for a long time.

It wasn't long before Mr Brain was making his way over to my table. "May I sit your Majesty?", he asked.

He began to explain their intentions and I just stared at his features while he talked. His lips, his hairline, his manicure … oh he looked delicious. He offered himself and his wife to me in sexual servitude. Told me that the whole group of them had rented out the top floor of the beach side hotel. Said they were going back home to

North Mississippi on Sunday. He left me their room key and paid for my food, asking me to come whenever I felt comfortable.

The next day I was awakened by a text: *Good morning Majesty the theme tonight is paint the town Red.*

I waited until well after lunch and made my way to the hotel. I dressed in all black like the omen, no bra ... no panties ... backpack ready, pepper spray handy. When I got off the elevator, there was a desk and a thick black curtain and I was greeted by Ms Pinky dressed in a soft pink body stocking. She took me around and I took in all the sights and sounds of a real swingers party. Each room was a wonderland! There was string light hung in the blue and purple, themed cocktails, red lingerie far as the eye can see, three massage tables, a black out room, strip trivia live ... sex acts everywhere.

We floated like butterflies until we got to their room. It was filled with whips and chains and nasty thangs. Fox tails, and floggers and crops, oh my! Ropes and buckles, a St Andrews Cross used for bondage. I was trying to hide my naivety, while Mr. Brain fixed me a drink as we sat down for our parlay.

We discussed hard limits, everyone's safe word, they showed me all the tools of the trade, some of which scared me ... a Wharton's

36

wheel, a tens unit ... yikes. I decided to stick to the flogger and the crop. I watched enough porn to navigate those too. They talked with me about my level of comfort, and we discussed the preferred jargon of play....

Humiliation.

They wanted me to express a sadistic persona, perform impact play upon them.

Slap them.

Pinch them.

Spank them and speak to them in a vulgar ugly manner. They submitted themselves to perform a long list of sexual acts for my pleasure. They said it gave them great joy to be dominated by a woman, and how they wanted to worship me sexually. I agreed even though I didn't know what the hell I was doing. Something in me started burning, I felt like I was charging into something else. They both sat on the floor at my feet, nose to the carpet. Hmm, submission had begun.

Duchess: You ... pinky, take mr. brain's clothing off. I want him completely naked.

Pinky: Yes Majesty.

Duchess: Now get down on your knees right here in front of this window.

Pinky: Yes Majesty.

Duchess: I want the whole world to see how nasty you are.

Pinky: Yes Majesty.

Duchess: and you, so called Mr. Brain, walking around like you da man, you da man? Hah! Na you da bitch tonight.

Mr. Brain: Yes Majesty.

Duchess: Pinky, get over, and suck my bitch's dick.

Pinky: Yes Ma'am Majesty.

I grabbed a handful of her hair and mushed her face down on his dick.

I circled them like a shark and used their flesh like a drum with the crop. I whipped them both with the flogger as I instructed them through various levels of foreplay. Their light skin began to turn pink, red, black and blue ... a rainbow of kinky pleasure. I could feel my own dew start to fall in between my legs. Before long I wanted more.

I instructed Mr Brain to lay flat on his back in a supine position so Pinky could ride his dick as I used his face as my personal Sybian throne. I smothered him with my pussy and slapped Pinky on her face, and then on her tits and thighs. I raked my nails along his torso and pinched his nipples. I grabbed her by the throat and cranked her whole body like a floor jack on his dick.

When I glanced over and saw the three of us in the reflection in the window, I became overwhelmed and I gushed out all over everywhere. I had a huge squirting orgasm.

I kinda fell back to rest on the floor and gather myself while Pinky licked my juices off his face and chest. They both began to crawl over to me like timid little kittens.

"Here kitty kitty you wanna drink this pussy?" I said, out of breath. "Come on."

"Yes, Majesty," they said in unison. And then I heard a firetruck singing in the distance ... a trill rhythm that disturbed my ecstasy ... as it got closer and louder. I looked over at the alarm clock and it said 5:55am. I was wet again, and I'd had another sadistic wet dream.

About the Author:

Duchess Cashmere, The Griot Erotica. Producer of The Cashmere Room Podcast & Pillow Talk, The Live Experience, and along with her husband, Deuce, The Mister, is the co-founder of The Cashmere Room LS Collective. She tells sexy stories & performs pussy poetry like you've never seen before. She hosts Lifestyle Parties in/around the MS Gulf Coast that specifically cater to a POC audience and that are BDSM friendly. Her podcast and live performances are NSFW but perfect for pillow talk with your favorite lover. You can listen to the podcast, watch performances or book Duchess Cashmere for your sex positive conference, poetry showcase, or Lifestyle.

Surprise for Mommy's Boy

by Lola Lawrence and Rhett Lawrence

I walked quietly into the room and shut the door. The rich burgandy and black of the room set a mood. A smile tugged at my lips, dark and sexy, just like her. I breathed deeply and could smell her. The musky spiced vanilla of her perfume lingered like a blown kiss. I felt a throb in my pants. Oh, what this woman did to me.

Laying against the pillow was a note. Petite cursive letters scrawled across the paper and I ran my fingers over them, hoping to touch some part of her. "Be a good boy for Mommy and take all your clothes off. Sit on the side of the bed with your eyes shut and maybe Mommy will give you a surprise."

It was signed with a big, red lipstick print. Good lord her lips... My mind went back to our first meeting. Looking across the crowded bar patio and seeing those lips around the cork end of a cigarette. How I loved watching her smoke. Red tipped fingers delicately holding her cigarette as she gracefully brought it to her lips. The tight jeans hugged each curve and when she caught my eye, I remember blushing. Black heeled boots made the earth shake or it could have just been me quivering to my core. Those smokey gray eyes captured me as she leaned over my table. Her tits were barely contained by the deep V neck of her shirt. She put another cigarette between those lips and softly commanded I light it for her. I completely belonged to her after that.

Shaking my head, I needed to focus not fantasize. Excited fingers undid the buttons of my jeans and I pushed them down, kicking them off. Boxers and t-shirt followed. I briefly considered being naughty and leaving the pile on the floor. I smirked knowing the punishment that might follow but I wanted to see what Mommy had in store. So like a good boy, I neatly folded my clothes like she wanted. Sitting on the deep burgandy comforter, I waited.

It felt like an eternity. The soft Egyptian cotton felt delicious against my naked skin. My hands caressed her pillow, as I brought it to face. Inhaling deeply, it smelled like her hair. My cock twitched in response. The hold this woman had over me. Suddenly, I heard the click of impossibly high heels on the wood floor. The bed shifted and I felt her against my back. Her lips were against my ear and she whispered, "Such a good boy waiting for me...are your eyes shut?"

My heart was pounding as words tried to form on my tongue. All I could manage was a fervent nod and I heard her seductive chuckle.

Mommy's hand crept around my waist, fingers lightly caressing my skin as she slid it down. Her thumb began rubbing the head of my cock and a gasping shudder vibrated through my body. "Mommy has a surprise for you today...." Her lips kissed my ear as she squeezed my tip. "I brought you a playmate. Open your eyes."

My eyes flew open and sitting across from me was a very pretty woman. My eyes widened up with excitement as I looked at the sexy toy Mommy got me. She was slim and covered in satin. The corset accentuated how tiny she was. Blonde waves fell to her breasts and I itched to stroke the lace on her thighs. Pretty pink panties sat low on her hips. My eyes traveled further and I was in sudden disbelief. Seeing the outline of a bulge in her panties made my mouth water as I turned to Mommy with the biggest grin on my face.

Mommy got up and moved in front of me. I groaned looking at her. Black lace clung to her curves, a stark contrast to the plaything next to her. Mommy's red lips wrapped around a cigarette and her red nails flashed in the lighter flame. Her free hand reached over and started rubbing the girl's cock. Seductive, hooded gray eyes focused on me and she took a drag off her cigarette. Smoke curled around those red lips and my dick began to throb.

Come on little boy.... show Mommy how you please a cock..." and she pulled the pink panties down, exposing the girl's thick dick. Sliding down the bed, my knees hit the floor. I crawled to Mommy and she grabbed my chin, guiding me up. The girl opened her legs and I leaned up between her thighs.

Red tipped fingernails lightly grazed the girl's dick as my mouth hovered in front of it. Mommy began stroking her slowly, making the girl's pink lips open into moans. My eyes wide open, I thirstily stared and admired the beautiful hard cock that was throbbing in front of me. My hands travelled up her legs to rest on her thighs, and I watched Mommy's hand grip her cock. Those red nails against the paleness of her were mesmerizing.

As Mommy stroked, softly, I kissed her tip and wrapped my lips around her. Swirling my tongue around her head, the moans coming from her pink lips thrilled me.

"That's it, my good boy. You love how she tastes, don't you?" Mommy chuckled and my body just reverberated with the sound of it. Glancing up I saw Mommy take a drag off the cigarette. Delicately she held it between her fingers and my cock throbbed so hard to feel those pouty red lips against my skin. My mouth went a little faster, licking and sucking her while Mommy's hand glided down her shaft. Mouth following her trail, Mommy's fingers and and my lips intersected, and her finger slipped into in my tongue. I moaned a little, finally getting to touch some part of her.

Mommy's nails gently raked through my hair and a smile played at her lips. My tongue danced around her finger and the head of the cock. Mommy withdrew her finger and I whimpered in protest. Suddenly, I felt her hand pushing on the back of my head and my throat was full of dick. I struggled to get a rhythm and I made lots of gagging sounds which seemed to delight Mommy.

"Oh, look at my good little cock sucker! You look so cute gagging on her cock." She almost purred as she held my red face down.

The girl's pink lips parted and she lifted her hips to go deeper. Mommy raised an eyebrow and commanded, "Fuck his mouth. Now."

She obeyed, her dick sliding in and out of my mouth. Mommy kept stroking my hair pausing only to lean over and put out her cigarette.

Finally, Mommy released her grip and I pulled back, spit running out the sides of my mouth. My teary brown eyes looked up to Mommy's dark gray ones. Her finger stroked my cheek lovingly. "That's my good little boy. Keep sucking that dick while Mommy makes you feel good." As my lips neared her dick, Mommy got on the floor. In the corner of my eye I watched her disappear underneath me.

My cock jumped at the feel of pouty lips encircling it. I moaned around my toy's dick as Mommy's red lips teased my head.

Her lips felt incredible. Soft and wet, her tongue hypnotized my dick until I was wracked with shivers. I did my best to focus on the delicious cock in front of me, but Mommy was making it so difficult! Mommy's nails dug into my hips as she slid that mouth up and down. She would bring me to edge and my cock would get so rigid. Then she'd stop and I felt the chuckle in her throat at my groaning.

My eyes glanced down long enough to spot red lipstick on my shaft. A shudder ran through my body at the sight. How I loved her red lips. Mommy sometimes let me watch her get ready. My favorite part was kneeling at her feet, watching her slowly put on her lipstick.

Mommy's lips released my cock, and sternly, she said, "If you want this cock to cum, you better get busy and make her drip on your lips."

This refocused my mind and as Mommy began teasing my head again, I doubled my efforts on the cock in front of me. Pumping my mouth in rhythm with pace Mommy was setting. My muffled moans harmonized with the girls as I sucked harder. Then I felt her trembles, her calling out.

I pulled back and just as Mommy demanded, I let her hot cum drip all on my lips. My hand kept stroking her through her orgasm until she was a quivering, cum covered mess. I smiled triumphantly. Mommy's eyes shone with pride and she pulled my hips down until I was straddling her face. Her red nails flashed on my skin as she forced me to fuck her mouth. Her mouth was so wet and her tongue perfect against the length of me.

Shaking thighs and my moans through gritted teeth, I knew my orgasm was close. "Mommy! Mommy! Can I please cum?!" Frenzied, I called out to her.

Surprisingly, Mommy pushed me off, leaving my cock swollen and wet, the tiniest dribble of semen leaking from it. I whimpered, fascinated as I watched. Both frustrated and incredibly turned on, I looked at Mommy who was now laying on her pretty bed. She lit up another cigarette.

"Come to me little boy."

I crawled up the bed to her, presenting my still hard cock. Mommy's free hand began spreading my cum all over, and it felt so good. My lips parted in a half moan, half growl. Taking a drag, she slowly opened her lacey thighs. "Breed with Mommy..."

About the Author:

Lola lives in Arcanum, Ohio, and writes poetry, erotica, and other stories. Both her debut poetry collection and a collaboration novel with this anthology's editor will be released in 2021.

Dancing for the Girls

by M.H. Macdonald

"Stick those titties out like a good little cum slut!" Amy encouraged, a tawse gripped firmly in hand, as she prowled around foofoo like a wild cat toying with prey, studying his every pose, from every angle. "Head up, titties out, facing your audience, smile!"

As scantily bare as ever, but for the tiny little pink chastity cage, pink leather collar and shaming-bells at wrists and ankles Nikki attired him in; foofoo obeyed, keen to please; his bare flesh dotted with livid red marks highlighting how ready Amy was to discipline. Hands on his head, weight evenly distributed on both feet, and based in the centre of the soles of his bare feet with their freshly painted toenails, moving only slightly on the spot, foofoo thrust his chest forward, extending the tiny nubs that were his nipples out as far as he could and smiled like a Las Vegas show girl as his shaming-bells tinkled. Concentrating on all the moves and poses Amy demanded meant he kept forgetting his Vegas smile, which kept earning him fresh stripes.

"Now, slow turns foofoo, display and flaunt yourself, let the audience see your body."

Hips writhing, as powerfully muscled thighs did most of the work, the chastity cage jiggled from side to side as each hip raised. Serving as impromptu percussion to his move, his shaming-bells continued to jingle and his bare feet slap, as he exhibited himself to the watching critical eye of Mistress Amy.

"Ass out, when foofoo has his back to the audience." Amy barked the order. "Flaunt it foofoo, I want the girls wanting to smack that oh so smackable ass all your daily squats have given the pet!"

Contorting himself to Amy's commands, foofoo briefly risked a pleading look at Amy while he complied with exactly what she had just told him, writhing on the spot, rehearsing his moves for what he would do for real to a small but boisterous audience later. Feet apart, head up, titties pushed forward, butt pushed back; he stood awkwardly, shivering as a chilly early morning wind blew about his nether regions, raised goosebumps evident on his arms. It was supposed to be summer, but it certainly had not arrived yet. From the corner of his eye, he briefly caught a glimpse of Nikki observing the proceedings from the comfort and warmth of her living room, sipping coffee or perhaps tea from a mug.

"Yes! Like that, nice and wanton foofoo!"

Hands behind his head, he turned and turned, writhing on the spot, his bare feet propelling him in a small circle, showing off every inch of his lean body, as he wiggled his male bits and his butt.

"Remember foofoo, Nikki wants to see a big cheesy smile, let everyone know how happy the pet is to see them." Amy reminded.

"Whmpr," he answered through clenched grin.

"Very good, now let's repeat that, this time, up on the pet's pretty painted toes." Amy instructed. "I am thinking still how we can get some pointed toes action into the pet's routine but first things first, let's get the pet nice and lewd for the girls, get them in the zone from the off, to score some early brownie points for the pet in his routine."

Contrastingly, dressed in jumper, jeans and cosy Uggs, Amy certainly wasn't feeling the chill like his bare skin was out on

Nikki's patio. As tight as his chastity cage was day to day, he could almost feel his cock rattle around inside the usually tight cage, so great was his shrinkage from the chilly temperature and his physical exertions. His bare feet seemed to suck the cold from the tiles up into his very core. There was a case he had once made to Nikki, with his working-livestock status under Nikki's domain, that as farmers gave horses overcoats in winter and dogs were given coats too, that as her working-livestock he could be at least be provided with some blanket or some sort of covering on cold days, through the winter. But it was a case Nikki had held little truck with, her view being that if he was cold, he should work harder as his way of keeping warmer and that by doing so, he would be more productive at his menial toil. Her only lenience to the Winter months, was to give him more pellets in his feeding pan and extra straw for his bedding at night.

Foofoo was long experienced with the humiliation of having to learn off by heart and then perform small voiced routines based on nursery rhymes like 'I'm a little teapot', complete with actions; to Nikki initially but soon enough to his mortification to an audience of the various vixens too. Frequently after such presentations, Nikki would deem he had not performed with sufficient passion, and so she would make him repeat the whole routine all over again. But through having him learn to dance, Nikki had upped the ante, by having him dance for an orgasm. His chance to cum, directly related to the votes his efforts earned from the various vixens in attendance at their raucous girls nights or weekend get togethers. Assessed on passion, creativeness and laughter levels he would get either a thumbs up or down. So far, he had failed miserably in convincing a sufficient number of the vixens through his performances, and he had been danced seven times! He remained without an orgasm for over three hundred days and counting, 306 to be precise, scarily, fast approaching the one-year mark. His frustration however wasn't just from the length of time but the daily torment, teasing and ridicule he had to endure for Nikki's amusements too!

"Oh foofoo, look at you in your bells, what a picture you'll make this evening when your little nub is let out, the head painted brightly for the girls." Amy smirked. "If only Tyler was out here, I suspect she would be enjoying your practice, the pet knows how much she loves seeing you all miserable and feeling sorry for yourself."

"Whmpr,"

"Oh, well, she'll just have to wait till later to see what a little cum slut foofoo is won't she."

Foofoo's eyes widened in alarm and he paused his rotations, shaming-bells coming to a shrill and abrupt halt.

Amy giggled, "Didn't foofoo know, poor pet, Nikki never informs foofoo of much does she, heehee."

"Whmpr, whmpr!"

"Poor, poor pet, yes Tyler is attending and foofoo knows, however well and amusingly he flaunts his tiny little cock for the girls, Tyler will never give him a thumbs up for the little thing to orgasm, right? I mean, when it comes to Tyler, foofoo best start praying, as that is pretty much the only way his little nub is getting any satisfaction, if she has anything to do with it!"

"Whmpr!" came back the forlorn response.

"Don't give up hope foofoo," Amy smiled, pinching his cheek in a firm grip that enabled her to shake his head patronisingly. "There will still be enough of us to perform to, that are more open minded about such things. If we think the pet has shown us, he really, really, really needs to cum and dances his titties off for us, giving us a good giggle, foofoo stands a good chance, well a fighting chance at least, I reckon of finally adding some of his own to all that sperm he likes to gobbles up!"

"Whmpr!" hating the slightest hint or suggestion that he was thought to like cum consumption.

"I mean," Amy mused, letting go of his cheek with one final shake of his head. "Missing out on an orgasm last time round by a single vote, on what must have been the pet's sixth or seventh time of trying, shows how close the pet got with his performance last time round, so close!"

"Whmpr!"

"Aww poor pet, I bet foofoo really felt that in his balls afterwards, three quarters of the way to an orgasm, all that heated passion but no chance to blow." Amy chuckled, reaching down to fondle, providing just a few caresses to make sure foofoo was nice and uncomfortable in his cage. "Look, I know that foofoo really wants to squirt his goo, how desperate and horny the pet is to do that

"Now, I have pretty good idea how much cum foofoo has consumed through the years, from what Nikki has shared and from all those condoms from the guys I've slept with; so much cum, the pet must really find it yummy. Personally, I hate it and never swallow but I've been more than happy to save my fucks for you foofoo. So, the way I see it, a cum slut like you foofoo can't be demure about these things if he wants a cum of his own, that means I want to see the pet being extra lewd, showing us his aching need!" Amy said, drawing away her fingers, her nails leaving his ball sac last, with a lingering tickle as she ran them across his tight undercarriage.

"Arch your back, foofoo, I want the pet's head up, smiling and the pet's rear raised, his ball sac nicely exposed, that way the girls will see how plump they are, understand how long it has been for foofoo." Amy instructed. "Now dance those little titties off like the pet actually wants an orgasm!"

Foofoo started his rotations again energetically, bare feet slapping against the patio, back arching, feet more widely spread for the exposure demanded from him. He got glimpses of Nikki again and again as he rotated, still standing at the window, now on the phone, seemingly laughing.

"Better, foofoo, better." Amy encouraged. "How does the pet feel, manly?"

"Whmpr, whmpr!"

"No? Good!" Amy laughed. "I hope the pet appreciates that I'm out here this chilly morning helping him devise a dance routine that will make the pet's audience giggle and laugh even more than last time!"

"Whmpr!"

"Well show me what a good little cum slut you are!" Amy barked, using the tawse for added encouragement. "Work it foofoo, work it!"

Still rotating and arching, foofoo emitted a few gasps and cries, as abruptly the leather tawse began to land across his rear encouraging him on each turn.

"I must say it didn't go unmissed foofoo," Amy informed. "That the pet incorporated an extra emphasis towards Mistress Verity, I mean bringing a red rose to her on all-fours between his teeth is hardly subtle foofoo; though an amusing way for the pet to let Verity know how he has the hots for her, so I am sure she will give the pet a thumbs up. That is unless, Tyler's whispered in her ear…"

"Be thankful I'm not the jealous sort foofoo," Amy pouted with a playful smirk. "I could have had my feelings hurt after all our practice time together. I've worked really hard helping break down every last shred of proud masculinity that lingered on in the pet and through the medium of dance assist the pet to realise what a cum slut he is; I mean doing all that he has so far and all that he will, just for a taste of his own cum for a change, means the pet is a certified bona fide cum slut!"

"Whmpr!" he yelped as another strike of the tawse landed down on lean but soft flesh.

"And, while we all know foofoo has a special beta-crush on Verity, my tip for later for the pet is to include more beautiful, memorable, moments like taking Verity the rose between his teeth, if he wants to earn his cum at long last. One moment for each of us, let us all know how special we are to the pet and I bet foofoo will be well on the way to a majority vote!" Amy advised. "Get my drift, make us all feel special like the horny cum slut did for Verity. I know it will be humiliating but this is the pet's life now, Nikki has unmade you as a man, rebuilt you as a domesticated working animal, so I'm sure you'll cope and take it in your stride foofoo."

"WHMPR!" foofoo panted.

"Ok goody good, that's it foofoo embrace your inner tart, nice and slutty; we'll keep at it till foofoo secretes precum as a little tell-tell sign he is all set, so think your sexy thoughts foofoo, think of the submissive things the pet would like to do with the beautiful Mistress Verity." Amy encouraged. "Titties, ass, smile, and repeat till you leak foofoo; come on cum slut, you know the drill by now!"

"The girls all know every time the pet leaks, it means an attempted but failed arousal, the tiny but firm cage doing its job, keeping the cum slut denied." Amy tormented. "Making the pet's little nub even more useless and insignificant than the day before. I do wonder foofoo, if what Nikki tells me is true, that long restriction in a small chastity device like the pet wears, will eventually result in atrophy and shrinking of the penis? It makes sense, use it or lose it, and Nikki sure doesn't let the pet use it, so I reckon it's probably true foofoo. Not that the pet has much to lose in the first place, but won't it be exciting to find out foofoo?"

"WHMPR! WHMPR!" foofoo emitted.

Amy chuckled, watching foofoo's movements with a beady eye. "I suspect we will you know, find out eventually, as honestly foofoo, you belong in chastity, a pussyfree virgin. You may get the odd vote in favour for the pet to experience an occasional cum but none of us are voting to let the pet out of chastity, that's a given, no going back ever and there's no point in pretending otherwise."

"And do remember, I've seen it unlocked and unleashed foofoo, it is too tiny and given the chance would cum way too quickly for it to be any use to a woman. Just a few inches when erect. It is useless and serves no purpose, the choice between a proper sized cock and foofoo's comical nub, obvious. No, for it foofoo is better growing as a beta-male submissive, while his cocklet shrinks, his manhood vanishing away, the longer he stays locked." Amy mused, sharing out loud thoughts that made her horny when it came to supervising foofoo, while foofoo's mostly naked, lean form continued to prance about before her.

"Just an itty-bitty tiny thing, of no significance to the opposite sex, an embarrassment for the pet really, foofoo should hold little hope that…"

"Awwww foofoo you shouldn't have!" Amy exclaimed, giggling, her guidance about hope forgotten. Instead, fascinated at the sight of a long stringy, gloopy thread of clear precum dangled down from the end of foofoo's pink chastity cage. "Did the pet leak his precum for little old me?!"

"WHMPR!" came back the humiliated response of a horny male, gagging for some action; helplessly getting off to his own humiliation, in the sexually submissive frustration of the beta-male kept in a long-term state of chastity.

"Foofoo will make Mistress Verity jealous if he's not careful." Amy teased. "Poor pet, getting all hot and bothered by my girl talk, and there's me rabbiting on and making the pet dribble and leak like this; all from being such a meanie about how small his little nub is!"

"WHMPR!"

"Awww pet, I'm sorry, I really am but it really is that tiny foofoo, we all agree it's the smallest any of us have seen on an adult guy." Amy nodded sagely. "Anyways, a leaky pet means, you're ready to point those pretty painted toes for the girls, freestyle I think for now, you greedy little cum slut …"

About the Author:

Heralding from the UK, Ms MH Macdonald writes prick teasingly mean, but oh-so chaste, femdom frolics inspired by the notion 'Real Women Don't Do Housework' ensued via zero tolerance subjugation of the male as little more than working livestock, toiling away, pretty & chaste, providing menial work around the house, sans clothing or rights.

Ms MH Macdonald's fondness for things femdom (though her hearing of that term and knowing it was 'a thing' did not happen till years later) go back as far as her first proper boyfriend. Whenever he started to complain or whine about being too horny and blue-balled after some kissing and cuddling, Ms MH Macdonald discovered she liked to drive him nuts all the more, just because she could. So, what seemed like a surprising discovery at the time, was something she grew to love more and more and perhaps even to crave.

Ms MH Macdonald started publishing her Modern-Day-Cinders tales in 2019 and gets excited by spending the cash from the sales on new pairs of shoes for herself and ever smaller chastity cages for her sub. Her favourite things to say to her sub are either

'BooHoo!" or "Not today" and she has the ambition to gift him the

experience of a 'dry year' at some point in the future …

Date Night

by Hope Parker

I sent him a message from the hotel bar. *Room 212. The key is at the front desk. Leave the door open.* I nursed my martini, knowing I wouldn't take more than a few sips of it.

Yes, Ma'am, he replied. *I'll be in our room in ten minutes.*

I didn't watch the door but took note of the time. He wouldn't be late. When ten minutes had passed, I left a tip on the bar top next to my unfinished drink and walked to the elevators. My light pink spring trench coat hid the boned corset underneath. I wore thigh-high stockings with garters instead of pants and the most comfortable red-bottomed stilettos I owned clicked against the tiled lobby. It had a been a long time since we'd played and I reveled in my sexuality.

When I reached our room, the door was propped ajar with the bolt. I couldn't see into the room. *Perfect.*

I pushed into the darkened space, locked the door behind me, and smiled when I saw him. He knelt next to the king-sized bed, his powerful thighs resting on his calves, feet tucked under him. His body was sculpted from long days on construction sites and I couldn't wait to feel his calloused and rugged hands on the soft flesh of my body. The branches of his Joshua Tree tattoo snaked around his back, a testament to his personal journey. His head was bowed and hair trimmed short. It was practical, the way he took care of himself. As I requested, he was naked.

"Up, pet," I commanded.

He followed directions, facing the bed and not daring to look at me. I took off my coat and hung it in the closet by the door. I wanted to take my time. Make him wait.

When I reached him, I ran my hand along the inside of his thigh until I cupped his balls. I squeezed and fondled them for a moment, loving the way he quivered as I touched his sensitive skin. I moved to his other leg and traced my finger upward, barely giving his cock a second glance. I wasn't interested in playing with that yet.

I followed the ridge of abs up his chest, breathing in the subtle scent of lumber and Irish Spring soap that drifted off his skin when I touched him. I tipped his chin up and allowed him to meet my gaze. He wouldn't be allowed to see me again until our scene was complete.

"Good job. Are you ready to play?" I asked. His eyes widened in appreciation when he saw my fitted corset and the high heels that made me just taller than him.

"Yes, Ma'am," he replied, a wide dimpled smile filling his face when I cupped his cheek.

I reached into my purse and pulled out a blindfold, ball gag, leather cuffs, and cock ring.

"On the bed. Face up," I said. He settled flat on his back with the same smirking grin he had while he was standing.

"Since we're trying something new with the gag, are you comfortable snapping as a safe word?"

I grabbed his arms and set them above his head before putting on the leather cuffs. I made sure I could fit two fingers in between the leather and his wrists, feeling his wild pulse underneath my fingertips. The tangible evidence of his excitement grounded me to him in this moment and I let the same anticipation sweep through me.

"I am," he replied.

"Keep your hands right here. I don't want to see them move an inch. There will be punishment for breaking my rules." I pushed his arms back into the pillows and admired his body spread out before me. He was a good boy and rarely disobeyed. He liked the test the limits but never enough to require serious punishment.

This was the first night that we were delving deeper into the world of sensory deprivation. I moved the blindfold over his eyes, noticing the hitch in his breath as my hand grazed his cheeks. I gave him a brief caress and reached for the ball gag. He was blindfolded, completely still, waiting for my next move.

"What's your color?" I asked after I saw the slight tremble in his chest.

"Green, Ma'am," he said. "I'm good."

Exhaling, I brushed a kiss across his lips and teased the seam of his mouth with the tip of my tongue before I put the ball gag in his mouth and told him to lift his head so I could secure it. I chuckled at how he lay at my mercy and began to make my way downward to his cock, which was already erect.

"Is this where you want me, pet? Want me to make you feel good? Because you know you have to earn that," I crooned. I barely touched him until I reached his erection. Then I bent forward and blew on it, making him twitch. He whimpered behind the gag but his body remained still. I traced my fingernails up the beautiful veins in him and felt a rush of attraction as wetness pooled in my core.

A drop of salty precum beaded at his tip and I swiped my tongue across it, laughing at the hiss that escaped around the ball gag and how his leg jerked. I smacked the inside of his thigh.

"I'd keep yourself together or you won't have any part of what I have in store for you tonight."

He took a deep breath and settled down. I stretched the cock ring around my fingers and maneuvered it over his cock and balls, making sure it was tight over his entire package. His hips tightened and he fought against wanting to move, doing his best not to squirm.

"You're being such a good boy and handling our new toys so well," I said. Deciding to reward him for his effort, I began to suck him, noticing how much harder he had gotten after the ring was put on. I bobbed on him, laving his shaft with my tongue and hollowing my cheeks around his cock head. He kept his hips on the mattress and I tasted the salt and clean essence of him that I craved so much. When he tightened his core, I popped off. He shuddered but didn't come. I had long ago perfected the amount of time I needed to suck him off to make sure he didn't come but that I didn't ruin his orgasm either.

He was breathing hard. I silently slid my wet panties down over my legs and threw them into the corner. I retreated to a chair positioned a few feet from the bed and began touching myself, smacking my own pussy so he could hear how wet I was. He hated not being able to participate in pleasuring me. I watched the rapid rise and fall of his chest, his hard nipples. I ached to get them in my mouth.

I started to moan. "Oh, pet, you look so pretty trussed up for me. If you keep being good while I finish getting myself off, I may just let you eat me out. Would you like that?"

He nodded. A dribble of drool escaped the corner of his mouth. My favorite part about the ball gag was the forced humility. His body reacted to what was happening, and he was powerless to stop his physical responses. I didn't care when he drooled around it. He was never sexier than when he was under my command. I pushed myself to orgasm, imagining it was his tongue instead of my own fingers.

When I came down from my high, I took in his painful looking erection. He had to be ready to burst. We'd had most of our fun. After a little more teasing, I'd give him his release. Before I tended to him, I took off the corset and heels, leaving my stockings and garters on. I returned to his side by the bed and removed the ball gag. I kissed the sides of his mouth before giving him a hard kiss and opening my mouth to his. His tongue entered my mouth and I savored the familiar taste of mint and cinnamon from his favorite gum. I pulled away and gripped the headboard, positioning myself over him so that my pussy lined up with his mouth. I was still soaking wet and had recovered enough from my orgasm to have another. The second I lowered myself to him, his tongue lapped at me.

"Good boy," I whispered as he showered attention on my core. He alternated licks, first focusing on my slit and then moving up to my clit, doing whatever it took to have me gushing in his mouth. This wasn't how I wanted to finish again. I continued to let him eat me out until the surge of nerves deep in my core started to rise.

"Do you think you've earned your orgasm?" I panted, as caught up in this moment as he was.

"Yes, Ma'am." His reply was instantaneous.

I agreed.

I kissed down his body, rubbing my cheek against the hard stubble of his face, and giggling when the soft tickle of his chest hairs brushed my nose. My lips found his nipples and I sucked hard on each of them. I followed the ripple of muscle down his body until

I kissed the head of his cock. His thighs were trembling. It was time to give the man what he needed.

I squeezed his hips and made sure his cock ring was still fit well around him. Satisfied, I seated myself over him and sunk down onto his erection.

"You feel incredible, baby. Make as much noise as you want but don't move," I demanded as I began to ride him. I ground my hips against him, rubbing my clit against his pelvis with every stroke. Without the gag, he hissed and cried out.

"May I…can I come?" he stuttered when our bodies had reached a fever pitch and both of us were ready to topple over the edge.

"Yes!"

He groaned as his hips rose up to chase his pleasure. I pushed him back down on the bed and rode him until I'd finished. When we were both done, I collapsed onto his chest. I settled there for a moment, listening to his thudding heartbeat and tasting the tang of salt on his skin when my lips pressed to his chest. He started to go flaccid and I rolled off him, removing the cock ring to give him more relief. We were done for the night.

Then, I removed the cuffs and released him from our play.

"We're done now, pet. You're my favorite boy. Great job tonight," I whispered. I kissed him once and removed the blindfold.

His gaze met mine for the first time since we started our scene.

"Thank you, Ma'am. That was fun." His eyes were bright and happy, his tone light and sincere. When he flashed me that dimpled smile, my belly swooped and I fell in love all over again. His hand reached for the back of my neck and he pulled me to him for a searing kiss.

"Come on, let's go get cleaned up and then we can order dinner," I suggested. We were back to life as usual.

"Fine, we'll do it your way, honey," my husband said, wrapping his arm around my waist to walk with me to the bathroom.

I started the shower and we let it steam before stepping into the warm spray.

"So, what hotel should I book for next month's date night?" he asked.

About the Author:

Hope Parker fell in love with an unconventional hero in high school lit class and has had a passion for romance novels ever since. Her contemporary erotic romances explore themes of forbidden love, couples who test each other's limits, and those who will do whatever it takes to stay together. Her first novel, Atlas Calling, was released in September. In 2020, she received her Master of Fine Arts degree in Creative Writing. She lives on a small hobby farm in Tennessee, where she resides with her husband and son.

The Doctor is In

by Victory Von Stryker

Doctor Von Stryker sat in her office preparing for her next patient, aged 35, with a chain-smoking habit. He was coming in for hypnosis as his preferred method of treatment.

The Doctor crossed her legs, reflecting on their previous appointment, and read the last note she made after that visit: *Patient X has a tendency to speak inappropriately. Needs to be taught a lesson.* She giggled. That was a note she didn't want anyone else reading, nevertheless; it was true. Time after time, over and over, it never failed. Doctor Von Stryker had become a leader in her field, a Master at helping others conquer inner demons. Still, some guy would demean her achievements, calling her Doll, or Honey or Sweetheart, as if it was his genuine right. It never ceased to amaze. This time Doctor Von Stryker had a plan to get even. Oh, yes, she would still lead him out of his haze of nicotine addiction, but there would be a few changes to his treatment plan. She smiled wickedly.

Just then, there was a knock on the door. Using her most professional manner, Doctor Von Stryker welcomed her client, directing him to the leather chaise. The patient, let us call him Cameron, sank into the couch's buttery softness. "Looking good, Doc. I like that skirt." He tossed the comment at the Doctor, as if she should be impressed.

Strike one, thought the Doc. Outwardly, she ignored him. Seating herself in her favorite chair, she suggested, "Let's get started. How did you do with your journal this week?"

She raised one brow, tapping her pen lightly on her knee. Cameron quipped, "Nice legs, doll."

Ignoring the Doctor's disapproving scowl, he continued. "Well, Doc, it's like this. I did cut back from 4 packs a day to 3 packs, last week. But see, I forgot to write it down."

Strike two. Victory checked another imaginary box, and paused a minute to calm herself. This man was seriously trying her patience. She reflected, "So what I'm hearing is you made some progress, but you neglected to do your homework."

She brandished her pen, stopping to write in her note pad. "We're going to have to address this need you have to avoid doing the work."

Appropriately chastened, Cameron hung his head. "Sorry Doc."

He missed her evil grin, as the Doc smirked, "That's better."

Cameron settled deeper into his snug berth. If he understood the surprises hidden below him, he might not have relaxed so easily. After months of practice with Doctor Von Stryker, his brain was trained to respond to her soothing tones. Said brain began to subtly shut down.

The Doctor coaxed, "Cameron, remember to focus your gaze on the Prism in front of you. Look at the light refracting from the surface. Let your mind go. Pay attention to your breathing. Take deep breaths. In through your nose, out through your mouth. Victory led him through each step, asking for consent and submission to her control. He gave it willingly and with complete trust. The Doctor began by following the normal routine. She instructed him to picture a poison label, with the skull and cross bones. The familiar pattern, the imagery, her musical voice. Cameron was lost. His spirit floated, deeply entranced. He was under the Doctor's spell. She had him right where she wanted him.

Victory whispered, "Cameron, can you hear me? How do you feel? Where is your comfort level?"

Cameron melted into the cozy leather. He nodded, answering cheerily, "I feel great, Doc! More rested than I have in weeks." His chest rose and fell with each healing breath.

The Doctor praised, "That's a good boy. I want you to take off your clothes and lay back down. Will you do that for me, Cameron?"

He inhaled sharply and disrobed without hesitation. Dropping his clothes on the floor, he quickly resumed his supine position, displaying his body for his Doctor. She circled the chaise, examining his frame from top to bottom. She patted his head, indicating her approval. She even opened his mouth to inspect his teeth and gums. Her right hand traveled the length of his body, gripping his muscled calf, eyeing his growing cock. "Nice specimen, excellent lines. You are quite the fine stallion. Cameron, your arms are so heavy. Why don't you drop them by your side?"

His hands fell like bricks. The Doctor revealed the restraints hidden beneath him. Soon Cameron was shackled, completely exposed and at the mercy of Doctor Victory Von Stryker. She straddled her helpless client, and crooned, "Now, Let's get to work."

Doctor Von Stryker admired the beauty splayed before her. Cameron stood several inches above six feet. His hair was thick and golden, like the sun, his eyes brilliant turquoise pools, his skin tanned and flawless. He was perfectly sculpted with the lean thighs of a runner. His erect member stretching to ten luscious inches long and thick as a fist. He was indeed the ideal plaything, and in that moment, he belonged to Doctor Victory Von Stryker.

She stripped away her blood red blouse to reveal a black lace bra, and flung that away as well. She hiked her skirt higher. Her natural D cups swayed as she dug her knees into Cameron's hips.

Rising above him, Victory palmed his cheek, turning his face to hers. She explained, "I'm taking a firmer hand with you, Cameron. We're taking things in a new direction. You need to realize I am the expert. You will submit to my control. You have not been following directions or doing your homework. You have been disrespectful, oppositional, and frankly, obnoxious. I am finished with your attitude and your backtalk. Beginning now, it all changes. You are trapped with no place to go. You may be an attractive man, my dear, but you have relied on your looks far too long. Today, I'm going to mold you into a decent human. Do you hear me, Cameron?"

Cameron was both shocked and excited. His heart pounded. Sweat trickled from his pores. His lovely prick began to rise.

Victory reveled in the powerful emotions consuming her body. She gathered a fistful of blond locks, pulling Cameron in for a quick nip on the nose. The doctor dismounted. She stepped out of her pencil skirt, leaving on her black panties and kitten heel shoes, and faced her victim.

Armed with a shiny, new riding crop, she teased, "Do you like what you see?"

She pushed her tits in Cameron's face, daring him to taste, then moving out of reach. The Doctor reproached, "Not so fast, little boy. You have some bad habits that need breaking, and I am just the Doctor for the job. When I'm finished, you're going to be polite, gracious and courteous. Isn't that correct, Cameron?" The Doctor punctuated her statement with a sharp whack to his dick.

Cameron yelped at the punishing surprise. He lowered his eyes, and mumbled, "Yes, Doctor, I'll try."

Victory pointed her weapon. "No, Cameron, you won't try. You will succeed. I will not accept anything less."

She unlocked a nearby chest, and chose a few instruments, arranging them across her desk. Then she grabbed her riding crop and stalked her prey. The Doctor faced her bound captive and detailed her new treatment plan.

She explained, "Cameron, it is inappropriate for you to call me Doll. You know that, right?"

She paused, waiting for affirmation. Cameron's head dropped lower. He muttered, "Yes, ma'am."

"Speak clearly and refrain from remarking on my appearance. I am a Professional. Your Doctor, and you will conduct yourself accordingly. Do you follow?"

Cameron pleaded, "I didn't mean no harm, Doc. I was only trying to show my appreciation."

This time the crop snapped across Cameron's balls. He winced at the sting, tears bathing his face. He writhed uselessly against his restraints. There was no escape. Doctor Von Stryker instructed, "Cameron! You have earned your punishment. You will strive to obey. You will address me as Doctor, Madam or Mistress. You will submit to my every whim. If you do not, you will suffer the consequences. Do not say a word. As a matter of fact, I'm tired of the sound of your voice. I have just the thing to ensure your silence."

She showed Cameron the bit gag/nipple clamp combo she held in her hand. She gloated, "I have selected a few tools especially for you. When I'm done, you won't dare think about misbehaving. If you do, you'll remember the agony you will suffer today. A nagging fear, tugging at your brain, forever warning you to stay in line."

Cameron paled as Victory buckled the leather to his neck. When she attached the nipple clamps to his budding flesh, she warned, "If you try to spit out your gag or if you attempt to talk, it's probably going to hurt. If you endure your trials like a good boy, I will reward your compliance."

The Doctor trailed her fingernails along his chest, watching as goosebumps decorated his muscled torso. Cameron felt strangely relaxed, even optimistic, as he relinquished his will.

Cameron took to the bit willingly and with devotion. His mind emptied. He felt weightless. Every experience with Doctor Von Stryker left him renewed, but this was something more Though restrained, he was free! He surrendered his burdens to the Doctor. His arms ached and his muscles burned, but he was alive! He gazed into his Doctor's eyes, waiting patiently for further instructions. He smiled dreamily, craving the discipline he knew he deserved. The Doctor presented the next implement in her behavior modification arsenal.

"Meet your new friend, the Violet Wand. Cameron, I'm not going to lie. This is going to hurt. Your lesson for today is that disrespect yields agony. Good manners and obedience lead to untold rewards, pure ecstasy. Just remember, this long journey of pain will end in pleasure beyond compare."

The Doctor ruffled Cameron's hair, laughing at the mix of terror and anticipation lurking under his lashes.

Victory pointed the wand at Cameron's chest. "I'm not your Doll." *Snap*!

His left nipple suffered a direct hit, and his body jerked in surprise. Cameron's jaw clenched the bit in his mouth, and tears soaked his cheeks. The Doctor gently wiped them away, caressing his skin.

She pointed the wand once more. "Don't call me Babe, Cameron. It is inappropriate." The wand crackled as it lit up Cameron's right hip. He shook with pain from the wand's searing touch.

The Doctor patted his head before adding, "Cameron, you will never comment on my appearance." She zapped his balls, sparking his flesh.

Cameron writhed under her disapproving glare, both fearing and desiring her next move. Her nails grazed his burning sack. She pressed her cleavage in his face as placed a cold compress against his brow. "Hang in there. You are doing so well."

Then her tone turned stern once more, as she summarized, "No more Doll, No more Babe, No more leering stares!" The Doctor stung the arches of both his feet. Every nerve wailed in anguish. Cameron bit down hard on the gag, wishing he could scream.

The Doctor massaged a path towards his groin. "Very good, my dear boy. Such compliance deserves a reward. I have a special treat just for you."

Victory grabbed another toy from her desk. She lubed the remote controlled, anal plug, watching Cameron's eyes widen.

"Don't worry, pet. You're going to love this." The Doctor pushed the plug as far as it would go and set the vibration to a low hum. Cameron moaned under his bit, absorbing the new sensations invading his asshole. Doctor Von Stryker turned her attentions to his rock-hard dick, her silky hand pumping him vigorously. The combination was more than Cameron could stand. He exploded with an intensity he'd never imagined, drenching his torso in salty rain.

Victory's eyes sparkled with delight. She crooned, "Excellent, Cameron! I'm so proud of you!"

She kissed his temple, taking a moment to cuddle him in her arms. The Doctor bathed her patient and applied a healing balm to his wounds. She erased all traces of her new treatment plan. She released Cameron from his restraints and told him to get dressed.

Easing him back into the comfort of her leather couch, the Doctor whispered, "I'm going to count back from 10. You'll wake feeling rested and refreshed...."

Cameron blinked as he rose from the couch. Doctor Von Stryker perched on the edge of her desk, the very picture of innocence. She asked, "How do you feel?"

Cameron blushed a deep red, but didn't know why. "I feel great, Ma'am. When can I schedule my next visit?"

The Doctor checked her calendar, smiling devilishly as she planned their next adventure.

About the Author:

Mistress Victory Von Stryker is a pen name for her writing and Online Personality. She is a Real Dominatrix living in the Carolinas, working under a different name. She has a degree in Clinical Psychology and has always been intrigued by what makes a person tick. When she exited a bad, abusive marriage around 10 years ago, she decided it was time to take matters into her own hands, make things fairer in her own special way.

She began writing as a child, it has always been her favorite emotional outlet, and now she writes fictionalized stories based on her life as a Bad-Ass Domme Queen.

Diana, Goddess of the Hunt

by Brenda Blacklove

"You might find your cock getting hard right about now. You might want to touch it so badly, but I'm not going to let you yet."

I looked over and he was definitely hard, and he was dripping precum, too. I licked my lips and thought about wrapping them around that velvety head, but that could wait.

"That's right. Deeper and deeper into relaxation. Think about how good it feels as you listen to the sound of my voice, wrapping around you, going deeper and deeper. Just enjoy the sensation and the sound of my voice as you relish the feeling of having a hard cock."

It felt a little ridiculous to hypnotize him into not masturbating. I very much longed to see him jerk his cock, to see him grip its firm base and slide those guitarist fingers up and down, as I knew he would be jerking off to me.

But I knew that keeping him turned on would only help me.

I needed him mindless, under my control, spellbound.

I had to resist the urge to tell him to touch it for me. He was a perfect subject with a beautiful body and a gorgeous cock, though, and it made me wet to just sit there and watch him with his eyes closed, his lashes fanned across the dark circles, and totally under my spell. His body was loose and limp, his hands at his sides and his legs splayed out on my couch.

He had come to me for months now – at first, for jerk off instructions, and then as he grew addicted to the sound of my voice, for jerk off addiction recovery hypnotism. But he definitely got aroused while I went into the induction.

I needed that. I drank up his addiction with hunger. He would come back to me after this session, too. I knew he would.

I decided to take it a step further. After I counted down, I had him open those beautiful, intelligent eyes of his.

I walked slowly towards him, my high heels clicking on the hardwood floor, my hips swaying seductively. He was in a dream state – he looked at me through half closed lids, his face relaxed and dream-like. I could see his pupils dilate, and I could tell his eyes were drinking in my entire body, as if he had travelled through a dry desert and my body was a beaming oasis.

It was time to test him.

"Perhaps you're wondering how you found yourself in this situation. Under my spell, things are not what they seem."

I could see the veins in his neck pulsing. My eyes wandered across his lightly tanned body, soaking in all the intricate details: his broad chest, the muscles, that intoxicating line of body hair that ran down, down. I inhaled sharply, letting his rich, soapy scent fill my lungs. Oh yes, I wanted to drink him up. He would taste so good.

"Tell me now, slave. Wouldn't you just love it if I touched you right now?"

"Yes, Goddess Diana. Please."

He bucked his hips just a little, the precum bead growing thicker. I ran my fingernails down his chest, marveling at the red streaks left behind.

"I'm going to kiss your neck now. You might find that it feels so good, you'll want to embrace me. I'll give you permission to do that, but you must not be afraid."

I saw something flicker across those eyes, something like fear, but it was quickly washed away by his arousal. I leaned in and nuzzled his neck, enjoying the texture of his prickled skin. I kissed and sucked at the flesh. It tasted sumptuous, sensual, like opium and salt. I let my teeth prick the flesh gently, and once I felt the hot trickle of blood, I licked it away.

He seemed to like what I was doing, so I removed my dress. I longed to feel his body against mine anyway. I removed my bra and panties and stood before him in only my garter belt, thigh high stockings and heels. I positioned myself over his cock and took him inside me slowly. I could feel him raising his hips so he could fill me up, but I was in control. The blood trickled down his neck in little red rivulets, and I could resist no longer. I let him fill me up all the way to his balls and I leaned in to drink his blood.

As he pumped into me, I drank. My instinct was to suck him completely dry, but I couldn't ... no. The blood was so delectable and tempting, though, and I wanted to tongue every last drop from his warm body.

But I had to keep him alive. I had to keep him under this spell.

I pulled away and put my fingers over the little holes my teeth left. I looked down on him then, into his glazed, half-open eyes, down his sculpted chest. God, he was beautiful – but I couldn't get too attached. Not to this one. Not to any of them.

I rode him harder until I could feel my muscles clenching and the intensity build. I put my fingers down to my clit. There was just a little bit of his blood on them, but I'd clean everything up before I woke him out of his spell.

He could feel me getting closer and he finally made a face that wasn't so passive, so out of it. His breathing quickened and he held me tight by my hips, but I was still in control. I bounced up and down on him until I came hard, until my thighs were wet nearly to my knees. I could feel him contract and his cock seemed to get even bigger, and he shuddered and groaned when he came.

We stayed like that for a moment. Now was when he was most impressionable, so I said, "Bring me more, my darling slave. Bring me more."

I cleaned him up, got him out of the trance and sent him on his way.

My need was sated for the time being. But it would only be a matter of days before it overcame me again. I knew it would come on like a rush, sudden and biting into my core--that familiar hunger pang for blood. I dreaded it already. Instead of periods, it was the hunger. I didn't know which was worse. I barely had any memory of my past life, but it was a woman who came to me and made me what I am today.

It was back in the eighties, back when the word "dominatrix" was still a terrible taboo, back when yuppies ran the world and Reagan advocated for morals and values. I came across a men's magazine in a porn shop with sordid pictures of beautiful women in leather and lace, their hair teased until it looked like it was its own sentient being. When I flipped through the glossy magazine and saw these beautiful women in power poses, dominating these cowering men, I knew this was the career for me.

My mother had passed away from cancer. I had just gotten out of a terrible relationship and had kicked the selfish prick out of bed in the middle of the night. The memory of it still inflames me, but the things that happened after it are as fresh as newly brewed coffee.

My specialty was always hypnotism. People came to see me for smoking cessation at first. But once I incorporated it into my work as a dominatrix, business boomed, and two months later, I wanted to kick myself for not starting sooner.

But then, *she* walked in my door.

Her presence stunned me. She was gorgeous, almost unreal with her blue-black hair, alabaster skin and dark blue eyes.

"I want to feel wrapped up in your power," she told me in a sultry voice, her ruby red lips curling into a slight smile. "Show me what you can do." I thought I saw a glint of sharpness in her gleaming white canines, but I wasn't sure. I was so drawn in by her eyes – they were an unnatural shade of blue so dark, reminding me of the mysterious depths of the ocean. The paleness of her skin was utterly fascinating and smooth, almost like a marble statue. I longed to reach out and caress her. Would she feel warm and inviting, or as cold as stone?

It didn't take long for me to find out. She was upon me fast, so fast I didn't even see her move. She smelled creamy and clove-like. I couldn't place it at first, but then it hit me. Funeral lilies. The memory of my mother's recent funeral hit me like a hammer. It had been around the time of the breakup, and I choked back an exasperated gasp.

"Are you alright, dear?" she asked. Her voice echoed through my brain and I got a strange, dizzy feeling. She put her hands on me and I could feel how icy they were, but something about her touch felt so inviting, so right. She smiled and leaned forward, nuzzled my neck, her hypnotizing whispers caressing my skin. I moaned into her funeral-spiked black hair. There was a brief prick of something on my neck, but the sensations that came after it were so delightful, I quickly forgot about the pain. I felt sensual, and any reservations or anxieties I'd had about my mother or the breakup or work ... they were all gone, and all I could think and feel involved this strange woman.

She pulled away momentarily, and my vision blurred and became jumpy like a stop-motion film. She offered me her wrist, which confused me – that is, until I could smell it. It smelled like the most delectable choice of steak, meaty and faintly metallic. As if by instinct, I put my mouth to it. The taste did not disappoint, and the cool sensation of her skin on my lips contrasted with the rush of warm liquid made my sex pulse with taboo anticipation.

"Now you will really have power. More than you ever thought before," her voice purred into my ear, sending shivers through my body. The shivers soon turned into quaking as her lips moved down my body, her icy hands trailing all over my skin to remove my clothing. She travelled to the apex of my thighs, her hands on my ass to pull me closer. I could feel her tongue snaking deep inside me, filling me up like no man had ever done before, and I was washed away by a climax that seemed to go on for eternity. My legs shook as her tongue thrusted in and out relentlessly. I could feel warm liquid covering my thighs and I threw my head back, my hands in her luscious hair to brace myself.

When the waves of ecstasy subsided and my clit grew sensitive, I looked down at her. My heart leapt to my chest at what I saw. Her lips were covered in blood. I floundered and pushed her away, but she just laughed.

"You're mine now. I chose you because you're special. You can reel them in …"

She disappeared like a ghost, like a dream. I ached only slightly, the pain in my neck and crotch only a minor annoyance for the rest of the day.

Something strange happened once she left. I had the memory of my mother dying and the awful breakup, but the usual physical symptoms that came with the memories, like crying, grief or even anger, were gone. In fact, I felt like she took all my emotions, just like she drank them away. I could describe those emotions, I just didn't feel them anymore. The only thing left was a general sense of more energy and elation – pure elation, uninterrupted by my past or the emotions of others.

I was with a client when the hunger came on. It rushed inside me and wrapped around me so fast it nearly knocked me over. I could smell the sweat on his skin and could hear the blood rushing through his veins, down to his cock, through his beautiful body. I wanted nothing more than to sink my teeth into that salty flesh and drink his juices. I had him under, hypnotized fully so that he could experience a memory of his ex-girlfriend pegging him with a strap-on. He wore jeans and a t-shirt, but I could see the outline of his erection and it made my mouth water.

She left like a ghost and came back the same way. Something danced in the corner of my eye, a figure outside the door. I found I couldn't resist standing up and letting her in, and the subject was none the wiser. In fact, his cock seemed to strain even more against his pants.

She showed me where to bite while they were under, how to drain them to the point of either no return or just enough to make them into our slaves. As slaves, they were more useful to us. They could leave for a few days and return rejuvenated, their blood renewed and ready to be drained once again.

"You can make them do anything," she purred into my ear as we braced ourselves on either side of him. We both ran our hands under his t-shirt, over his muscled chest as he breathed deeply. She told me they could either be drained on the neck or that sweet spot on the thigh, which was much less noticeable. The pinpricks were so minute, by the time they got home they were nearly invisible.

"You can hypnotize them to bring you more and more," she said.

And I did. It was easy. And they flowed through my space one after another, mindless and willing to surrender to me, to the pleasure of succumbing to someone's hunger. They passed through like gypsies, one after the other, bringing more and more. My appetite grew and grew, never quite sated.

Until she came in.

"I heard about your power," she said.

And I was sure that when I smiled, she could see the white glint of my canines.

About the Author:

Brenda Blacklove is a pen name used by horror fiction author Clare Castleberry. She grew up in the middle of nowhere with a police officer father and an artistic bar-owning mother, which fueled her imagination with stories and left lots of time for reading and writing. She lives in New Orleans.

Stage Fright

by Keary Hayes

It was an entirely new sensation, one that left Lewis feeling exposed and on edge, as though at any moment his *secret* might be discovered, but at the same time it was also exciting, a tingling thrill that kept him constantly on edge. Lewis had not expected *this* when he had agreed to Her offer, but he could not deny that he was beginning to enjoy the things She was making him do.

It had started innocently enough two weeks ago, when he'd matched with a mysterious but beautiful woman on his regular dating app. Her profile had been aloof and almost enigmatic, but it was Her photos that had really captured his attention. None of them had been overtly sexual, but Her eyes had been dazzling, bright, brilliant blue, and they had seemed to stare *through* him, as through reading his soul through the screen, and then there had been Her lips, always brightest crimson.

He'd clicked 'yes' on Her almost immediately, then promptly tried to forget about Her. She was beautiful, and She probably had numerous matches. Why would She click 'yes' to Lewis? Sure, he wasn't unattractive, his features symmetrical, perhaps even classical, but they were also a little too delicate. Where other men were tall and muscular, he was slim, and short, almost petite. A woman like that could have any man She wanted, so why would She pick him?

She had clicked yes though, and Lewis had been ridiculously happy when they'd started chatting. She'd been captivating in conversation, prying secrets from Lewis that he'd not told *anyone* before, teasing out confessions that he'd never even admitted to himself, and he had found himself drawn to Her, unable to resist, so that when She'd offered him a simple, playful deal in exchange for a date he'd jumped at the chance.

The deal was simple. For one date he had to obey one instruction. It had seemed odd at first, obeying Her without question, a woman he barely knew, but it had also left him feeling breathless and excited, tingling in a way that left him craving more.

There had been three dates, and three instructions. The first was easy, if a little unusual, and Lewis had obeyed with only a little resistance. He had worn panties, a pink pair She had sent him, silky and soft, and he had found himself *enjoying* how they felt, Her subtle teasing, and had quite liked how he looked in them. The second date had required him to shave his legs and body, and again, wear panties, a black pair this time, lacy and tiny and snug. Finally, on their last date, there had been one more addition. As well as panties and smooth legs, Lewis had been told to wear a metal cage on his cock, fitted with a padlock to which only She had a key. At first he had laughed, knowing he could never go that far, but, as the date drew closer, he had grown curious, fascinated by the idea until, eventually, he had given in, knowing that it was his only way of seeing Her again. It had been emasculating, humiliating, locking his cock away, giving Her that power over him, but he could not deny how excited it had left him.

That had been four days ago, and Lewis was still caged. Tonight was their fourth date, and that was how he had found himself at work, shaved smooth under his trousers and shirt, his cock locked away in a metal cage, aching, desperate for some release, wearing a pair of cute, white panties decorated with pretty pink bows.

The whole day he had been on edge, terrified someone would discover his *secret,* would notice the scent of his feminine moisturiser, notice the way he kept squirming because of his cage, delighting in the feeling of his smooth, soft body, catch a glimpse of his panties peeking out above the waist of his trousers. His heart was racing but still, he was … *enjoying it.*

Lewis jumped when his phone alert sounded. It was the sound he had set for Her, as per Her instruction, so he would always know when She was messaging him and he could make sure to respond as a priority. He pulled his phone out of his pocket and opened Her message, anxious and excited as he wondered what Her fourth instruction was to be, and Lewis wondered just how far he was willing to go for Her?

A car will arrive at five o'clock sharp. It will bring you to me and I will give you tonight's instruction in person. I look forward to your obedience.

*

The car pulled up at one minute past five o'clock and stopped just in front of Lewis where he stood waiting. He had been waiting there for five minutes to be sure that he didn't miss his ride. The car was sleek and black, anonymous and almost intimidating. The back door swung open and Lewis took a deep breath, his heart racing. Was he really going to just let Her lead him into the unknown? What did She have planned?

His cock twitched in is cage, locked away. Only She had the key to release him. She held so much power over him already. Was he really ready to go *further*? Did he even have a choice?

Lewis exhaled, forced himself to calm. He could not deny how much he enjoyed Her company, just spending time with Her, making Her smile, and he could not pretend that he had not *enjoyed* doing what She told him to. Lewis grinned, made his decision, then stepped off towards the car, slipped into the back seat, and pulled the door shut.

The driver was silent as the car drove through the city towards the unknown, and Lewis was left in the back alone to imagine what lay in store for him. His hands were shaking, a potent cocktail of nerves, anxiety, and excitement, and he watched out of the window as he tried to force himself to remain calm.

Streets passed. The flow of traffic thinned. The sleek buildings of glass and steel that made up the commercial district of the city were replaced with redbrick warehouses and sprawling lots of cracked concrete and tarmac. The car turned off the road, passed through a gate in a rusted chain link fence, and drove around a rundown looking warehouse with boarded up windows.

There was a deep thrumming as the car passed the main building, like music, then it faded as the car drove round to the back. It stopped outside a set of loading bay doors.

She was stood outside, waiting patiently, dressed in tight black jeans tucked into knee length heeled black leather boots, a white blouse under a black corset. Her blue eyes were sparkling, Her chin length black hair tucked back out of Her face, Her lips were the same bright crimson they always were, with Her nails painted to match.

Lewis felt his heart skip, his belly fluttering. He opened the door and climbed out to greet Her. In the distance was the sound of heavy music.

"You're late," She said, smiling. "Come on. We've got to get you ready."

Before Lewis could argue or speak, She turned and stepped off through the open doors. Lewis was left with no choice but to follow Her into the unknown, the scent of Her perfume left in Her wake making his caged cock throb.

"Sit," She said.

She gestured to a simple chair next to a table on the far side of the room. The room was plain, with bare brick walls, a single mirror in the corner, a sofa on which sat several bags, and a table with a small silver case on top.

Lewis did as She instructed, sitting in the chair. He sat still as She moved around him, circling him, inspecting him, grinning – her smile was the same as always, stunning, mischievous, beguiling.

"It shouldn't take too long to get you ready," She said, "After all you are already so attractive."

Lewis blushed. She often complimented him, telling him he was *attractive, charming*, and *cute*, and he had come to enjoy the rush of emotions Her words conjured in him.

"However, you'll need to change. What you're wearing is not suitable for tonight's… activities."

Lewis nodded. She smiled at him, grinning.

"And as for tonight's *instruction* … well, it's simple enough. You are to obey me, at all times, and refer to me as Mistress. Are you willing?"

Her grin spread as She watched Lewis's reaction. He paled, flustered. He nodded, without a moment's hesitation.

"Yes … Mistress." He said – he blushed, heart racing, his caged cock throbbing, hard.

Why was he enjoying Her telling him what to do? Why did obeying Her feel so good?

"Good. Now, how about we set about making you pretty. We can't have you embarrassing me in front of everyone after all now, can we?"

The question was rhetorical. Lewis knew he was not expected to answer. Still, the words left him flustered and confused. *Pretty*? Everyone?

Lewis sat motionless as She worked. She opened the silver case and took out make-up palettes and brushes. He remained silent as She set about making him *pretty,* keeping still as She applied fake lashes, eyeliner, mascara, eye shadow, dark make-up with bright pink highlights. He did not resist as She painted his lips pink, with a glittery, glossy topcoat, and he held his hands out for Her as She painted his nails to match. As She stepped back to look over Her work, smiling, clearly satisfied, Lewis felt his heart skip.

"Now clothes," She said. "Strip so I can dress you."

Lewis shivered, a cold sense of dread, but he knew he could not disobey. He nodded.

"Yes Mistress," he whispered, and set about complying.

Lewis stripped naked, blushing as She watched, then dressed in the items She gave him, his blush only worsening.

She dressed Lewis in a set of bright, hot pink lingerie, to match his nails and lips, a pair of small panties, a suspender belt, a small corset around his waist, a pair of pink silk stockings. Lewis had never worn anything like it before and for the first time he found himself glad for the cage he was locked in. At least with that on She would not see how aroused he was becoming, the sensation of wearing such sexy, *naughty* underwear over smooth skin so thrilling and exciting. Finally She handed Lewis a pair of hot pink high heels.

"Put these on, then we can add the final touch."

Lewis nodded, did as he was told. He slipped the heels on and tottered for a moment before finding his balance, realising he needed to wiggle his hips as he moved to keep his balance, his ass wiggling in a way that felt pleasant and *naughty*.

"You're a natural in heels. Somehow I knew you would be. Now, the last detail, then you can see how you look."

She stepped close, looming over Lewis even in his new heels, looking down into his eyes. She smiled, and slipped a thin pink collar out from behind Her back.

"You'll wear this for me, won't you?" She asked.

Lewis's head was spinning. He nodded without even hesitating.

She slipped the collar around his neck and there was a click as a small silver padlock locked it around his neck. On the front was small metal ring, and She reached out to attach a long silver chain, a leash. She held the other end in Her hand, and She giggled, obviously pleased.

"You look so *cute*," She said. "Do you want to see?"

Lewis nodded.

"Yes Mistress," he whispered.

She tugged on the leash, led Lewis over to the single mirror in the corner. Lewis's eyes went wide at the sight of his reflection. He was … *beautiful*.

He was stunning, feminine and cute, pretty. He was so pink, his make-up emphasising his delicate features, his lingerie and heels making his smooth, slim body seem svelte and sexy. He blushed and his head spun. He could not remember ever looking so … amazing.

"Now, are you ready to join the *party*?"

Party? Lewis's heart skipped. A party, dressed as he was in pink lingerie, led by Her on a collar and leash, tottering in heels, wiggling his ass in panties. He could not say no, not to Her. Lewis took a deep breath and nodded.

"Yes Mistress," he said, smiling at Her.

*

The warehouse was loud and busy, one vast cavernous space filled with people and music, chatter, laughter, the only light coming from the numerous dim bare bulbs that hung overhead.

Lewis walked behind Her as She led him on his leash, his locked collar, leading him slowly as he became accustomed to walking in his pink heels, his hips and ass swaying, wiggling. He was glad for the dim lighting, exposed as he was in his hot pink panties, stockings, suspenders, corset, looking cute and feminine in his make-up, but as he moved through the room he began to relax, noticing that he was not alone in being so *provocatively* dressed, and he was not the only person being led about on a leash.

There were men and women in leather, latex, lace, blacks, bright colours, collars, heels, men and women crawling like pets, gagged, others standing or kneeling like furniture with their heads hooded. The whole scene was completely overwhelming, and it made Lewis's caged cock throb.

He kept his gaze down, shy, timid, his heart racing, a sense of shame at being so exposed, humiliated at being paraded in girly underwear, having his cock locked in a cage, the key held by Her, but still … it left him feeling breathless, almost giddy, a sense of wonder and excitement that he did not understand. Lewis stopped as She stopped just in front of him, almost tumbling in his heels, still precarious.

"Darling! How *are* you? You look stunning and… is that a new toy? Oh, she's utterly adorable. You always did have the best eye for finding them."

A woman, shorter than Lewis, dressed from neck to toe in black latex, wearing dangerous looking heels, her face painted with black make-up, a short white blonde pixie cut, stood in front of Her, glancing at him. He blushed did not speak. Had she said ... *she,* in reference to him?

She laughed, kindly, friendly, and nodded, tugging on Lewis's leash to bring him closer.

"I really can't take all the credit for this one. They were already so cute and irresistible when I met them, and just practically begging for someone to come along and claim them, though I don't think they really knew it." She said.

Was She talking about him? His head was spinning. She had called him cute and irresistible, but also ... had She *claimed* him? Is that what the collar was? The cage? Why did that idea thrill him? Why was he smiling at the thought of being *owned* by Her?

"And I heard you're in charge of the *performance* tonight."

She smiled, nodded.

"I am. I have a little something special planned, but no spoilers." She grinned.

Lewis felt his heart skip. *Performance?* The other woman glanced at him, grinning, and winked.

"Well, I'll look forward to it," she said. "And good luck, to both of you."

Lewis could not remember ever being so aroused and embarrassed. His panties were wet from the trickle of precum leaking from his caged cock, and his face was burning from the constant blush.

She had led him through the room on his leash, making him strut in his heels and lingerie, stopping often to talk with people She knew, laughing and chatting as he stood demure and polite behind Her, acutely aware of how exposed he was in his skimpy pink lingerie, heels, collar. And though he was not the only one it did not make him more comfortable – the way other men and women looked at him made him squirm, their gazes roaming his smooth body, smiling, lust and desire.

Never once did She leave him though, his leash always in Her hand, and She spoke about him with flattering words, making him smile as he stood behind Her like Her pet, Her toy. Others too complimented him, telling Her that Her toy was *pretty, sexy,* even *beautiful*, and though these were words Lewis associated with girls and women, he found a certain thrill in having them applied to him.

As the evening wore on, She made Her way through the crowd, stopping close to the stage. As the lights went down, She turned to face him, smiled.

"It looks like we're up. Now, try to stay calm, though a little fear is always fun, and just follow my lead. I know you can do this. Just trust me, and it'll be fun, for both of us."

Her smile, Her deep red lips, hooked him. Her bright blue eyes saw him, not just the surface, the face he presented to the world, but the *real* him. He nodded, smiling.

"Yes Mistress," he whispered.

As music swelled, She turned, and led him by his leash and collar up into the stage, his heels clicking loudly. She stopped in the middle of the stage and bright lights came on, dazzling him, blinding him to the audience that stood beyond the front of the stage, watching him.

"Welcome," She said. "Many of you know me, but few, if any of you know my lovely assistant. This is Lucy, and tonight, for your entertainment, I'm going to accept her confession and submission, and I will, if she behaves, *claim* her as my personal property."

She turned to face Lewis, stared at him, tugged forcefully on his leash. *Lucy, submission, property, claim*? His head was spinning, heart racing, a swell of excitement and shame. She stared down at him and he forgot about the stage, the audience – there was only Her.

"Kneel for me Lucy."

There was only a moment of hesitation. Lucy smiled, nodded.

"Yes Mistress," she whispered, and obeyed.

Lucy knelt at her Mistress's feet. There was silence. Lucy took a deep breath.

"Mistress … I …" Lucy blushed, faltered, head spinning, momentarily lost for words.

She took a deep breath, forced herself to be calm. She wanted to please her Mistress, *needed* to please her.

"Mistress, I beg of you, accept me."

As She smiled, pleased by Lucy's words, her submission, Lucy grew more confident, her heart swelling. The room was silent, rapt, watching her, witness to her offering herself to Her, her complete and utter surrender to the beautiful, powerful, beguiling woman who was waiting for her confession, her formal submission, and the words flowed without thought, coming from a place deep within Lucy's soul, from a part of herself that she had never known before, a glorious, wonderful part of her that She had shown her, that belonged to her Mistress.

"Accept me as your toy, your property. I beg you … let me serve you, let me pleasure you, worship you, let me stand by your side as you doll. I offer you everything I am, as worthless as that is. Train me, teach me, so that I am better able to satisfy you. I beg of you Mistress. Without you I … I am nothing." Lucy said.

Her voice carried, loud and bold, out from the stage. She stared up at her Mistress, smiling, waiting for Her reply. Finally, She nodded.

"Very good. I accept," She said. "However, you forgot to say please, so first, before I formally *claim* you … I think a little punishment is in order."

*

Lucy lay strapped down to the bench, head facing the audience. She was trembling, but could not deny the bubbling, fizzing excitement.

Her Mistress moved around her, examining the straps, then stopped just to the side, looked down at her. There was a swish and a crack and Lucy realised that her Mistress was holding a riding crop, and it all fell into place. *Punishment.*

"Are you ready to receive your punishment?" She asked. Are you ready to become my girl?"

Lucy took a deep breath. She was. She really, really was. It was wild, and fast, and crazy, but she knew that she could never say 'no' to Her. Lucy nodded.

"Yes Mistress."

She smiled, nodding, obviously pleased.

"Good. Now, try to relax. After this comes the *fun* part."

She moved round to behind Lucy. Lucy waited, the moment stretching on, then it happened and her breath caught – the crop fell, the swish, the crack, the sting and it fell across her ass, striking both cheeks at the same time.

Her body lit up with pain, a hot brightness swelling inside of her. Before she could react, it fell again, then again. Each strike was different, a new sensation, some striking one cheek, some both, some light, others hard, some thudding, others stinging.

The crop fell over and over and Lucy stared out into the brightness of the stage lights, aware that she was watched by a rapt, silent audience, and the thought thrilled and humiliated her in ways that left her giddy.

Her heart was racing, breathing hard, and the crop fell, striking her ass, over and over. She seemed almost to float, up and out of her body, set free. She was buzzing, the pain becoming a unique pleasure that flooded through her. Lucy lay strapped to the bench, at Her mercy, and felt liberated in a way she had not felt before. The crop fell once more then stopped.

"You did well," She said. "And now … I think you deserve a reward. I'm going to *claim* you, here and now in front of everyone, so that they can see what a slut you want to be for me."

Lucy smiled, giggling, a rush of endorphins. She was going to be Her *slut*.

"Thank you Mistress," she whispered.

*

There was silence as She worked, slowly, hands roaming Lucy's restrained body, stroking, squeezing, caressing her thighs, ass, hips, lower back. Lucy shuddered under Her touch, her caged cock throbbing, leaking precum, biting her bottom lip in an attempt to remain quiet.

She slipped down Lucy's panties, tugged them off over her heels, then stuffed them into her mouth, packing them tight so that even her loudest moans were quiet whimpers. Lucy did not resist. The taste of her precum was salty on her tongue.

"Now, are you ready to become my pretty toy Lucy?" She asked.

Lucy nodded, strapped down, staring straight ahead, the audience hidden behind the bright lights. She did not know what her Mistress had in store for her, but she wanted so desperately to please Her.

She felt her Mistress move in between her legs, nudging them apart, her soft, smooth, stocking clad thighs parting, and then something cold and wet dribbled over her ass, her cheeks hot after her *punishment*, the slickness running down her crack. Warm fingers traced down, teasing at the entrance to her ass, just barely entering her.

Lucy moaned, the noise muffled by her panties, and she pressed back, the sensation new and wonderful. She wanted more, head fuzzy, giddy, so that she was almost drunk on pleasure.

"You want to be my girl Lucy? My slut? My pretty doll? My property?" She asked.

Lucy moaned, a desperate *yes,* that was muffled. The fingers slipped away and something hard and thick ran down her crack, slippery, pausing at her asshole. Lucy's eyes went wide. It was a cock, a strap-on. Her Mistress was going to *fuck* her.

Lucky smiled. She wanted it, needed it. Lucy pressed back as She pressed forward and the thick head of Her cock stretched her, pressure building, forcing her open, claiming her ass for the *first time.* Lucy moaned, pleasure and pain and need, and then, wonderfully, suddenly, the cock slipped deep, filling her ass, fucking her.

Her hands roamed over Lucy's ass, squeezing, then roamed up to her hips, gripping her. She pulled back, slipping her cock out, tugging at Lucy's entrance, her body shuddering in pleasure, so sexy and feminine, Her toy, Her doll, Her pretty girl all pink and pretty.

Lucky whined, desperate to be filled again, then gasped in muffled delight as She fucked Her cock deep, hard, thrusting her hips forward to fuck Lucy's ass. Lucy gasped, and spread her legs, curving her back, lifting her ass, offering it, eager for *more.*

As She pulled back, thrust forward, fucking Her doll, Lucy worked her hips, chasing the joy that was fluttering in her belly, her caged cock throbbing, leaking. She was lost, and she submitted utterly to her Mistress as She claimed her body and soul.

"You like that Lucy? Like being my pretty fuck toy?" She asked.

Lucy nodded, eyes glazed, expression a mask of pleasure, whimpering quietly, teeth biting down on the gag of her panties. Lucy worked her hips, thrust back, fucking back as her Mistress fucked her.

"Lights please," She said.

The lights dimmed, suddenly, and with the dazzle gone the audience was suddenly visible, the dozens of faces staring up, watching Lucy get fucked in her ass by Her, a pretty toy dressed in hot pink lingerie and heels, collared, caged. There was a swell of shame, humiliation, embarrassment, but it only fed her pleasure, her joy, the bliss of being fucked, *owned*. The fluttering in her belly grew bright, intense, the sensation of Her cock fucking in and out of her tight hole, being Her *slut*.

Lucy moaned, loud, only the gag of her panties keeping her from screaming. She was being watched, by dozens of people, their eyes on her as she was taken, fucked, dressed so pretty and cute. The thought thrilled her, burning hot, bright, and her caged cock throbbed hard. Lucy thrust back, riding Her cock, and then, suddenly, without warning, she came, cumming hard as She thrust Her cock deep into her ass, claiming her as Her doll, Her property, Her pretty toy. Lucy shuddered, her cock drooling a trickle of cum as her whole body was wracked with a climax more intense than any she had ever known.

"Cumming already? You are a filthy slut," She said.

Lucy whimpered, too blissed out to speak, gagged by her panties. She squirmed, still full of Her cock, wiggling her hips, savouring the sensation of being *full*.

A hand roamed over her back, stroking gently, squeezing her ass, hard, her cheeks still sore after her *punishment*. Lucy moaned, pressed back into her Mistress, relishing Her touch.

"You did well though, and you pleased me, performing like such a *good girl.*"

Those words, *good girl*, made Lucy blush. She looked out at the gathered audience. They had all watched as she had submitted, been *punished*, been *fucked* in her ass for the first time, and she had *loved* it.

"However, you came without permission," She said. "So I suppose … I'll have to arrange another *punishment* for you."

Her hand swatted Lucy's ass gently, making her yelp. Another *punishment.* The thought made her tingle and ache, a craving she had not known before.

Lucy moaned as She leaned over, Her lips close to her ear, Her body pressing into her back. She reached out and pulled the panties out of Lucy's mouth.

"But for now … let's get you cleaned up. You did just perfectly. And I can't wait to introduce you to people properly, now they've seen what a good *slut* my *special girl* is."

Lucy smiled, basking in the glow of her climax and her Mistress's praise.

"Thank you, Mistress," she whispered.

She was already looking forward to their next *performance* together.

About the Author:

Keary is a young writer from London, England who enjoys cooking, music, and long walks with her dog. Having spent her formative years lost in books and comics, she learnt to escape from dreary reality by taking flight into lands of fantasy.

Experiencing her first tinglings of kink while watching cartoon heroes and heroines being tied up by the villains, she has always found power play interesting.

Fascinated by the many and varied forms of love and sex, and infatuated by themes of Domination, transformation, feminization, cross-dressing, sissification, and submission, Keary set out to share her fantasies through erotica.

Keary believes that the route to happiness and joy lies in accepting yourself and your nature.

Keary can be found rambling about current works and other nonsense under @Keary_Writes on both twitter and instagram. If you enjoyed this story, you may also enjoy her novellas and short stories, all currently available on Amazon!

Three Layers Removed

by LN Bey

"You're late," I distinctly heard, through the wall, through the fog of a dream (something about endless cubicles in some vast office somewhere) and I was instantly awake. My heart was already pounding, in fact.

They were at it again. It had been a while.

"*Very* late."

I heard the rounded, muffled syllables of his reply, which might have been: "I'm so sorry, Mistress." He was farther from our mutual wall than she was, and harder to understand.

"Approach."

Pause.

"On your knees."

Yessss. They *were* at it again.

The walls in this apartment building – in the entire complex – have always been thin. I lived in another, larger apartment here for two years, and always heard the couple next door arguing, and maybe half-heartedly fucking. You learn to tune it out. But now, in my downsized studio, I occasionally hear … this. And I have waited weeks for it.

There is no schedule to their meetings, that I can discern. If there is one, it is far too complex to understand, and whether it is he who initiates their sessions or she who summons him, I have no idea. But I do know it's been longer than usual.

"Undress," she said. "Remove all layers."

I see my neighbor, Sonya, around – in the parking lot, the hallway, at the mailboxes. She always gives me a nice little smile, a nod, maybe a "hi," and I do the same back to her. She *has* to know I hear these meetings, just as she's surely heard me and the few hookups I've brought in; just straight sex, maybe, but a few of the girls were fairly loud. Does she care? Does she *like* knowing that I know? I've heard her having regular sex a few times, too, though not with this guy – but I usually drift back to sleep, those nights. It's just not the same.

Sonya is attractive, though not a staggering porn-star beauty. She has beautiful dark brown hair; she maybe carries a few extra pounds. She wears casual business; I've gathered she works up on campus, in some office but not especially high in the hierarchy. She looks good, and always seems very nice.

But that's the thing – meeting her in the hall, commenting on the weather – you don't get this sense of … *authority*, that I hear every few weeks or so. When I hear these two, when I picture her in nothing but a leather corset and knee-high boots – and there has been audio evidence to suggest that she sometimes wears nothing but a leather corset and knee-high boots – Christ, is she hot. I mean, at least from over here, on this side of the thin, uninsulated drywall.

"Crawl," she said. "Elbows and knees. Keep your ass higher than your face, as is proper. You will then lick my boots."

Sonya has a generic Midwestern accent (I think she's from Iowa?) but on these nights she adopts an almost Germanic crispness and formality, and I swear her voice drops an octave.

Lying on my back, I realized my cock was hard as steel, its tip extending my boxers up like a ridiculous tent pole. I admitted defeat and slid them off – *my* only layer.

"Cleaner! You think you're finished? Did I give you permission to stop? I should make you lick the soles. Maybe I'll take a walk around the parking lot first. Would you like that? Waiting here with your ass in the air while I say 'hi' to the neighbors, dressed like this?"

Oh, Jesus.

"I said, would you like that."

"No, Mistress" – now I can understand him; he's closer to my wall – "I'm sorry. Please, let me continue."

"On your back. You're going to suck my heel like it's a cock."

I heard, or rather felt, the clunking of him changing positions.

"Faster. *Suck* it. Head up and down. Maybe I'll get you a real cock to suck. I have a cute neighbor. Maybe I'll knock on his door and ask him over. And there you'll be, kneeling naked, ready to take him in deep without a moment's hesitation."

You know those weird goosebumps when you realize you're being talked about? I froze, as if she knew I was listening.

There were several things to process all at once: she's noticed me, and thinks I'm cute; she's at least theoretically considered bringing me into this alternate world of theirs. Or, this might be total bullshit for his benefit and I don't matter one bit.

And – importantly – would I do it? I listened for stilettoed footsteps heading toward her door. Nothing.

What *would* I do? My blood was absolutely on fire, electric, at the thought of her approaching me. But I've never wanted a guy sucking my dick. And I've definitely never wanted to suck another's. Nnnnnope. From the safety of my room, I'd never really thought this through. Just listened with my heart in my throat. And jerked off.

Speaking of which: I grabbed my hard cock and squeezed, tight, then let it go. I didn't want to rush this. I ran my fingertips over my balls, a tingling teasing, and up the shaft. I left it, for now. I rolled over onto my stomach, and as carefully and quietly as I could, got up onto my hands and knees and slowly, gingerly, pressed my head, my ear, against the wall.

"Go fetch the cuffs, all four, and the whip, and the collar with the short chain attached."

"Mistress, I've brought my own collar?"

"I don't care what you brought. I have not heard from you even *once* in a very long time now. Until you earn it again, you will wear the collar everyone else wears."

Of course, I knew that there was no "everyone else." Did he? Did it matter?

"Crawl!" A solid smack, on the ass from the sound of it.

I heard a rumble of knees on hardwood and then the high rattle of loose buckles. I reached down and teased my cock again, trying not to make the bed move.

"On your stomach. Hands behind your back, as high up as you can reach. You'll be bound *tight*, tonight."

There was grunting, and buckles, and finally a pained groan.

"Mistress! Please!"

"Shut up. Is this too tight? Are they too far up your back?"

"Yes, Mistress. Please. I … I can't breathe."

"You get *one link*. I'll lower them one link. I'd *like* to dislocate them, but I won't. There. Better?"

"Yes, Mistress. Thank you."

"Do they still hurt?"

"Yes."

"Can you take it? Or do I need to lower them again?"

"I can take it. Thank you, Mistress."

More buckles – the ankle cuffs?

"Up on your knees."

I squeezed my cock; felt its heat, its pulse.

"Stop hiding it. Spread your knees, hips forward. Just because you won't get to use that thing on me, doesn't mean I don't want it on full display." This was what they did; sometimes he got to jack off at the end of the night, sometimes not. (Meanwhile, I always did.)

I heard the clicks of her heels on the floor, pacing. I wondered what the people downstairs from her thought.

"I see we've made a change," she said.

I listened more closely. I heard no response.

"What shall we play tonight?" she finally said, in a new tone.

"Mistress, I've been thinking about … schoolboy?"

More pacing.

"No. I am tired of … of pretending to punish you for things you're only pretending that you did."

"You could punish me for something I really did?"

"Did I say you could speak?"

"No, Mistress. Apologies."

This guy. If my drinking buddies from the office could hear this. But then, if they knew I was leaning against the wall naked, trying to refrain from jerking off …

"We are going to play …"

The heels moved slowly – I think she was walking around him in a slow circle.

"… interrogation."

"Mistress?"

"You will not call me Mistress. You will call me … Sir. Or Commander."

"Yes, Mis – Sir."

"Hm. I kind of like that. Maybe I'll get the strap-on, then you *will* call me Sir."

"Yes, Sir."

"You're going to talk, prisoner. You're going to tell me everything I want to know. Have you ever fantasized about being captured and bound, and *forced* to talk?"

No response.

"I said –"

"Yes, Mis – yes, Commander."

"Good. Because I've always fantasized about having someone under my *complete* control, and doing whatever I wish until they tell me what I want. Are you ready for that?"

"Yes, Commander!" This was always fascinating, the setting up of their games. I tried to picture them in a prison cell somewhere, like they were imagining.

"Maybe you've been shot down over enemy lines. Maybe I'm the Viet Cong or the Japanese. Maybe we're spies, in Berlin, or Moscow. In any case, you're a long, long way from home, and you're *aaaall* alone. No one can help you. And there are things I want to know."

Now I stroked my cock, yes. As far as I knew – they never talked about it – this was not a paying relationship. They did this for pure fun.

"Yes, Commander."

"Shut up, worm."

At first, months ago, some of the names she called him kind of repulsed me. It seemed kind of … *rude*. I guess I got over it?

"Of course," she said, "the problem is, it is well known that people will say whatever they think their captor wants to hear, under severe enough torture. But what is it you think I want to hear?"

"I … I don't know, Commander."

"Oh, is that right?" she said, more quietly, and I pressed my head against the wall as tight as I could, hoping that some apartment's toilet didn't flush or someone's air conditioner didn't kick in.

"I think you do."

It's the anticipation, from my room, you see. Getting the gist of their routine, but never knowing exactly what they're going to *do*, next.

Although it always involves: "Ass up. Face to the floor. As if you have a choice, bound like that."

Heels clicked rapidly. Around behind him?

"We're going to warm you up for your questioning. Don't bother to thank me for each one, there won't be time. Besides. You're not my slave tonight, you're my prisoner." There was a pause.

"Brace yourself."

What followed was a shockingly loud and fast whipping. She must have been swinging it back and forth, backhand, forehand, over and over, ten, fifteen, twenty strokes; I lost count but it was intense and forceful.

He groaned at first but began crying out, "Ah!" "*Ah*-huh…" He finally shouted, "*Oh!* Mistress," far too loud in such a paper-thin building.

"What did you call me?" She hit him again, twice, and he actually started whimpering.

"Commander! Please! I …"

I wondered about their safewords. I always had. I'd never heard him utter any odd phrases that brought the action to a halt; sometimes "please" worked, sometimes it didn't. I'm not especially knowledgeable about these things; I sometimes watch some kinky porn and pick up discussions online, usually after listening to these two the night before.

"Shut up. Shut *up*, slug. Don't like it, don't come back – oh wait, you haven't in a while now, have you?" I heard her grunt, along with him, like she was pulling him up by his collar onto his knees.

"Kneel up *straight*!"

They both regrouped a moment; I did not. I was pure anxiousness, my body sizzling. *I* kneeled up straight.

"Tell me what I want to know."

"David Patterson, Sergeant, serial number seven, eight, oh, seven –"

I heard a slap against skin. His face? That has never struck me as sexy, even in videos. So why was my cock even harder, in my hand?

"Talk."

"Sergeant David –"

"No!" Another slap. Then the snap of leather against flesh. I still had to smile a bit; he'd watched enough old war movies to know the "name, rank, and serial number" routine.

"Talk, asshole. Tell me." I heard a much louder stroke of the whip. He groaned.

"The, uh … the battalion is in the forest, by the river, ready to cross the –"

"No!" *Crack!*

God *damn,* that one must have hurt. How would I do, at this? Not a real interrogation, but just this game? It sounds like it *hurts.* It's fun to watch in videos, but Jesus … Yet here I was, doing my best not to whack off to real people doing it.

But I wasn't succeeding; I couldn't stop. I could feel that first inkling of orgasm, deep in my balls, behind my balls. I forced myself to put both hands on the bed, cock throbbing with every heartbeat.

"The other spies are … my contacts are all hiding in the cabaret, on the Street-a-strasse, behind the trap door under the bar. They're all there, Pierre, Jean-Paul …"

Crack!

"Oh, god. Mistress. Commander, please."

But she didn't stop: *crack!*

"Do you really not know what I want to hear?"

"N-no, Commander. Please. A hint, a sign. I'll talk, I swear Commander, I'm ready to talk."

"Stand up."

There was shuffling, struggling. I heard the clinking of whatever clips or links held his ankle cuffs together, the thudding of bare feet. He cried out in pain again, a sad moan.

"Got you by the short hairs, don't I boy. Helping you up. *By the short hairs.*"

He was groaning, panting. She was silent.

"Still don't get it? Turn around, keep your balance. This is going to hurt."

Another series of fast, hard strokes as he cried out. I had to admit, this was making me a little uneasy. He didn't seem to be having fun – wasn't this supposed to be fun? But I also had to admit: I was riveted. *Riveted.* I wasn't going to move my ear from this wall if she started pounding on it.

"You like that? Now face me. I know you like your entire front whipped." Okay, so he *was* still into this; it was just more intense than anything I'd ever heard them do.

I grabbed my cock again. People *do* this, I thought. For real, not just in their heads or for viewers online. I shifted my weight so that I could keep my head against the wall and stroke my cock *and* my balls, both hands busy, balanced on my knees on the bed.

He began whimpering from the repeated blows.

"Short … *hairs* … David," between the harsh strokes.

Was she pulling on them? I tried to picture one of her hands yanking them upward, the other flailing away. I ran my fingers through my own pubic hair, made a fist, and pulled as I jacked my cock with my other. Pulled 'til it hurt. Plus a whipping? That would be too much!

"Red, Mistress, red!"

So there *was* a safeword. The whipping stopped.

He sounded nearly in tears. "Mistress. I have not shaved it in weeks because I took on a lover."

Took on a lover, I thought. Such antiquated, formal language, another layer removed from reality. That's what these two did: their speech was never quite real, along with their actions. Although he was gonna feel those welts for a while – *that* was real enough.

"That's better, asshole. Tell me. Tell me about her. Tell me why you never even called. It's been *six weeks*, slimeball."

"It … didn't work out."

"So now you're crawling back to me. Without *once calling me*."

"No. Yes! I mean … She's … she was … not into this. This. She's …"

"Normal?"

"No. Well, yes. I'm sorry, Sonya. She … wouldn't have approved of any of this, even a shaved cock."

"That's ridiculous."

"You and I would think so, but we forget. Out there … some people don't even watch porn. Or read it."

"You hooked up with a girl who won't even watch porn."

"Y-yes."

"And what attracted you of all people to such a nice, wholesome girl?"

Suddenly, something felt different. This was all fascinating, but wasn't especially … arousing. This was the couple next door having a fight. It's the kind of thing you listen to the first time or two, then it gets boring, irritating, even. My cock was still hard, but less so; I was squeezing it to maintain it until, I hoped, something more interesting happened.

"She *is* … nice. But she didn't meet my needs. I couldn't tell her anything. I couldn't take it, Sonya. Mistress. I called you. I've left her."

"You're not cheating on her, and me, lying to us both? That would piss me off even more than ignoring me for six weeks."

"No! No, Mistress. I made a mistake. I am yours. If you'll accept me." There was that formality again. "Please."

Then those stiletto heels, clicking around the room. I heard a chair being pulled across the hardwood floor.

"On your knees."

That's better.

"You know what to do."

I had the feeling I knew what they were doing, but there was still the frustration of guessing, which was always part of this thrill. I assumed he was going down on her, she seated on the edge of the chair, legs spread, he kneeling before her, naked and whipped and painfully bound. I started jacking furiously; I couldn't help it.

"*Deeper*, bitch," she said. "You are a slovenly slave. By now you should know every *nuance* of when I want you to go deep, when I want you to return to my clit. Have I trained you that badly? Is this my fault?"

"Mmph!"

Bingo! God damn. I imagined him kneeling humbled at her feet, licking her pussy, doing everything he could do to please her. Cock throbbing helplessly in the air. I imagined myself in his place, so completely different from anything I've experienced.

"Don't even think you're going to get to come tonight. I will until I'm exhausted, you will wait until tomorrow. *If* you're lucky."

A helpless moan, nearly a whimper. Then a groan from her – not her high-pitched straight-sex pant that never interests me so much, but a deep, guttural *grunt*. Was she grabbing his hair, pulling him into her?

Sweet Jesus. I tried to back off. Wrists chained high up the back to the collar, too tight to be comfortable. Knees on hardwood, entire body stinging, and all your attention on *her.* Pleasing her, making it up to her, doing whatever she said. I let go of my cock, I was *right* on that edge. I could feel the muscles behind the balls contract, ready to spill, ready to shoot. But I stopped, enjoying that tension but not wanting to come – at least until she did.

"What shall we play next time, slave?" she said. "*If* I let you come back."

I grabbed my cock again and began thrusting my hips while I tried to hold my head still so it wouldn't slide against the wall (or did I care, at this point; *want* her to hear?).

"I know … I'm going to try you as a witch. Yes. Our own little Inquisition. Not a warlock, mind you, but a witch, a little slut witch. Oh, you'll confess to me. You'll confess *all* your sins. Sins! My little witch bitch. I'll strap on the cock, then you'll call me 'Father,' yes …"

Good God. I was going to come, soon, even though she was pushing hers back, making him work. The closer I got, the more I wondered if it would be possible to make my interest known to her. Make a noise against the wall, give her a little bow at the mailboxes, outright tell her I listen; offer myself.

The thought set me on fire, but the more I pictured it, the more the actuality of it crept in. (Why was my brain deciding to be practical *now*?) How awkward would life be if she said no? Or worse, if she said yes and then it didn't work out? Then what? *Ugh.* I tried to put that thought – of reality? – out of my head.

"Or maybe I'll sell you, auction you off to the girls from the office. Would you like that, slave?"

"Mm-mmph!" He sounded desperate, both appalled and eager.

"There, *slave*." Yes. Back to their game; my brain reignited. When that first little moment of reality had intruded, earlier, when they'd used real names, talked about their outside lives, their relationship ... I'd kinda lost it. Kind of lost interest – like just now, picturing an awkward morning-after reality involving *me*.

But now that they're at it again, full swing ... *yes!* I pressed my ear tighter against the wall as I stroked.

"Not that you're ready. You need *all* new training in how to eat pussy. You're clearly out of practice – didn't that vanilla girl let you go down on her?"

Okay, wait, wait, the real world again. This time he made no sound, desperate or otherwise. Was he just embarrassed, not in a fun way?

And it occurred to me, even though I don't want this distraction right now: their night was almost ruined by reality, too. It had poked a hole in *their* fantasy.

"How could I possibly hold an *auction* after work some Friday night, all the girls here in our office clothes; you serving us naked, then standing there exposed, at attention, while I take bids? Hmm?"

Now he whimpered again.

"Not without a *very* rigorous training first. Very thorough, very strict. Very painful ..."

They've *always* played these games, always. Prisoner and guard, stern teacher and recalcitrant student, captured spy. Owner and slave. The beatings are real, of course, but they've never been the end in themselves, just the result of their imagined situations. *That's* what gets them off.

"Oh yes. I'd sell your ass. Literally."

They stay one step removed from reality, from their boring daily lives (as well as from whatever it is they're imagining, because nobody wants to be a *real* prisoner).

They stay a layer removed, in their intense little world.

But wait – look at me, here, on the other side of this wall, getting off on *that*. I am listening, and stroking (stroking *so* hard), to people acting out their fantasies – while having my own, *about them*. I am fantasizing about their fantasies.

I am two layers removed!

But you know what? I don't care. Because I am absolutely on fire, every inch of me. I have been since the moment her voice woke me up, just like I will be next time. I gotta get *off*, right now, and hearing the two of them does this to me every time.

And then what about you?

There you are, in bed, or at your desk, or at the beach or on the bus or subway, reading this story printed on paper or on some digital screen.

Is this your kink, too, eavesdropping? Placing yourself in the fantasy? It must be, if you've stuck with me this far.

Which means you, my friend, are *three* layers removed.

Do you care?

I do not. Not enough to think any more about it, anyway, because I am getting close, very close.

Just listen to them: Sonya – Mistress – is moaning that low moan that means she's on the edge, and poor David, in pain and kneeling down, is finally remembering exactly how she likes it and he's building her up to a good one, one that will drive him, and me, and you, insane.

She's planning on selling him, auctioning him! To people who might see him around town, later. *Think* of that. Do you think she will, really? What will those friends of hers do to him, if they go through with it? Will I be here to hear it?

Will you be here to read it?

Oh, God – she is about to have an intense one, and she told him she'd have more, all night, all damn night. I don't know about you, but I will too, my ear against the wall, coming on the sheets because I'm not moving.

And I am so close. *So ... close.*

About the Author:

LN Bey is the author of the erotic novel *Blue* and the almost-a-novel collection of erotic stories *Villa*, if it ever, ever gets finished. LN's short stories have been published in *No Safewords 2*, *Erotic Teasers*, *Best Bondage Erotica 2015*, and other anthologies. LN's reviews and essays on BDSM can also be found at www.lnbey.com.

Endless Pleasures

by E.M. Scarlett

Natalie stood over her slave, saying nothing and allowing her disapproval to wrap around him until it could be all that he was aware of. The only sounds in the room were Adam's ragged breathing and the sound of her leather crop hitting gently against the side of her knee-high black leather boots in a hypnotically rhythmic fashion. When the naked man on his knees before her began to shift awkwardly, no doubt in an effort to get more comfortable as she made him wait it out, she tightened her grip on the handle of the crop but made no move to strike him with it. Yet.

Just as it looked like he could no longer fight the need to say something, she finally spoke.

"Did I give you permission to touch yourself, Adam?" she demanded.

"N-no, Mistress. I'm sorry. I just …"

The sound of the crop whistling through the air cut off his words just a moment before it landed hard against his thigh. Adam's cry of surprise brought a slight grin to her face, although she was not happy to have to punish him. In fact, it was so rarely ever needed because he usually obeyed all of the rules that she laid out for him. But Natalie could not overlook these times where he made a mistake and broke one of his rules. Adam belonged to her and had willingly handed over full control to her, and now it was her duty to make sure that he honoured that agreement. She had been beyond disappointed when she'd arrived home early from a meeting and found him with his hard and leaking cock in his hand, and she would make sure that he understood it was completely unacceptable.

"That is enough!" she said firmly. "I did not ask you for an explanation, pet. Just a yes or a no will suffice. And we both already know that you did not have permission to touch yourself."

Adam knew better than to respond this time. Nothing more than a whimper escaped his lips as he lowered his head.

She crouched down in front of him, bringing her face almost to his eye level as she spoke again.

"Who does this belong to, Adam?" she asked in a softer voice. Reaching out with her free hand, her fingers touched gently at his cock to indicate what she was referring to with her question. It twitched slightly at the touch, eager for her attention.

"It belongs to you, Mistress. It is your property."

"That's right, baby." she smiled. "It is my property and you are not allowed to touch what is mine without permission, are you?"

"No, Mistress. I am so sorry." he whispered.

Natalie watched as his face flushed crimson, knowing that her slave meant every word of his apology. He was usually such a good boy and she had no doubt that the shame he felt about his disobedience could possibly be punishment enough all on its own.

"I know you are, baby, and I accept your apology. But we need to find a way to make sure that something like this never happens again. Do you have any ideas how we might be able to do that, Adam?" She flashed him a beguiling smile as a look of panic washed over his features.

"No, Mistress," he answered, a little too quickly to fool her.

Natalie laughed softly at his attempt to bluff his way out of the punishment that he must have known was coming his way. She stood once more and, with a swift underhand motion, the crop flicked up hard against his semi-erect cock.

Natalie patiently waited a few moments for his groans of pain to subside before speaking again. "Now now, pet. Don't disappoint me. I know you are smarter than that so I will allow you one more chance to answer my question."

She stood over her slave, watching the turmoil play over his face, and she gripped the handle of the crop a little tighter in case she should need it again. But it seemed she would have no need for it this time.

"Maybe a … a cock cage?" he stuttered, his voice barely above a whisper.

A wide smile spread across her face at his almost inaudible words. "Oh my!" she exclaimed; her voice full of enthusiasm. "Why didn't I think of that? What a smart boy you are for thinking of such an effective solution to our little problem."

Adam opened his mouth as if to say something but decided against it and simply let out a groan before pressing his lips together again. Of course he would know that she'd pushed him into giving the exact answer she had been looking for, but she didn't care. The mind games were her favourite part of being his Mistress.

"Now wait here, baby. I just happen to have something that will be perfect for you." She smiled down at him before turning towards the wooden chest at the end of her bed that she kept filled with all kinds of toys and implements. She carefully picked out the items she would be needing and placed them on the floor in front of her slave – a steel chastity cage and a small padlock. Once the items had all been laid out, she lowered herself to perch on the edge of the large wooden chest.

Natalie grinned wide as she watched him squirm at the sight of the implements laid out in front of him, his blue eyes wide and his face pale except for his flushed cheeks.

"Is there something wrong, my sweet pet?" she asked, her tone playful and mischievous.

Adam took a moment to clear his throat before speaking. "No, Mistress. I just didn't know you already had a cage. It is a surprise."

She smiled down at him, enjoying his look of shock. "I love the thought of keeping you locked in chastity, knowing that I would have full control of your cock. And I crave total control, pet. I know I already have control over your orgasms, but now I want to take it even further. I don't want you to even be able to get hard without my permission. The cage arrived only this morning, so your little indiscretion earlier was timed perfectly."

He kept his eyes lowered; his rapturous gaze trapped by the sight of the cock cage. His only response to her words were a loud whimper and an eager twitch of his cock. Natalie chuckled and rolled her eyes a little. If he got any more excited, it would become almost impossible for the chastity device to be put on.

"Yes, Mistress," he moaned. His squirming had become much more pronounced now and his cock was almost half-hard.

"Good boy. Now put the cage on for me."

Natalie watched as he reached out nervously to pick up the cage, the device looking small in his large hands as he turned it over to inspect it from every angle. He looked up at her several times as he pulled the ring over his cock and testicles and as he struggled to slide the cage over his cock, as if looking to her for guidance, but she didn't offer any. It was only once the padlock had been clicked into place that she told him what a good boy he was and leaned down to tug gently on the device, making sure it was secure enough that it wouldn't slip off.

As her fingers played over the cage, a heat began to grow at her core. The feeling of power she had over her slave now that she had his cock locked away and entirely under her control caused droplets of arousal to seep into her lace panties. She couldn't seem to pull her hand away from him, somehow entranced by the steel wrapped so snugly around him. How amusing that she got more turned on by his cock now that he couldn't do anything with it than she had ever been before.

"That's perfect, baby. Just the right size for you. Now I know that you won't be able to touch what is mine."

His hips rolled eagerly, causing him to hump against her hand, and Natalie could already see that his cock was swelling within the steel bars of the cage.

"How long will I have to wear it, Mistress?"

"Until I decide that it is time to take it off, Adam. And who knows how long that might be. You need to be taught that I will not accept any deviance at all from the rules I lay out for you."

The needy little whimper that emerged from his lips sounded pathetic and it only added to the heat building within her. She was breathless with desire at the new level of control that she had, and she couldn't imagine wanting to allow him freedom from chastity any time soon. Natalie gave another tug on the cage, a harder one that forced a soft grunt from Adam's lips. When the cage still didn't budge, she gave him a satisfied smile and finally released her hold of his caged cock.

"But how will I please you if I am caged, Mistress? I can't be a good slave to you if I am not able to please you," he whimpered.

Natalie let out a soft laugh at the weakness of his argument. "Now, baby, you will be a good slave by obeying me, and that means wearing the cage. The knowledge that I have got your cock completely under my control pleases me greatly. If you are talking about pleasing me physically, then we both know there are plenty of other ways for you to bring me to orgasm. After all, how many times have I ever allowed you to actually fuck me anyway?"

She let the question hang in the air and his face burned a bright crimson as he thought about the answer. It would be a miracle if he could remember even a handful of times that she had allowed him to be inside her.

"Only a couple of times, Mistress," his voice was small, defeated, as he realised that he would not be able to talk his way out of this.

Natalie didn't bother to reply. She simply spread her legs as she sat on the wooden chest and pulled her short red skirt up so that he would be able to see the skimpy black lace thong she was wearing underneath. Immediately his attention was rapt on her and that spot between her thighs that he constantly craved. While Adam watched her, she traced a finger up and down along her wet slit, teasing herself until more of her wetness soaked into the flimsy material.

With her free hand, Natalie cupped the back of his head and pulled his face between her thighs, until the tip of his nose was almost pressed up against black lace. "Take a deep breath, pet. Smell how aroused I am at having my property under lock and key now."

He let out a loud moan as he inhaled her scent, his hips instantly starting to buck as his need left him humping his caged cock against nothing but air. His tongue darted out from between his parted lips as he attempted to taste her through her thong, but she pushed him back quickly before he could make contact.

"No, pet. Maybe I will let you have a taste later if you keep being a good boy for me. But right now, I want you to please me in another way."

She smiled down at him before standing up and lifting the lid of the wooden chest once more. It didn't take her long to find what she was looking for – a large, realistic looking rubber dildo attached to a harness. Holding it up to show him, she took a few moments to enjoy the obvious battle between panic and arousal that was being waged within him at the sight of the strap on. While she had been giving him some training with a butt plug which he'd been enjoying, she hadn't yet taken his anal virginity and the size of the dildo must have seemed intimidating to him.

Natalie chuckled softly and shook her head. "No, pet. I won't be fucking you tonight, although we both know that is in your future. Tonight, you will be the one wearing this."

The wide-eyed, open-mouthed look he gave her was almost comical and she grinned wickedly at him. "You will be able to fuck me so much better with this than with your actual cock, pet. It's much bigger than you, plus you will be able to keep going for as long as I desire. Just think of how many times you will be able to make me orgasm with this."

His face flushed even brighter with the humiliation of her words but, as she looked down, she could see how his swelling cock pressed against the bars of the cage in a way that must be uncomfortable, and a glistening drop of his desire leaked slowly from the tip of the cage to the floor beneath him.

"Yes, Mistress. I crave to pleasure you as any times as possible." he moaned.

"Good boy. Now stand up for me."

Adam quickly stood before his Mistress, his movements lacking any kind of grace as the humiliation and his need left him weak at the knees. Natalie held out the harness for him to step into and then pulled the straps to make it a tight fit around his waist. She took a step back and grinned wide as she admired the sight of him wearing the large strap on dildo.

"Please, Mistress. Please just let me fuck you with my real cock. I promise that I will please you." His voice was little more than a needy whine, and he shifted back and forth from one foot to another, obviously uncomfortable with this little turn of events.

"No, Adam," she responded firmly. "You were disobedient today and you do not deserve such an immense treat as being allowed to be inside me. Do you understand that, slave?"

"Yes, Mistress," he whimpered. "I'm so sorry."

Natalie gave a curt nod of her head then stepped closer to him once more, waiting until he lifted his eyes to her face before smiling at him. "Besides, look at how big this cock is compared to yours. Why would I want your cock inside me when I could have this?"

He only whimpered in reply, but then she hadn't expected an actual answer to her rhetorical question. Slowly she ran a fingertip along the length of the dildo, making his hips buck forwards as if it were his cock she had touched. She couldn't work out if the tortured groan that ripped from him was caused by the verbal teasing or this more physical teasing, but it made little difference either way.

"Go to the bed and lay on your back, pet. It's time for you to start showing me how sorry you really are for your indiscretion earlier today."

Adam moved quickly to obey, getting settled on his back on the bed with the large dildo jutting upwards from his body in a lewd way that had her aching to be filled with it. A small amount of silver could just be seen peeking out from beneath the harness, a reminder that his actual cock was now locked away safely and that he would receive no physical pleasure from this act at all. She quickly pushed her panties down over her hips, allowing them to fall to the floor before stepping out of them, eager to take her own pleasure from her pet.

Natalie kept her eyes on Adam's face as she crawled onto the bed and straddled his thighs. Slowly, she traced her fingers over her pussy lips, moaning at the sensation of touch against such needy flesh. When she pulled her fingers away from under her red skirt they were glistening with her need, and she couldn't help but notice Adam's instant look of craving as he saw her juices coating the fingertips.

She smiled and pressed the wet fingers into his mouth while positioning herself over the dildo, lining up the head of the toy cock with her slick entrance. His lips sealed around her fingers and he began to suck at the same moment that she slid down easily onto the dildo, filling herself with it. A loud moan escaped at the intense feeling of fullness and she allowed herself a moment to adjust to the size of it within her.

Adam continued to suckle greedily at her fingers, his tongue lapping at the digits within the warmth of his mouth. He had always been addicted to the taste of her sweet nectar and he was happy for any little taste she allowed him. She slowly dragged her fingers from his eager mouth.

"Just think, baby, if you had been an obedient slave, you could have spent your evening lapping between my thighs until I was completely satisfied. Your lips and chin could have been dripping with my pleasure and the taste of me would have been so intense on your tongue. But instead, you acted selfishly, and now I have to take my pleasure from you in another way entirely. One you won't enjoy at all."

She grinned down at him and placed both hands flat on his chest, keeping his back pressed into the mattress as she began to move her hips slowly. Closing her eyes, she savoured the feeling of the thick cock moving in and out of her, the veins on the realistic toy causing blissful sensations as they rubbed against her inner walls. Beneath her, she could hear Adam whimpering loudly and those needy little sounds fuelled her desire, but she kept her eyes closed, staying focused on taking what she needed.

Natalie moved her hips faster, growing breathless, slamming down harder and harder onto the dildo each time, forcing a soft grunt from her pet. Knowing that the base of the dildo was pressed against his caged cock didn't make her go easy on him. Her hips bucked wildly against his and her palms pressed down harder against his chest, fingers curling slightly until long fingernails were digging into his skin. Her moans flowed freely now, the heat in her core building more with each thrust of her hips and spreading out all over her body, consuming her in a fire of passion.

"Fuck me, pet," she moaned out. "Thrust up into me and make me cum."

Within seconds, Adam had his feet planted into the mattress and his hips were thrusting up hard, pushing the dildo hard and deep into her. A cacophony of moans and grunts filled the room as they fucked wildly, the headboard adding to the disjointed music as it banged repeatedly against the wall, marking the rhythm of their thrusts.

Keeping one hand on his chest while using the other to firmly grip his chin, she locked her hazel eyes on him, fighting back her pleasure a moment longer. "You are mine, pet. All fucking mine," she growled out through gritted teeth. "And I will have total control over you, even if it means never removing the cage. Am I understood, Adam?"

Her predatory possessiveness only seemed to excite him more as he began thrusting faster and deeper with each growled word from his owner. "Oh God. Yes, Mistress. Anything for you. I am all yours. I am your slave."

With his words ringing in her ears, Natalie allowed her orgasm to consume her. The overwhelming pleasure ripped loud, breathless moans from her lips and her body convulsed as she clenched hard around the dildo inside her. Adam's ragged moans mingled with hers as their bodies rocked in unison, and he continued his frenzied thrusting until her body shuddered one final time and she collapsed down on top of him, breathing hard.

"Thank you, Mistress, for allowing me to please you even after I had been so disobedient," he whimpered quietly.

She lifted her head from his chest and looked down at him, smiling. "This is what you exist for, baby. You exist only for my pleasure. And don't worry, I am nowhere near finished with you tonight. You are going to make me orgasm over and over. And soon you will come to realise that it is so much better wearing the strap on, because then you can fuck me as long and as hard as I need without things having to end. Because, let's be honest, we both know you can't last long enough to please me otherwise. But now, the pleasure that you are able to give me will be endless."

With a wicked grin, she began to rock her hips again, moving on the toy cock as she kept her sweat soaked breasts pressed against his chest, using the weight of her body to keep him pinned to the bed. And with each orgasm that Natalie took, Adam only begged to be allowed to please her more, forgetting about his cock locked away in its cage and focusing more and more on his place as a toy for her to use. Just as she had intended.

About the Author:

E.M. Scarlett is an author and poet who has only recently given in to her temptation to write smut. She lives on the south coast of England with her two children and, to the people around her, she appears to be an innocent and quiet woman. They have no idea that she is a switch writing kinky erotica based on both her personal experiences and her vivid imagination.

Harley's Peeping Punishment

by Ruan Willow

Kiara parks her car in the driveway once again. "Damn ex. Get your shit outta my garage. Fucker," she mutters as she drags herself out of the car. She slams the door and locks it.

She jumps back as a bush on the side of the house jiggles. The first step into the grass, her right heel sinks in too far so she just slips her foot out as she takes a step and flings the other one off.

As she creeps closer her heart pounds, her fingers clench. *Fuck. Someone is there.*

The grass is so cold, being October, making her stockinged feet feel more frigid with each step.

She approaches the shaking bush and freezes when she sees a tennis shoe sticking out. A man's grunt rips through the air.

"Who's there?" Kiara demands. Suddenly feeling confident, she marches over to see who is messing with her bush.

He peeks out. "Oh, Hi Mrs. Acker."

"Harley Jensen, what are you doing under my bush?"

"Oh, I promised Matt I'd help him out by taking this bush out for you. I had nothing to do today since my break has already started and Matt is overloaded with finishing up his paper, so I offered to help out."

"Oh, well that's nice of you. I can't wait to see him. Yeah. Bush's half dead and my ex never could bother himself to remove it the past five years. And now that he's gone, I want the bush gone too. So, thanks for helping."

"Could you … I mean, any chance you could help me for a minute? Hold the top of the trunk and push it while I saw?" His soft brown eyes twinkle as he smiles. He rubs a hand over his smooth brow before he smirks. "I could really use you for a minute."

"Sure, no problem." Kiara drops her purse and steps over Harley, straddling him so she can get a grip on the top of the bush.

He adjusts his body beneath her with a few groans and begins to saw the thick wood trunk of the bush.

The trunk begins to give as she pushes while he saws. She takes a step forward to push and he stops sawing so she glances down. She gasps, almost drops the bush. *OMG! I'm commando in a skirt ... standing over his face.* And his eyes are zeroed in on her bare pussy. She's too old to blush, but her cheeks heat anyway.

The bush trunk gives way and topples over landing on the ground with a thud. She scrambles away from Harley, his face fully flushed as he drops the saw, his tongue protrudes out of his lips.

"Um. Okay. Wow." She smooths her skirt, averting her eyes from his gaze as she suppresses a chuckle by covering it up with a cough. "Thank you for your help, Harley. You are a life saver. I'm sure Matt can finish."

Harley stares at her with his mouth agape. After a full thirty seconds of not moving, he sits up with a large grin on his face. "I've got it. I can finish."

"Ok. Great. Thanks." She turns and rushes to back to her heels, pulls the one from the dirt and slips them both on. *Concrete will surely put holes in my stockings.* She rushes inside before Harley even stands up.

Once inside, Kiara sets her petite work purse on the little stained glass topped table by her front door, dropping her keys into the maroon pottery bowl shaped like a football helmet. "I gave that boy quite an eyeful," she mutters. "Oops." She grins with a chuckle, raising both hands in the air.

She runs her finger along the edge of the ceramic dish, recalling the day Matt brought it home to her, almost dropping it as he had hurriedly slopped it out of his backpack one September day years ago. He had been eight and so proud of that lopsided helmet bowl.

She smiles as she slips off her heels, ignoring the dirt specks that fall and choosing instead to savor the soft rug with her feet, curling her toes into the lush mesh of the carpet strands.

Meowww ... Bander comes slinking up to rub against her leg as he purrs.

"Hi, Bander, baby," she says as she reaches down to rub her fingers behind his ears. "How was your day? Were you lonely?"

She drops her skirt, unbuttons her blouse, tosses it to her overstuffed white couch, new and pristine, a recent self-gift after the divorce was finally final. She swiftly unhooks her bra and flings it across the room. She shakes her hair out before heading for the kitchen strutting along in only her black thigh high nylon stockings.

"Finally, home, and all alone, so that means it's naked time. Air out my pussy, she's been stifled all day, Bander. It's a pure shame."

Open-air feel against pussy, mmmm … so refreshing, invigorating. She pours herself a glass of chilled Chardonnay from the fridge, the cool air hardening her nipples before she closes the door. As she takes her first sip, there's a clink at the window which causes her to jump and almost spill. She gasps.

Her hand flies up to her forehead. "Oh, damn. It's just that stinking tree. Matt needs to trim that tree too, Bander. It's driving me bat-shit-crazy to hear it all the time on the window, I keep thinking it's a burglar. The scud of living alone, Bander, shit like this. Maybe we need ourselves a dog. Huh? What do you think? Now that we have no men living here." She pets Bander as he strolls along the kitchen counter, slinking against her hand. "But you are a good man, Bander."

She sets down her glass of wine on the granite countertop and walks to the bathroom where she sets her lavender bath bomb ball on the edge of tub before turning on the water.

Clink. Clink.

Kiara freezes. *That's the same sound I heard in the kitchen. Fuck! Someone is out there!* Her breath catches in her esophagus and stays.

She picks up her hand mirror off the counter and swivels, as if she's admiring her own bare ass in the mirror when she first catches a glimpse of him. Her heart beats in her throat, tickling that spot she hates to touch with her toothbrush because it makes her gag. She examines what seems to be a face in her window.

Is he a murderer or just a peeping tom? Don't panic, Kiara.

She takes a step closer and notices a mop of dark brown curls that looks sort of familiar. The water streams into the tub in a hum as she pivots in front of the mirror. She runs her hand over her generous breast, cupping then pinching her nipple. She rides her hand down her taut tummy and slips her fingers under to finger her pussy. Moans slip out of her mouth as she thrusts her fingers in. She grins as the face in the window comes closer, his seemingly male eyes widening, jaw dropping, his face almost pressed against the glass, fingers of one hand actually touching the glass.

She spins to face him, looks directly into his eyes, and points. He jerks back and falls down. She runs to the window and hurls it open.

"Harley! Harley Jonathan! Is that you creeping as a peeping tom in my window?" Kiara screams out into the darkening black of the evening sky as her heart pounds.

"Harley! You answer me right now, little man! I see you!" she hollers into the air that is saturated with the sounds of horny frogs croaking.

"Y-yes, ma'am. It's me. Harley. And I'm not so little anymore. I'm twenty. Ma'am."

She smirks. "And I'm old enough to be your mother. Hell, your mother and I are about a year apart and you are peering at my naked booty through a window." She sighs. "And you've completely crushed my rose bush with your man-child buttocks."

"Oh, damn. I'm so sorry ... ma'am. I didn't mean to land on it. You ... you just surprised me."

Kiara giggles as she glances at his crotch. "I can see that. And. Well you certainly are outgrowing those pants at the moment."

He covers his crotch with his hand as he gazes at the woodchips at his feet. His jaw falls even further open. "I'll replace the bush. I promise. Just. Please don't tell Matt I did this ... please?" He stands up and brushes off his pants. "He will kick my ass."

Kiara laughs. "Yes. Yes, he will. Now get your ass in my house so you can view me in proper light. I'll pour you a glass of wine and we can chat."

She grins a naughty smile, *twisting him should be fun, I have about five different scenarios for how to proceed ... horny youngster.* She shuts and latches the window, then turns off the water and strolls to the sliding door of the deck where Harley is already standing, quivering, smiling, crotch set in a significant bulge. His eyes drop to her bouncing breasts and Kiara grins deeper. *This evening just got brighter.*

She unlocks the door and sweeps her arm towards the center of her house. "Be my guest," she says as she almost swats his man buns as he passes by her. She smirks. *Hmmmm. Let's save that for later.* "Want a glass of Chardonnay? There's about one glass left in the bottle. Or I think I have a beer or two in the fridge."

"Oh, I'd love a beer." He grins and his shoulders relax as his head cocks to the side, a grin spreading across his face.

"Oh, wait, crap, you are only twenty. I could get in trouble for feeding a minor alcohol." She bites down on her lips to keep from smiling.

"Oh," he says. His face falls and his shoulders sag. "I guess so."

"Ah, I'm only joking, honey. You are a man. Your almost twenty-one anyway, right? Matt just turned."

"I know. Went out with him. He got trashed." He grins but it disappears into an open mouth as Kiara frowns at him. "Oh. Oops. Guess a mom doesn't want to know that."

Kiara keep her laughter in her head, and a frown on her face as she hands Harley the beer.

"Thank you, kindly," he says with a nod.

Kiara purposefully stares at his boner pushing out the front of his jeans. "So, you like looking at my tits and ass, huh? Pussy?" She resists poking his cock and takes a sip of wine instead. "Love me a boner in some *man* jeans, though. Nice job." She winks at him as he blushes.

"Oh?" He grins and stands up a bit taller.

"Hell yes." She smiles at him. "You know, my divorce is final now. Kicked that neutered man to the curb. Loser would barely fuck me anymore."

Harley's mouth drops open. "What? No way … that's impossible."

She sighs. "Sadly, it's true. Maybe once a month, and that's if he didn't have damn whiskey dick killing his boner to a limp noodle."

"Damn. If I was married to you, I'd fuck you twice or three times a day." He takes a seat on the couch after she passes her arm over it.

His gaze drifts down from her eyes, to her very erect nipples, down her tummy to her shaved pussy mound.

She stifles a giggle as his eyes remain at her crotch. She pulls her leg up onto the couch bending it so he can see her dangly lady bits. His mouth falls open further as she swipes her finger across her clit. "Poor ignored baby she is. You wouldn't ignore her, would you?"

"Um. Hell no. Never. I'd lick her and suck her as much as you wanted." His eyes don't move from her hand as she plays with herself.

"Good." She sucks her lower lip into her mouth as his stare finally travels up to her face. "Drink up, babe. Cheers."

She holds up her wine glass to click his beer bottle and he takes a nice long chug. As he pulls the bottle from his full lips, his mouth spreads into a grin.

"You want to play a little naughty game with me, Harley?"

His eyes flare open. "Do I? Hell yes, I do." His jaw falls, his tongue rests on his lower lip as he takes in her full body.

"Good," she mutters. "Will you go over and stand facing that bookshelf while I go try on a new piece of lingerie? I want to know a man's opinion about it."

He takes another swig of beer before stumbling quickly to the bookshelf.

"Careful now, don't spill. And would you be a dear and strip your shirt off for me, just so we both have some skin showing. Makes us more even."

"Oh, sure, I will do that … Kiara. Anything for you."

Her eyes take in his boner, pressing at full hardness against his jeans as he removes his shirt.

"Mmm. I see that, Harley. Good boy. And yes, I've told you that you can call me Kiara."

She hurries to her room and pulls out her new mesh mini dress, pulling her nipples out to poke through the holes. She adjusts it over her hips and grabs her leather handcuffs from her bedside drawer.

She saunters back into the living room, slips on her work heels, flippantly eyeing the dirt specks and struts over to where Harley is pretending to read the book titles. "Can you be a hun and put your hands behind your back? I love to see man muscles when they are clenched up like that. So damn sexy."

"Oh, sure thing, Kiara." He brings his hands together behind his back and she takes the beer from his hand, places it on the coffee table.

"It also presses out your sexy chest. I love that." She snickers silently as he opens and closes his hands. She says, "I'm going to touch you, but don't worry, I won't hurt you." *Yet.*

He sighs and his head tips back a bit. "Oh, my Gawd. Kiara, I'd love that so much. You have no idea."

She gently grabs his wrists and gently slips the cuffs on, pressing them closed quickly to lock them.

He jerks his trapped arms up. "Wait, what? Oh, fuck. Oh, shit! Handcuffs?"

"Is that okay with you, Harley? I think it's *so* hot."

"Yes. I mean, I've never been handcuffed before, but, yes. it's okay." He drops his chin towards his chest.

She pushes his arm to pivot him to face her and they meet each other's gaze. "You like this outfit? I just bought it."

"I love it. Oh, fuck. That's the sexiest thing I've ever seen. That's amazing!"

"Aw. Thanks Harley. You really are the sweetest." She reaches around and smacks his ass. "Now lie down on the couch so I can show you my pussy up close. She wants to meet your mouth."

His jaw drops as he scrambles to lie on the couch.

"Now, you tell me if you are uncomfortable, alright, baby?" Kiara unzips his pants and runs her finger up the gap in the zipper, all the way to his tip, which has wet his brief boxers. "A little wet up here, huh?" She runs her finger over the wetness, then leans down and licks it.

"Oh, fuck, oh, gawd. Oh, fuck." He musters out between gasps. "You are my dream woman, Kiara. I've always thought so. Honest."

"Oh, I've caught you staring at me over the years, honey. But now, it's time to teach you a lesson about peeping toms."

"I'll be good. I promise. I'll do anything."

"Oh, I know you will, Harley. I'm going to make you." She pulls open a drawer next to the couch and digs until she finds her nipple clamps.

His eyes expand wide as she holds them to her nipples, but then shakes her head, grins, and secures them to his erect nipples. He jerks against them as she tightens them. She attaches the chain and gives it a jerk. He winces.

"Such nice big man nipples you have, Harley." She grins an evil seductive grin.

He gasps, cries out as she tugs it again harder.

"You shouldn't go peeping in windows." Her voice now stern. "If you want to date me, see my naked body, you should ask me out like a proper man." She yanks the chain again. "Got that?"

He lets out a whimper, nods, his eyes raging with both lust and fear. "Kiara ... I ..."

She pulls the chain again and he yells out.

"Oh, fuck me," he mutters as he squirms on the couch, hands beneath his ass.

186

She straddles his stomach, which causes her baby doll dress to creep up, so she lands open wet pussy on his belly. She rides his stomach up and down smearing her wetness across his abs.

"Yum. Your hard tummy feels good against my pussy."

He nods, his eyes fixated on her crotch grinding on him. She reaches back and slips his underwear off his cock.

He gasps. "Oh, hell yes."

She drags a finger up it to the top of his cock and presses her finger onto it. "No cumming for you, baby. Your punishment for window peeking without my permission." She lifts her legs to lay her heels at his throat then presses one to the tender hollow of it. "No cumming or I will spank your bottom with a large wooden paddle. Don't think I won't."

"Uh," he sputters, his mouth remains open as if he will say more.

Little boy eyes in a man's face look back at her as she nods. "Comprehend, Harley?"

"Y-yes, ma'am." His gaze flickers back and forth between fear and want.

She crawls up his chest, swivels placing her pussy right above his mouth. She lowers herself down and commands, "Lick me. Suck my clit. Do it."

She slams herself down, placing her vagina flush against his wide-open mouth. As he begins to lick her pussy lips in loud slurps and lip smacks, she leans down with a sigh and simply pokes at his cock with one finger. Then she smacks it. He recoils with a groan, pushing his ass into the softness of the couch, his knees rising.

"Spank you, naughty boy." She grinds her pelvis against his mouth and moans. "Yes, yes, Harley, just like that. Good boy." She presses her tits to his belly.

He groans as he licks and pulls both her labia lips into his mouth in turn, flicks his tongue along her clit.

"You can't use fingers, so you'd better get crazy and forceful with that tongue because you aren't stopping until you make me cum."

He shifts his head up and down along her pussy as he nods. She leans down as if to sixty-nine with him and his whole body tenses then jerks as he whimpers. She breathes on the head of his cock then takes it in her mouth as he groans out, muffled by her pussy covering his mouth. She sucks for five seconds then pops off his cock, then she reaches back to yank the nipple chain.

"Don't you dare cum," she commands as she pokes his cock with a knuckle. "Maybe I'll let you cum next time, if you ask me out properly and take me to dinner."

He nods aggressively underneath her.

"Good boy." She pokes at the base of his cock with her long maroon painted fingernails and runs her pinky nail along the curve of his ball sack. She sits up and grinds against herself against his face, moaning. "You like butt plugs, little boy? I've got one for you." She heckles as she rides his face. "I've got lots of toys for horny boys like you."

He mumbles against her pussy, his mouth full of her.

"I oughta spank you red for peeping at me like that. You do that before, Harley? Tell momma the truth." She lifts herself off of his face and hovers. "Well, have you?" She turns to face him and sits spread-eagle across his chest, pussy pushed flat against his slight bit of chest hair.

"Well. I … may have before yes." His lower lip quivers before he sucks it into his mouth.

She presses both her heels against his temples as she gropes her nipples and pinches them, hardening them to nugget peaks. "How much?" she asks as she pulls on her nipples. "Don't lie. I'm a mom. I'll be able to tell by your eyes."

He swallows and shifts his chocolate brown eyes back and forth before he whispers, "Um. A lot."

"Alright." She hops off of him. "Flip your ass up. Head in the crack of the couch. *Now.* It's spanking and latex time."

He scrambles to obey, positioning himself as she said.

She pulls his jeans down exposing his ass and gives him three hard smacks. "Wait here. Don't move. Don't cum. I'm going to spank you and send you home. But first I'm going to put latex on and let you see me before I redden your boy-man bottom."

Kiara chuckles heartily as she skitters off to her room. As she wiggles into her black latex bodysuit, she stops before pulling it up to insert her bullet vibrator with a tail into her pussy, since Harley didn't make her cum. She pushes the little button and a very low hum strums as she feels it nestle and rub against her G-spot. She fits the little tail over her clit and grabs her paddle from the closet. She fingers the words "Kiara's paddle" burned into the vastness of the bigger portion as she approaches Harley. "Thanks to my ex, I have a perfect paddle to handle your big man butt. You ever been spanked, Harley?"

"No, ma'am." His voices quivers and Kiara wavers. "But I want you to do it." He nestles his face into the couch.

"Look at me, Harley." She spins for his gaze. "Have you seen me wear this before?"

"No."

"Okay, I believe you." She rotates her index finger. "Now head down, ass up."

He settles into position, his handcuffed hands the peak of him atop his ass.

Kiara grips his cuffed wrists with one hand for leverage and raises the paddle high in the air. She sails it downward and smacks his right butt cheek.

He yells out. Then mutters, "Holy fuck."

She raises it again and brings it down hard on his left butt cheek. She reaches under him from behind and strokes his cock. "There there. I'll make it better, baby. We'll save the plug for next time."

He moans as she strokes his cock for about twenty seconds. Then she hauls the paddle into the air and lands several spanks in a row across both butt cheeks, making sure she strikes over his hole. She presses her finger against his puckered anus and he shudders. She giggles and pushes her finger hard against it, but not in. She squats down behind him, reaches up to give him a single cock stroke.

She removes his pants from his ankles then stands and unlocks the handcuffs.

When he stands and faces her, his eyes are filled with so much lust.

Maybe he will push me on the couch and fuck me. I could use a decent cock in me. It's been way too long.

"You are so sexy and amazing. I deserved that." His cock sways as she pushes him towards the front door. "You are a goddess."

"Out," she commands. "Think about your behavior." The toy inside her makes her almost double over. She suppresses a moan.

"Out there? Naked?" he asks with a look of horror as he covers his dripping, engorged cock with his hands.

"The night air and the walk home will do you some good." She hurls his balled-up clothes out the door. They land in the middle of the yard. "Get dressed only before you see your mother, but not in my yard." She swats his butt as she forces him out the door.

He jogs to his clothes, his reddened ass cheeks bouncing slightly.

"Thank you," he calls turning around just before he reaches his clothes.

"Be a good boy, Harley."

She turns back into her house and shuts the door, a huge grin on her face and a very wet pussy ready to be fully pleasured. She kicks off her shoes, they tumble and tip. She heads for her bed, a plethora of toy usage ideas swimming in her head.

About the Author:

Ruan Willow is the erotica author pen name for a multi-genre author and voiceover narrator living in the United States. She loves wine, working out, and sex, of course. She enjoys cooking, being outdoors, yoga, and prides herself on being a bit of an amateur photographer. Her passion is writing about love on multiple heat levels. She recently launched a podcast, *Oh F*ck Yeah with Ruan Willow*, and a new Amazon author page showing new releases, including a collaboration with BD Hampton.

Three Trances

by L.K. De Blas

The door-phone buzzes and you look at the display. An all too familiar voice says, "I'm outside your door."

You slowly sigh at the prospect of having another conversation with your ex.

There had been no helping it. As you were forced to move to get the dream job, there would be no maintaining the relationship. She had tried her best to make you stay, but your mind was made up and so you had left.

There's an impatient knock at the door and you move to open it, but just before you turn the handle, you wonder if it's a good idea.

But really ... what's the worst thing that could happen?

As you slowly open the door, you see her. Your Ex. Stunning as usual, but with a radically different facial expression than last time. Her tearful and misty eyes, replaced with a sultry smirk.

You notice something pulsing and glowing in her right hand.

As you shake your head and move to close the door, she puts her foot in to block it. "There's something I need to show you." You shake your head again and make to close the door again.

With unnatural speed, she forces her way in the door, grabs the back of your hair and shoves the glowing object in front of your eyes.

You lose your balance and start to keel over, all the while focusing on the pulsing object filling your vision.

It's a superbly cut jewel that has an inner light that swirls like a miniature galaxy.

An unearthly calm settles on your mind, even as you are falling towards the ground, and as you hit the floor, your ex-girlfriend straddles you and holds the jewel in front of your eyes. Every shred of your attention is sucked into the wonderful depths of the jewel.

As she sees this, she starts to move it back and forth. Your eyes following every minute movement.

"That's right. Just follow the light and listen to my voice. You can do that can't you?" Completely transfixed, you subconsciously nod and follow the path of the jewel.

Running her hands down your body, you feel every caress magnified a thousandfold. A tide of pleasure rises and swamps your entire being in ecstasy.

"That's right. Find the center of the jewel. Ultimate pleasure is there. I am there."

Her words worm their way into your mind, bringing you ever-growing levels of pleasure.

"And you want to find me there don't you?"

You nod one last time and your vision fades as deep trance takes you.

*

You regain consciousness in your ex-girlfriend's apartment. A haze slowly lifting from your mind.

As you see her approaching, you notice something in her hand. Not the jewel from before. But a red crystal.

She starts swaying it in front of your eyes.

It is even more captivating than the jewel from before. Dangerously seductive.

As you quickly try to look away, she forces the crystal into your vision again.

The haze that had momentarily started to lift, settles again on your mind as you gaze at the crystal. She gently sways it from side to side, making sure that your eyes follow every minute motion.

"Now that's much better isn't it?"

You find yourself nodding as the crimson crystal is now pleasantly holding your attention again. Dissenting thoughts seem to fade and you slow your breathing.

"That's right. Just keep breathing and watching, while you listen intently to my voice."

Still holding the crystal in front of your eyes, she steps behind you and begins to run her hands down your body. The caress of her hands more skilled than anything you have ever experienced before.

"While you look at the crystal, you can feel yourself going deeper, can't you? It's warm and red colour seeping into your mind now."

As you register her words, you feel the landscape of your mind subtly tinting crimson.

Like trying to stay awake in a tedious lecture, you ache just to let go and go deeper.

"It would be easy just to let go and close your eyes, wouldn't it? Just to surrender?"

While you unconsciously nod, a rushing feeling of arousal starts to build in the center of your body, "But not yet. You have to go deeper don't you?"

With each sway of the crystal, you find it harder and harder to resist its call.

While you try to plumb the depths of the crystals haunting beauty, you feel yourself responding fully to her touch now. She smiles wickedly and whispers in your ear:

"Now that's right. Are you ready to go all the way down?"

You whisper a breathless "Yes." and your vision fades again.

*

You regain consciousness on the floor of a dark and cool room. You try to move, only to realise that you have been shackled to the wall behind you.

As your eyes adjust to the dark, you see a woman sitting across from you. Your Ex-girlfriend. Hauntingly beautiful and suspiciously calm given the circumstances.

As you start to get to your feet, she turns to face you.

Fixing you with a steely gaze, you are frozen to the spot as she starts to speak.

"I was wondering when you'd be back. You went terribly deep for me."

Her voice has a sing-song quality that is both otherworldly and frighteningly compelling.

"You don't even remember do you?" she says with a predatory grin as she stalks slowly toward you.

With each word she utters you find as if a fog descends upon your mind. Hazy recollections of sensual pleasure and an irresistible voice surface in your thoughts.

As if reading your mind, she cups your chin and lifts your head, and with a smile and a sing-song giggle, she starts to speak again.

"Ahh, you are starting to remember. I see your body already responding again."

Your body floods with tantalising arousal as her words wash over you.

"Well then, let me take you back to that wonderful state that you so clearly crave."

Still holding up your head, she brings her fingers up to your eyes and giggles again. "Time to go deep again!"

She snaps her fingers and your mind sinks into a void of pleasure that is strangely familiar now.

You are now hers and want to stay forever.

About the Author:

L.K. De Blas writes mesmerizing hypnokink stories, and makes fantasies come true one keystroke at a time.

No. 13, Baby

by Jay Willowbay

"Many happy returns, sweetie! You made it … 13 weeks!" she giggled, slipping off her shoe and running her soft foot over my caged cock. "Not that you had any choice in the matter."

Indeed, I did not. She'd kept me this way for the entire autumn. 91 days. Three long months. A quarter of the year. From ending the summer with one last orgasm at the end of August, to now with the advent calendars and Christmas decorations going up. 13 weeks.

First, I'd endured a sexless September. Thirty days without release, unthinkable once upon a time, but now this was the easy part. At this point, all the other subs joined in for Locktober, so my Twitter feed was awash with them and their plight, making me intensely vulnerable as collateral damage to the teasing they received, given my own one month head start.

On October the 11th I passed the 40 days and nights which so troubled Josh Hartnett in the movie where he gave sex up for Lent, and I was still less than halfway through my ordeal. Ten days later, some exec at the movie studios decided it was Wonder Woman day, meaning I was further teased and tortured by videos and images of Lynda Carter, Gal Gadot, women in cosplay, and even cartoon representations had me swooning, aching, drooling, sinking, wanting, needing, begging, almost to the point of sheer insanity.

My memory of subsequent days is a little hazy. I guess I must have had some level of functionality, but my head was in a whole other place. As it was another ten days later, when the Locktober subs were counting down to midnight, that I had to suffer all those sexy Halloween costumes without any prospect of release for at least another month. Witches, vamps, Elviras, Morticias, Catwomen, Batgirls, Harley Quinns, and Poison. Fucking. Ivies. Ohhh, how they haunted me, and even constrained as I was, I was dripping ectoplasm all night.

Come No Nut November, but not cum me, I tried to elevate myself above carnal matters by throwing myself into my writing, creating a brand new novel for Nanowrimo. But Mistress was having none of that. I was allowed, I was commanded, to think about sex night and day, all the more because I couldn't have any. So she banned me from writing any other genres except femdom erotica. Every day I had to produce another chapter in which a sub luckier than I enjoyed the happy ending which so agonisingly eluded me. I suffered more for those 50,000 words than I ever had for any other writing project.

Which brought to the December, the beginning of advent, and her divine foot teasing me further, but this time with my suffering behind me, and my reward looming large.

"You probably want to be let out of that thing, don't you? You probably want to cum today."

Mistress has always had this wonderful knack of making the bleeding obvious seem profound and prophetic.

"Yes, Mistress."

"You understand that there will be a catch, don't you?"

"Yes, Mistress."

"Because you don't deserve to get anything for free, do you, pet?"

"No, Mistress."

"Good boy. Then I offer you a choice. Either you can stay where you are for another 13 weeks, and then I will let you out, to do as you please. *Or*, you can agree to take part in another challenge, and I let you out right now, and you will be cumming by lunchtime. But if you then fail the challenge, there will be consequences. Severe consequences."

That didn't sound good. But what consequences could be worse than doubling down on the torture I had already suffered? I figured it wouldn't hurt to ask.

"What are these consequences. Mistress?"

She laughed, and the sound was both seductive and chilling. "That, my sweet pet, is privileged information. I will only tell you if you accept the challenge, and by then it will be too late to back out. Otherwise, you can choose to spend the next 13 weeks aching in your cage, wondering what would have happened if you'd been brave enough, *man* enough to accept my challenge, and let me have my fun. You *do* want me to have fun, don't you pet?"

"Yes, Mistress, I want you to have fun."

Her dazzling smile glowed with satisfaction and triumph, and made me flutter and twitch more in my cage. But still she pressed. "*And ...?*"

"Yes, Mistress, I accept your challenge."

The smile changed. Still beautiful, still seductive, but now laced with a cruelty which somehow aroused me even more, even as the fear took a grip of my mind and body. I wondered what I'd let myself in for.

*

"So, here's what's going to happen," she began, perfectly matter of factly, neither sadism nor seduction in her tone, like this was a business meeting, and she was dictating the terms of a contract to her subordinate. Actually, that's exactly what she *was* doing. "At exactly twelve o'clock, high noon, you are going to cum."

Exactly twelve o'clock? To the second? I think I can do that.

"It doesn't have to be twelve o'clock to the very second ..."

She always could read my mind.

"But it must be during that actual minute, after it has changed from 11.59, but before it goes to 12.01."

Oh my Goddess, that's too easy! I never realised she was such a soft touch.

"And then you will cum again at exactly 1pm, to the minute."

Brilliant, second helping's even better than the first.

"And then again at 2pm,"

Three times after 13 weeks caged, no problem.

"And three ..."

Okay ...

"Four, five, six, seven,"

Wait, what?

"Eight, nine, ten, eleven,"

Is she mental?

"And then, if you can cum once more at the stroke of midnight, you will have won the challenge. Thirteen orgasms in twelve hours, you lucky little pet!"

"But … but Mistress, that's a physical impossibility, isn't it?"

She giggled, "Probably. I've tried it with a dozen other subs, and none of them even got close. Bigger, stronger, younger, and more virile men than you they were too.

"Yes Mistress, most men are."

"That's true, and you're a good boy for admitting it. But that won't help you: either do the impossible by passing the challenge, or you'll be spending the next two New Year's Eves – and every moment in between – locked up right there in chastity."

Her next smile was dripping with seductiveness and sadism, as deft fingers worked quickly to free me. "Good luck!"

*

At 11.50am, I reached down to lazily begin stroking my freed cock, teasing it lightly with slow, gentle caresses. Damn though, after 91 days untouched, I might as well have been pumping it full speed for all I was worth. I throbbed and ached and felt the heat rising, my long-time longed-for orgasm bubbling rapidly to the surface.

Oh no, not yet! It's too soon!

Mistress sensed my vulnerability, and pounced like a predator. "Yes, my good boy, give it all to me, cum for me pet, cum for me!"

I closed my eyes, I knew seeing her would take me over the edge for sure, but even her words, her presence, everything about her was overwhelming my flimsy resistance, and knowing she was doing it on purpose, manipulating me, outwitting me, defeating me, was all too much.

Take your hand away you idiot, no more touching until it's time!

I took it away, but the damage was done, I was past the point of no return, and all I succeeded in doing was to ruin the orgasm. It seeped and blobbed apologetically over the helmet and down the shaft in fat, lukewarm drops.

Mistress laughed, loud, long, and uproariously, like a studio sitcom audience member who was taking nitrous oxide while being tickled. "Oh my fucking god, you pathetic loser! I've caught a few out like this, but never so quickly!"

I couldn't believe it. Such humiliation! What made me think I could last ten minutes after thirteen weeks in a chastity cage? I was a fool, I was a dupe, Mistress had played me like a drum! Clever, cunning, seductive Mistress, making sure I would be firmly under her control for another thirteen weeks, aching, throbbing, begging for her …

Oh, I feel a stirring …

I looked down, and there I was, bobbing back to life! I took it in my hand, rolled it around a bit, and soon it was fully hard. I still had three minutes, reserves of cum after all that abstinence, and a mental picture of Mistress mocking me. I rode that image with some rapid wrist action, and soon felt that familiar glow.

I checked the clock. 11.59, and accelerated a little, making myself ready. I felt Mistress's gaze upon me, unwittingly helping me out. I didn't need to slow down, I could go full out on this one, really enjoy myself.

It flicked over to 12 o'clock, high noon, and I was in business, I let it rip, knowing I would definitely get there within sixty seconds. And I made sure I was looking in Mistress's eyes – oh, those, beautiful eyes – when I reached my eruption, a rare show of defiance from me, which she might punish me for later. But for now she showed no anger, not a trace of disappointment, just a faintly amused smile as I threw my head back in ecstasy, and gushed out, pumping my seed over my chest in long, thick, luxurious torrents until I sank back, sighing blissfully and basking in the afterglow.

Mistress smiled, raising an eyebrow, and said: "Well done pet, you've cleared the first hurdle. But you probably shouldn't have cum so much, you'll be needing that later. See you in nearly an hour."

*

So I was still in the game, but I wondered if it had come at too much of a cost. My first orgasm had been both ruined and wasted, my second had been self-indulgent and excessive. I needed to have saved enough seed for another dozen ejaculations, and as horny and needy as I'd been feeling for the last three months, I knew it was a big ask. I needed to replenish.

As it was just gone 12 o'clock, I treated myself and Mistress to a lunch of cheese and ham sandwiches, crisps, and a sugary cup of tea with dippy chocolate biscuits. I rested, relaxed, and felt my energy returning. And at 1pm, I did exactly what I needed to do, but no more, looking at Mistress with a knowing smile as I shot out a modest load at 18 seconds past 1300 hours.

There then followed another hour of chill time, and another gently satisfying orgasm. This was a lifestyle I could get used to, nothing to do all day but lounge around in readiness for the next time I would cum. I felt like a lion, ruling over my pride, my harem, taking turns servicing each one and basking regally in between. I came at three, and four, and five, and had never felt so alpha in all my life.

I was starting a feel a bit sore though. I'd never used any lotion or lubrication, and my fingers were becoming raw and calloused. But my cock was worse. It was throbbing and swollen in a different way to it had over the 13 weeks. So I took a bath, to see if I could soothe myself under the warm water, and also slew off the crust, sweat, and grime that had accrued with my efforts. I also realised the physical toll that my exertions had taken, so I let the tiredness wash over, sank back and closed my eyes for a moment, building up my energy for the final push …

I woke with a start, in water which was noticeably much cooler. What time was it? Mistress was awfully quiet, had she let me sleep through the hour to fail the challenge?

I didn't think so. She would have come in at 6.01 to gloat, or even pop the cage back on me while I dozed. Had she?

I looked down. No. There must still be time. I jumped out of the bath and ran down the stairs, naked and dripping, to where Mistress was waiting, next to the clock. Her hooded visage gave little away, but the clock was showing red alert. 5.57.

I grabbed my cock, which was puffy and fat from the friction, but shrunken and withdrawn from the bath. I had to prise the foreskin away to reveal the head, and started pumping furiously at the frenulum, right where I stood. 5.58.

It was still only halfway up. I summoned up my finest mental images and recollections, Mistress in her PVC corset and thigh high boots, the first time I saw her in person, the first time I walked through her door. The feeling of her riding crop making stripes on my backside, and the backs of my thighs, and her teasing, purring voice rightly telling me how much I loved it. *Yes Mistress, i love it, i love You, i love it, i love You, yes Mistress* … 5.59.

Hardish now, but the fantasy was strong, the feeling was there, and my clever little wrist was working overtime, faster harder, faster harder, I could do this, I could do this, I could do this, I could this. 6pm.

Must go faster. Must cum for Mistress. Must go faster. Must cum for Mistress. I drew upon all my memories, all my strength, all my energy, all my desperation. Ignoring the ache in my wrist, the erosion of my fingerprints, the burning agony on my shaft and helmet. I sent a sad little splash of semen splattering on to my feet, and then turned to the clock just in time to see it flick from 6.00.58 to 59, to 6.01. I'd made it.

I washed my cock and undercarriage over again – very gently – sprayed some Lynx Africa under my arms, and put on some loose fitting lounge pants and a t-shirt. Then I seared me and Mistress a couple of nice, rare steaks with chunky chips and fried eggs, sunny side up, with lashings of full sugar Coke to wash it down and perk me up. Thus I was able to find reserves and 7pm, and again at 8, but by then, even having belatedly starting using lube, my cock was chafed right through, bleeding in places, and I was in absolute agony. I was going to have to admit defeat and bail out of the challenge before I manhandled myself into John Wayne Bobbitt. If I was all next year in chastity, good, the way I felt I didn't want anybody touching my poor, mutilated member ever again, let alone within the next year. I'd rather be locked up forever more, completely celibate, apart from occasionally begging for a pegging.

What?

Begging for a pegging!

I couldn't believe my own stupidity. How had I not thought of it before? Here I was, all fixated on my cock like a sad, selfish brute of a bloke, when if I'd been thinking like I sub I'd have been well aware that there's more than one way of making yourself cum.

I dared not even trouble Mistress and embarrass myself by asking to borrow one of her sex toys. Instead I cast my mind back to the very first episode of *Gavin and Stacey*, and remembered, toilet brush. Mistress looked at me with a little concern, but also a little pride I think, like a parent, or a teacher, or more specifically a pet owner, when their pup learns a new trick. I was a clever boy.

And this time I was so clever that I *did* think to use lube, and I even put a condom on the brush handle, just to try and make it a little softer and more forgiving for me. I came euphorically and easily at 9 o'clock, squeezed one out fairly comfortably at 10, but the 11 o'clock orgasm was a real ordeal, it took me pounding the toilet brush into my burning hole with my right hand, jacking my raw, bloody cock at top speed with my left, and summoning up every sexy thought of Mistress pegging me, teasing me, tormenting me, to get there just in the nick of time. It was a sad little dribble, but it counted.

I was wrecked though. I was ravaged, I was ruined. Physical and emotional fatigue had me in a zombie-like state. I hurt all over. I was bleeding from both my cock and my rectum. Contorting to push the brush in had given me cricked neck, and pain in both my upper and lower back. I had never felt less sexy or horny in my life, and I wished I'd never gone anywhere near this crazy challenge. But I hadn't come this far just to fail at the final hurdle.

I dosed up desperately on Viagra and painkillers, and as midnight approached I got to work again, a steady rhythm, accompanied by my mantra, *arse, cock, cum for Mistress, arse, cock, cum for Mistress, arse, cock, cum for Mistress,* but beyond a pleasant tingling and a dreamy glow, I wasn't getting any erotic surge. The midnight chimes started, which I figured still gave me 71 seconds. So through muscle memory and determination I stepped up my efforts, left hand, right hand, and erotic author's imagination all working overtime. I closed my eyes, gritted my teeth, and sprinted towards the finish. *Arse, cock, cum for Mistress, arse, cock, cum for Mistress, arse, cock, cum for Mistress …*

"Time's up, pet. You lose!"

What?

I opened my eyes, and looked to the clock. 00.01. She was right; I'd lost.

I collapsed down in despair and exhaustion, closed my eyes again, and only opened them again when I heard that familiar click. I looked down to see that, sure enough, Mistress hadn't wasted any time – she'd put me back in the cage already. But she didn't have scorn or disdain in her eyes. She knelt beside me and said, "I'm proud of you, pup. No one has ever come this close to winning before. I love you."

I was swooning and blissing out to her saying those three words to me for the first time when she kissed me on the forehead and said, "Rest now." And I finally accepted defeat, or maybe a ceasefire, in my battle to stay awake.

*

That was a few hours ago. I've just woken up. I am in a lot of pain, not least because my severely roughed up member is tightly confined within its cage, and that Viagra has finally decided to kick in. But I've never been happier. Mistress loves me, and I have made her proud. And I can learn from all the mistakes I made during this challenge, and make sure I do things differently, and next time I *will* succeed.

After all, I have over a year to prepare for it.

About the Author:

Jay Willowbay is a multi-genre author from the south of England, and when he's not writing he is a keen sportsman and musician. Editing this anthology makes another big tick on his bucket list, and it winning a Silver Pigtail was the icing on the cake. His second short story collection, *The Femdom Factory Volume 3*, will be released in summer 2021.

Come Down, Come Down

by J.D. Wagner

Liam hadn't really planned to spend his first summer after graduating university on a fishing boat. He hadn't really had plans, exactly, but he'd sort of assumed he'd bum around like most of his friends, maybe land an internship or find a half decent job after a month or two of well-deserved laziness and get started on things.

Then the world changed overnight, and all his plans were tossed aside.

He'd graduated on a zoom call, his mother baking him a cake while his father watched from his hospital bed. It hadn't been long before they'd held a small service at his graveside, everyone six feet apart.

Dad hadn't left a will, and his mother had warned that until his estate and pensions were figured out, they wouldn't have much money coming in.

It had been his uncle who had called him up a few days later and mentioned a "friend" who had been looking for some help, and not long after Liam had found himself buying heavy insulated rain gear, lighter weight "fair weather" gear, hearing protection, and clothes that would put up with the abuse before driving down to Kellybegs harbor.

It was some of the hardest work he'd ever done, and a degree in sociology didn't really prepare you for pulling all day and all night shifts hauling nets full of haddock and mackerel on board.

Still, as he stood on deck and watched the stars dance above the waves, he had to admit the job came with a hell of a view.

He'd loved the sea as long as he could remember, always fascinated by the beauty and mystery of it. As a child, he'd always wanted to go to the cliffs or the beaches to play, and he'd started learning to swim almost as soon as he'd learned to walk.

He couldn't explain why, but Liam had always felt soothed by the rise and fall of the waters, the sound of the surf like a melody that seemed to always be calling his name.

He'd considered a degree in marine science or oceanography in school, but he'd always struggled with the maths. He'd audited a few classes, but it hadn't been long before he'd dropped them, unable to keep up with the serious students.

It hadn't bothered him as much as he thought it would, but after a long think and a pint in a cliffside pub Liam had finally realized he loved the experience of the ocean more than studying fish or understanding the science of the depths, and no classroom could properly capture that.

*

So here he was, leaning against the portside rail, nursing a paper cup of coffee as the boat chugged towards a new patch of fishing grounds, experiencing it.

With no active fishing at the moment and most of the crew below decks checking email or playing cards, it was as if he had the entire sea to himself, and Liam loved it like nothing else.

He took a long deep breath of the salt-tinged air, letting it fill his lungs before slowly exhaling back out, and closed his eyes to better hear the sounds of the ocean on the wind.
On nights like this, he could almost imagine the rushing air and soft chop blending into a haunting melody.

Come down, come down, down to me love.

Come down, come down, and find me now.

Come down, come down, into the sea.

Come down, come down, and be here with me.

He'd heard the song since his second or third night aboard the boat, but hadn't said a word to anyone else. They already made fun of him for being a greenhorn, they didn't need to think he was crazy.

Still, each time he could hear it, he would swear he was picking out words, just a few at first, but more and more each time.

Come down, come down, down to me love.

Come down, come down, and find me now.

Come down, come down, into the sea.

Come down, come down, and be here with me.

Liam often found music getting stuck in his head, but this was different in ways he couldn't quite explain. The song seemed to rise and fall just as the waves did, stronger as tides came in and weaker as they went out. It went quiet when the seas were glassy calm, and thundered when the waves washed over the deck.

Come down, come down, down to me love.

Come down, come down, and find me now.

Come down, come down, into the sea.

Come down, come down, and be here with me.

Tonight they were sailing into a head sea. Every time he heard the waves coming in to break against the bow of the boat, one word seemed to repeat over and over, drumming itself into his head.

Come.

Come.

Come.

Come.

Come!

Without really understanding why, Liam tossed away the coffee, stripped down to the t-shirt and shorts he'd had on beneath his wet weather gear, and launched himself over the rail.

Come down, come down, down to me love.

Come down, come down, and find me now.

Come down, come down, my voice is the way.

Come down, come down, and you will obey.

Some part of his mind that wasn't occupied with swimming downwards recognized that this was strange.

Even in August, this part of the North Atlantic was cold enough to sap the life from a man in a matter of minutes, but Liam felt no chill in his bones. It wasn't the false fever of hypothermia, either. Instead, a gentle warmth that surrounded him, as welcoming and relaxing as an expertly drawn bath.

His muscles should have cramped and stung from swimming deeper and deeper without a respite, but he barely felt any exertion at all.

His chest should have burned as he suffocated in the dark, but he seemed to take in lungfuls of sweet, slightly salty air each time his mouth opened, the song sustaining and guiding him down, down, down until he was moving more by feel and instinct than anything else.

The saltwater should have begun to sting his eyes, but they simply slipped closed, letting his mind fully occupy itself with listening, his body moving without any need for his guidance.

The passage of time had become meaningless without anything to judge it by, but eventually Liam felt himself being pulled in new directions. Left, right, up slightly, left, and up again until his feet touched soft sand and the world re-oriented itself.

He took a few more steps and realized the ground wasn't just soft, it was *dry*, and his eyes snapped open as the song came to an end.

"Welcome."

All the unease and panic that had been gently kept apart from Liam's mind slammed into his skull, and it felt like his heart and lungs were suddenly moving at five times their proper speed, his chest heaving as he turned in place, taking in impressions of rocky walls and softly glowing plants and fungi that filled the cavern with an eerie light.

"What - what is - where -?" His voice was rising in volume and pitch with panic, and his damp clothes seemed to be growing colder by the second as beads of sweat began to form on his skin.

"There is no need for that."

The panic seemed to stop as if a switch had been thrown, and Liam found himself taking a deep breath, letting it out slowly before he turned to face the source of the other voice.

She was beautiful, with hair that seemed to fluctuate between shades of gold and red spilling down over her shoulders and breasts. Her blue-grey skin had a faint sheen that gleamed in the light, and

227

her eyes were a faintly luminous shade of green that seemed to pull his gaze deeper and deeper into hers the longer he looked.

"Yes," she said in a voice that seemed just barely above a whisper. "Yes, my love. That's it. Just look at me."

"I am," Liam whispered back as he took a few hesitant steps towards her. "I am looking at you…"

"And that's all you can do, isn't it? All you can do is look."

"All I can do is look," he agreed, and knew it was true.

"You can't stop looking, and as you look into my eyes you just want to look deeper and deeper, sinking down as you hear my voice."

"Sinking …" Liam slowly sank down to his knees a few feet from where she sat regally on a shelf of rock, his toes curling into the sand. "Looking ... listening…"

"Yes," she purred with approval, and Liam could feel his wet clothes growing tighter as his cock swelled in response. "That's very good, my love. Looking and listening, because you know that everything I say makes sense."

He felt a bit like he was drunk, but somehow combined with the giddy rush of a runner's high, unable to look away as she told him what to think.

"Everything you say makes sense."

"That's right," she confirmed, sending another thrill down his spine. "Everything I say makes sense, because you know that I want what's best for both of us."

"Best for both of us..."

"Mmmhm. So when I speak, or when you hear my song, you will listen and obey."

"I will listen and obey," he confirmed with a nod.

Her smile was like the rise of the moon over the water, and Liam knew he'd do anything she asked to see that smile again.

"And you have done a very good job so far," she said as she rose, revealing the shimmering scales that covered her long, sinuous tail. "You listened so well, and when I called, you came just as I asked."

She tilted his face up to hers as she leaned down, gently kissing him with lips that tasted of sweetness and brine.

Her tongue stroked out, and he opened for her with a soft moan as his eyes slid shut again, a blissful sensation flooding him as her free hand stroked down his chest.

"I don't think you need these right now," she murmured as her fingers played along the waistband of the shorts, and Liam shifted just enough to push them down off his hips, scooting himself out of them so he would stay on his knees before her.

That was how it should be, after all.

She released him just enough to let him pull the soaked shirt off of his head, and the briefs he'd been wearing fell to the sand in two pieces, the waistband sliced apart in a heartbeat without leaving any mark on his skin.

"Yes," she said with a satisfied little groan as her fingers deftly inspected his fully erect form. "Yes, this is just perfect, isn't it, my love?"

She was close enough now that he could see the razor sharp edges in her smile, but the warmth and want in her eyes turned it from a chilling sight to a funny little secret between them.

Liam tried to find the words to agree with her, but before he could speak his mouth was occupied with a pair of her fingers as she encouraged him to lick and suck, the other hand pumping him slowly, waves of pleasure washing over him with each pass.

"What is your name, my love?"

He gave the fingers one last suck, his tongue running along their length before he kissed the tips, and looked back up into her eyes. "Liam, Miss."

"Miss?" She giggled, and it was like little bubbles of seafoam fizzing and popping in his brain. "I think it's better if you just call me Áine, my love."

"Áine," he breathed out softly, then gasped and bucked as she ran her thumb slowly back and forth over his head. "Áine ... so beautiful ..."

"As are you, my lovely Liam. Now – be a good boy, and hold still."

He did as he was told as Áine's tail slid slowly around him, gently pushing him up and back until he was resting against the muscular appendage, her upper body pressing to his as she ran her hands down his sides.

"I'm going to take you now, Liam. Do you want that?"

"Yes!"

"Do you want to be my love? My pet? My own?"

"Please," Liam gasped as he could feel her gliding sinuously over him, making him shudder with anticipation. "Please, Áine. Please, let me be yours?"

Her smile grew brighter as she ran a finger against his lips. "Forever?"

He leaned to kiss the fingertip, then stared up into her eyes once again, letting his will sink away as he submitted completely. "Forever."

Áine's response was to pull his body tight to hers as she engulfed him, warm and wet and welcoming, her tail undulating against him.

He didn't need to do any work – she was content to handle that while he just melted into the pleasure of being fucked by Áine, moaning her name between his gasps and cries as they covered each others' necks and shoulders with kisses, her teeth leaving little tingling stings each time she broke the skin until Liam felt like his entire body was being electrified.

"Such lovely hands you have, my love." Áine's voice had become even more sultry as she praised him, her own pleasure coming in low groans and shivers as he did his best to return the bliss she was sharing with him. "So soft and gentle ...s o deft you are ... so strong!"

Áine's pace increased, and he could feel himself throbbing and churning in response, stirred up and aching for release, but not yet.

He knew instinctively that he must not yet. Not without her permission.

Áine tensed as she tossed her head back and let out a long note of pure delight, shuddering and pushing him impossibly deep into her as she rode him through her orgasm, the sound of her wordless song blanking his mind and leaving him unable to do more than push and thrust and pound against her until she finally sagged back against him, her lips brushing against his ear.

"Now, my love. *Now!*"

It had been the best part of a year since Liam had gotten laid, and it felt as if every pent up moment of that time was suddenly bursting from him, a white hot pulse that seemed to go on and on as his voice joined her song, blending into harmony as she hummed into his ear, wordlessly encouraging him to give her every last drop that he could.

The world disappeared as his eyes rolled back into his head, and as his body finally went limp he felt the sting of her teeth digging into his breast, followed by a gentle kiss against his forehead.

"Sleep now, my love. Sleep until I wake you."

As the world faded away, the last thing Liam remembered was being gently enfolded by Áine's tail, and her fingers running through his hair.

*

They found him washed ashore near Malin Beg, hundreds of kilometers and the better part of a month from where he'd gone over the rail, still wearing the same clothes he'd had on that night.

When he woke in a hospital bed, they told him he'd been suffering the effects of exhaustion and exposure, but showed no signs of drowning or starvation.

"A lucky escape," the doctors said, especially after Liam couldn't explain where he'd been all that time.

His uncle called a few days later to let him know the fishing boat's owner had paid him off for the full season, and two more besides. The message that he wasn't to come back – or to speak of what had happened – was clear enough.

He smiled as he hung up the phone, and lifted his hospital gown enough to reveal the raised pink scar that now marked his breast.

His family would have more than enough money now, and he would be free to do whatever he pleased as soon as the doctors wrote his discharge papers.

It wouldn't be long before he could make his way back to the ocean, and wait for her call.

About the Author:

Jaymie Wagner is a queer trans author, computer nerd, and giant robot enthusiast.

She lives in the Twin Cities area with her cats, a rotating cast of friends and lovers, and spends far too much time watching Adam Savage building stuff on youtube instead of getting her work done.

Jaymie can be found writing erotic microfiction on Twitter as "Fantasies Fractured", and her AO3 account is "bzarcher."

Marie Likes to Win

by The Barefoot Sub

Running her hands along her lingerie clad curves, Marie watched herself in the full-length mirror. Long, blonde hair falling over her shoulders, caressing her breasts. She knew she looked like a Goddess, black sheer lingerie highlighting her smooth lines and perky features. It wasn't in her nature to be anything less than pristine when she was completing a task for Sir. And as she picked up her satin night gown her eyes caught on his marks. "Sirs Property" emblazoned across her body in thick, bold marker pen, from her right shoulder to her left hip. Her eyes glinting with the joy of knowing she was his and was able to indulge in her fantasies for him, even without his being there.

Pulling the gown closed and tying the waistband Marie checked the clock: 21:22. They would start arriving soon. Scanning the room one last time, checking the number of water bottles, her bowl of condoms on the arm of the sofa, the wand …

Sitting herself on the cushions to send one last teasing email to Sir, and toying with her excited self she ran through the events yet to come.

He'd asked her to create a sexual task that would push her and please him. Followed by the usual picture, video and written feedback. She had chosen a group of men to entertain her in her submission.

There were three of them coming:

- Number 1: a friend, and semi-regular helper for tasks.
- Number 2: a sharply dressed banker
- Number 3: a rugged builder

2 and 3 were new to her, but of the recommended men, she had chosen them as they were taller than her, very well endowed and assertive yet respectful, just like number 1. As she lost herself to the evening's plans and the vibrations at her apex she heard a knock.

Straightening herself up as she opened the door the nerves hit. Fortunately, number 1, Pete, was first to arrive, and once she had run through the plans with him, and a camera tutorial, there was a second knock and the other two were let in.

The night went exactly as Marie had planned. She knew that Sir would be happy with the pleasure she received and the way that these three men enjoyed her. The reaction that number 3 had to her marks ... Cal, the tallest of the three, had traced his finger across her lettering; a wicked glint in his eye, enjoying the prospect of playing with another man's toy.

Marie had done Sir proud, and was feeling floaty from the countless orgasms and her submissive headspace as the men unloaded all over her flushed face. Once they had all gone home and she was curled up in bed with a cup of tea she emailed Sir with her news of the night. Marie hoped she would be given permission to meet with them again, either for tasks or her own gratification, and she smiled as she wondered what either of the new men would think of her if the meet was for her needs rather than Sirs?

As it turned out she didn't have long to wait to find out ...

The following week was one of rest. Having worked her hard, Sir always liked to give her time to recoup before the cycle would start again. No orgasms, no touching and certainly no cock! There was no permission to even ask for male company.

"Rest means rest, Marie!" and with that she put her lusty desires on hold.

However, the following week she was permitted to meet with a female friend. And socially she was always permitted to see anyone, so she invited Cal around for a cup of tea the evening after seeing Sarah. With other women, Marie tended towards being an assertive top, and this left her submissive self needy and aroused.

Inviting Cal around would be a fun way to torment herself. Her submission to Sir and his rules always at the forefront of her mind. Cal would be allowed to pleasure her, but she was not to touch him. He was allowed to bury his face in Sir's personal property, but she was not to taste him, or give him a free pass for entry. These two being what she truly wanted, more than anything else, but ... Marie's pleasure was the only thing that was important for Sir, and she was not to be secondary to Cal. He could be her toy for the night though.

When he arrived Cal had a certain swagger. Not arrogance, just an assertiveness that got to Marie. That air of confidence being what made her swoon over Sir, turning her to submissive goo. But that night Marie felt different. She couldn't be certain but it seemed as though Cal was trying to exert his dominance over her, and that made her cringe inwardly as well as laugh quietly to herself. She was channelling her inner Sir and the dominance that Cal brought felt like a challenge, a game for Marie to play.

And Marie never likes to lose.

Settling on opposite ends of the corner sofa, steaming cups of tea in hands, the conversation flowed as if they were old friends. A casual observer would never guess that this was only the second time they had met, and the first time she had been dressed in nothing more than lingerie and the words "Sir's Property". Marie stretched her long, lean legs out in from of her, bare feet grazing his thigh as they discussed curries and best recipes. He was caught off guard by this and their eyes met briefly. Her eyes sparkled as she wiggled her toes in invitation. He took her up on the unspoken request and lifted first one foot, and then the other. Strong, confident fingers working her soles, relaxing her and bonding them. As he was working on the right, she set her left down on the floor and wriggled down the sofa a touch. Her skirt subtly catching beneath her buttocks and riding up, exposing her dark knickers beneath. Letting her left knee fall wider in innocent relaxation she noted his eyes fall upon her shady crotch, felt the swelling of his cock beneath her right ankle as he continued to work his magic on the foot in his lap.

At this point she knew he was hers.

His fingers became less forceful on her soles and his glance kept dropping from her eyes to her lace clad cunt. She wondered if he could smell her arousal, or if that was just for her?

"Did I ask you to stop?" Marie hardly recognised the husky voice that leaked from between her lips. The tension was evident to both of them. Cal not quite ready to believe he had given up control just yet, Marie never feeling more like Sir …

"Sorry, I got distracted by …"

"By what exactly?" He regained the intensity of his strokes and she continued speaking "By my ideas on Bombay style lamb curry or …" running her hand to the hem of her skirt and drawing it up the final inch to expose herself fully "by the memory of what hides in here?"

"Errrr …" The blush she couldn't have imagined crept up from his neckline. She had him. She knew it, and now, as his plans slipped out of his mind so did he. She met his eyes again, this time challenging him as her hand slid down over the soft fabric, the last semblance of modesty covering her brazen, slutty and smooth mound.

Sliding first one finger beneath, then a second. Plundering her folds and withdrawing. Tasting her nectar before proffering the dirty digits to her prey. He leant closer on the sofa, wrapped his lips around her and used his tongue to clean them thoroughly. Marie relaxed back further, spread her legs a little further and innocently asked "would you like another taste? A proper one this time?"

His gaze now at that little patch of dark fabric, which was getting darker with every word she spoke. He nodded, lost in his desires. "Down on your knees then. Show me how much you want me …"

This was all the encouragement Cal needed, and he sank to the floor, crawling between her legs. He started to make love to her through her flimsy underwear, using his mouth. The frustration evident as he sat back, pulled her legs together and cautiously raised her hips to peel down the offending item of clothing. He looked up at her from beneath heavy eyelids, requesting her consent before acting on it. She let him, fascinated by his nervous desire to please her, and, when he lowered his face to her once again, she ran her fingers through his hair, massaging his head deeper onto her engorged, aching clit.

For the first time she witnessed a man breathing through his ears as he worked her diligently to orgasm. The waves of pleasure pulsing through her body as she used his face for her own fulfilment. Sated, she relaxed her throbbing body backwards, releasing her grip on his locks. His mouth pulling away as his eyes once more locked on hers. Strings of her awakening the only link between them now, trailing from his beard to their source. Marie wondered if there was any trace on his pale shorts, or if he was unmoved. He knelt back on his heels and she spied the dark spot of his own excitement on his crotch. He stood and removed those shorts, his composure regained, back in the driving seat. Or so he thought. Approaching her he pulled a condom from his pocket and with dark, lust-filled eyes and a smile on his lips he asked "can I fuck you now Miss? You taste so sweet, I want to bury myself where my tongue found a home …"

With a lascivious grin Marie shook her head, maintaining eye contact, challenging him to come closer, to kiss her so that his bobbing shaft was within reach, sucking her leftovers from his beard. As she finished cleaning his face her left foot searched out the discarded lingerie, gripped them in her toes and lifted them to her hand, rubbed them against herself. Enjoying the friction against her swollen labia.

"How much do you want me now Cal?" she asked, the words once more oozing from her lips as her juices had flowed not five minutes previously. She continued, knowing the answer but wanting to hear it from him "How much do you want to bury yourself in me?

To take every ounce of pleasure from within my tight, hot cunt? For your pleasure? Until you explode …"

"Oh Miss, that is all I want to do. I need to."

"What exactly do you 'need to' do Cal?"

"To fuck you Miss" and then he repeated her words "To bury myself in you, to take every ounce of pleasure I can get from your tight, hot cunt"

"So this is about your pleasure now, is it Cal?"

The silence was deafening. He wanted to know what to say. What was right. What was wrong. Not knowing that his fate was sealed before he had even arrived.

"Look behind you Cal, on the sofa." Pointing at the wand tucked behind the cushion, "please could you pass that to me?"

As he did Marie passed him the knickers. "Would you like to know what I want, Cal?"

The look of confusion quickly faded to curiosity as he nodded, seemingly unwilling to say the wrong thing again.

"I want you to watch me make myself orgasm. I will keep going until you fill my knickers with your seed. Once you have, I want you to put them on, and you will make us both a cup of tea." He nodded in agreement. His turgid manhood bobbing in time. "Then you'll wear them home, and sleep in them, I would like to see pictures of you in them before sleep and when you wake up. The more they have stuck to you the better. I want to see you again Cal, but only if you're a good boy who is happy to do this for me"

"But I don't wear anything to bed …" he faltered

"Not normally you don't, but tonight you will, won't you Cal?" And with that unanswered question lingering between them Marie lay back, locked eyes and took in the site of her quarry doing exactly as he was told.

The humiliation written all over his face as he watched her watching him. Knowing what he had to do to see her again. He wanted to, she wanted him to. And as she crested for her third orgasm under her own hand, she enjoyed the spectacular sight of two heavy balls erupting. Soiling her dark lace with ream after ream of white ribbons. And as his erection ebbed away, he slid them on, triggering a fourth and more powerful orgasm from the depths of her body.

Marie doesn't like to lose. But what she likes even more is winning.

About the Author:

The barefoot sub can be found over at A Leap of Faith reminiscing about her self-discovery through kink while also sharing smut that is yet to happen. You can find her over at Twitter, usually getting distracted by the filthy GIFs, and occasionally on instagram, where she is almost always covered in rope.

Window Shopping

by Pearl O'Leslie

There were men in the glass windows, each one lit bright and holding a chair or two or maybe a couch. Some held two or more men, talking to each other as they flirted with the crowd, eyes flashing lock and flick smiles to lure in customers. Some of them smoked, or ate snacks while they waited, or chatted with their coworkers.

Some were dressed up in suits, or flashy clothes. A brazen few wore next to nothing, little bits and pieces, or one affecting an artist's model look under a draped sheet, his trick apparently being to sustain the outline of an erection through it for hours while people gawked.

She passed by bar boys, and toga wearing preening gods, and even an old-fashioned sailor in see through white, giving only a little bit of a glance to rule them out.

She was looking for the right man tonight, drunk on possibilities for a very specific fantasy. She wanted one who was attentive, and yet craving attention, bold, but still able to hold onto a touch of coyness. A tall order, but anything and everything was for sale If you looked long enough and paid.

He was dressed a little like a police officer, but more tailored and fitted than the loose practical fatigue-like garb the real officers wore. It suited him, hinted at his business being a bit on the rougher side, as did the metal handcuffs he fiddled with while he trolled for a customer.

The length of his lean body was draped over the couch, buttoned shirt rolled to just before the elbow to reveal the taper of his wrist as it ran from strong forearm. As she watched, he caressed himself through his black slacks, hinting his readiness for her.

He was clean shaven, but the light hair on his arms suggested his body was not, her preference. As she kept watching he made eye contact, held it and smiled. There was a boyish enthusiasm there that ordinarily meant she would have taken him out, maybe to his room or one of the hotel rooms around the district for extra, and used him, savagely. But she wanted something else …

She pointed to let him know he had a customer as she stepped through the door of his building. All the rooms inside worked the same way, electronic barter booths to give them deposits for their protection. She would never stiff a man, and usually tipped well if their service had the right attitude and natural inclination for the work.

Her card elicited a beep from the terminal and the door unlocked. She stepped inside.

"Good evening beautiful." All successful men knew how to make it sound sincere, but he seemed genuinely happy she picked up.

"Hey boy. How about you kneel down and let me inspect?"

He did so gracefully, and she briefly lifted his hat so she could run her fingers through his short hair, checking his posture and giving herself a further tease for a once over, before putting the officer cap back with a preciseness, content with the adornment. He'd leave it on, she decided.

The little room he worked out of was big enough to have a bed and a shower, as well as a table with fresh towels. There were a few accoutrements of his specialization lying about, leather cuffs with pads, a gag, a cane and a thick strap. She passed on those, this time.

She brought him back to his feet and whispered her order in his ear. His eyes got a little wide, but he nodded. "Yes ma'am!"

By the time she had walked back out to the front of the building, he was already in the window again, palms resting on the glass, waiting for her. She liked the way he anticipated.

She gave him a little upwards wave to get started. Around her, other customers and tourists thronged back and forth, all on their own odyssey of gaze. But for now she watched only him.

He took a moment to collect himself. She liked that, showed he had to make an effort for her, nothing overly robotic or over practiced.

As she had ordered, he began to strip. There was no music, other than what played on the street, but she didn't care, watching his fingers on the buttons of his shirt. Undone, there was hair on his chest as she expected, and the right kind of muscle.

His finger circled his nipple, as his other hand stroked himself through his slacks again. She continued to watch, and smirked when she noticed another woman had already drifted over to join her.

The man in the window began to undo his pants, sinking back on the couch and revealing the length of a generously thick cock. She waved again to indicate he should move more of his pants down, wanting to see everything.

Another two women drifted over, stopping their conversation with each other.

His hand wrapped around the root of his cock, making an O with his finger and thumb, pulling with a slight curve back towards himself. He was touching his nipple again, tongue darting to lick his lip.

She continued to watch as he took his time, exposed for the entire street to watch. Over the next couple of minutes several more women gathered, all watching what was free for them to share.

He gave her a pleading look. She counted by the stop-start motion he'd had to add in, he'd gone just to the edge three times. She shook her head, making him wait, passing a fifth time before at last she nodded.

He spent in two bursts, one arcing onto his chest, the other landing in the trickle of hair leading down his flat belly. His head had tipped back, hat slipping at a cute, rakish and tousled angle. A perfect moment.

As his orgasm passed and he became more aware, he saw the five or ten women who'd been drawn in to watch and looked shy.

She smiled, walked back into the building, adding a tip to the terminal at his door. She didn't bother saying anything else to him, letting him watch her walk away down the street, still on display and dappled with his own come.

About the Author:

Pearl O'Leslie (O Miss Pearl) is a writer and female dominant. She writes because she wants the things she likes to be more available, and after starting a blog in 2011, rapidly discovered she was one of the more popular publishers of free online femdom stories, as well as the author of a successful dark erotic novel "The Pet Gentleman".

Blog: http://www.omisspearl.com

Twitter: https://twitter.com/OMissPearl

Razor's Edge Gifts

by Bentley Williamson

My phone is ringing. Three or four times now. I guess I will pick it up and answer, since that's what I get paid to do. It's not much of a payday but considering all I do is sit on my butt at my desk and talk on the phone, it's not too bad of a deal. I would never get a paycheck if it weren't for horny and lonely men. Sometimes these men want to talk to a lady, sometimes to a whore, sometimes something in between. It is my job to see they are satisfied at the end of the call so they will call back.

The company I work for only wants their money and if they are happy at the end of one call, they will call back. Usually multiple times in a month. That's what it's all about. The bottom line. The company I work for doesn't care about training their operators, if you can't keep a guy on the line, you are fired. If you can't make a guy call back, you better have another fish on the hook or you are fired. It is all about making money for the company, and clients for the operators. You are simply told to go with the flow for whatever the caller wants and take care of his needs and make him want to call back with a fresh credit card.

I talk innocent if they want, I talk to them as a mature and respectful woman if they want. On a rare occasion you will get a man who wants to hook up with someone who they can talk down to or treat badly. Some men want to treat you like a whore and they expect the same treatment back. I always make these phone calls go as fast as possible. I don't like them at all. They are dirty and make me uncomfortable, so I try and avoid them.

After a while, you learn to recognize people's caller ID numbers and you don't answer their calls. You just let it ring and it gets transferred to the next operator who's dumb enough to not look at their numbers. The men who like these kinds of calls are usually stuck in a marriage where they are unhappy with their wife. They usually want to treat a female how they perceive their wife treats or thinks of them. To do it in real life will only get them caught up in more problems than it is worth. At least doing it over the phone doesn't leave any specific trail for their wives to find, past the phone bill.

The men I like usually have the all-perfect wife who does nothing for their husband because she is too busy keeping up with the Jones down the street. For the man, it is cheaper to keep her and meet an escort if he can get away or make a phone call occasionally, when the need gets too big. I call these men, the Stepford husbands. He wants his wife to give him what she used to but she has spent too much time learning to look and act perfect that she is incapable of fulfilling her husband's needs any longer. That's where I come in. If he can't get away to meet a private escort, he can make a call. I get two dollars a minute out of the four dollars a minute they pay. It adds up if you can keep the ones you like on the phone. I am clean and discrete and if you get caught in the act, just hang up the phone. It hits your credit card as coming from a company where you would order online products for everyday uses, RAZORS EDGE GIFTS.

The phone keeps ringing and I recognize this number. I would like to get to know this man in person. He is always respectful and polite to me. He has called a few times and talked out his fantasy with a few different ladies who work here. None of them could ever give him what he needed over the phone, until he met me.

HELLO, MY NAME IS BENTLEY. THAT IS WHAT YOU WILL CALL ME, DO YOU UNDERSTAND?

Yes Bentley.

THAT IS PERFECT, I APPROVE.

Thank you, Bentley.

ARE YOU WHERE YOU CAN LISTEN TO MY VOICE AND RESPOND SO I CAN HEAR YOUR VOICE OR SHOULD WE TEXT BACK AND FORTH SO YOU CAN BE SURE TO GET EACH OF YOUR ORDERS?

I can listen Bentley, but I cannot speak back. I need to get my orders from you Bentley.

I WILL SEND YOU AUDIO CLIPS AND YOU CAN TEXT ME BACK.

Yes Bentley, as you wish. Would this be a bad time to tell you I just got out of the shower? All I have on is a loose towel and it is hardly covering me Bentley.

IT WOULD ACTUALLY BE A VERY GOOD TIME TO TELL ME THAT. THANK YOU FOR SHARING. DON'T SPEAK AGAIN UNTIL I GIVE YOU PERMISSION TO SPEAK.

Yes Bentley.

I WANT YOU TO GENTLY TAKE THE TOWEL AND RUB YOUR COCK WITH IT. WHEN YOU ARE ALL DRY, I WANT YOU TO HANG THE TOWEL UP AND FONDLE YOURSELF WITH YOUR RIGHT HAND. I WANT YOU TO STAY IN THE BATHROOM SO WE CAN KEEP THIS BETWEEN JUST US.

Yes Bentley.

NOW THAT YOU ARE DRY AND A LITTLE HARD, I WANT YOU TO GET SOME LOTION TO RUB ON YOURSELF WHEREVER YOU FEEL YOU NEED TO BE SOFTER FOR ME. YOUR SKIN MUST BE SOFT SO YOU CAN SERVE ME AND PLEASE ME THE WAY I LIKE. I WILL NOT ALLOW YOU TO NOT HAVE SOFT SKIN FOR ME TO BE PLEASURED WITH.

YOU WILL NEED TO PLEASE ME IN WAYS THAT ONLY I WILL ALLOW YOU TO DO.

Yes Bentley, I am applying the lotion now as you wish.

WHEN THE LOTION IS ALL RUBBED INTO YOUR SKIN, I WANT YOU TO GRAB YOUR SEMI HARD COCK WITH YOUR HAND AGAIN AND STROKE YOURSELF BACK AND FORTH. BE GENTLE, BE SOFT. ONLY USE GENTLE PRESSURE AS YOU STROKE YOURSELF. I WANT YOU TO BARELY FEEL THE FRICTION BETWEEN YOUR HAND AND YOUR COCK. I WANT YOU TO IMAGINE ME, NAKED AND IN FRONT OF YOU. I WANT YOU TO KEEP STROKING THE HARD MUSCLE YOU WILL BE SHOVING INTO MY WET PUSSY WHEN I ALLOW YOU TO TOUCH ME.

Yes Bentley.

I WANT YOU TO CUP YOUR BALLS WITH YOUR OTHER HAND AND THINK OF MY TONGUE RUBBING ALL OVER YOUR BALLS. USE ONE OF YOUR FINGERS IN PLACE

OF THE TIP OF MY TONGUE SO YOU CAN EXPERIENCE THE INTENDED FEELING.

Mmmmmmm, Yes Bentley. I can feel your tongue on my balls. Please give me more.

IMAGINE ME ON MY KNEES AND IN BETWEEN YOUR LEGS. I AM FLICKING THE UNDERSIDE OF YOUR BALLS WITH MY TONGUE AS MY DEEP BROWN EYES LOOK DIRECTLY UP INTO YOUR HAZEL GREEN ONES.

Yes Bentley. I see you staring up into my eyes as you use your tongue to flick my balls. I can feel my hand softly stroking my hard cock at the same time.

IMAGINE ME PULLING ONE OF YOUR BALLS, EVER SO GENTLY, INTO MY MOUTH AS I BEGIN TO CIRCLE MY TONGUE AROUND IT. THEN IMAGINE ME PULLING BOTH OF THEM JUST AS GENTLY, INTO MY WARM WET MOUTH.

Yessss Bentley. I can feel your tongue all over my balls. Your mouth is so warm and so wet. I can imagine.

AS I AM CARESSING YOUR BALLS IN MY MOUTH, IMAGINE ME REACHING UP AND GRABBING YOUR COCK, TAKING IT AWAY FROM YOUR OWN GENTLE TOUCH.

Yesss Bentley. I feel you touching my hard cock.

IMAGINE ME GRABBING YOU, PULLING YOUR COCK AWAY FROM THE GENTLE TOUCH OF YOUR OWN HAND. I PULL AND STROKE AND BRING YOU TO THE EDGE, BACK AND FORTH WHILE MY TONGUE IS FLICKING YOUR BALLS.

Ooohhhhh Bentley, I can feel your tongue and your stroke on my cock. I am close to an orgasm.

THEN I WILL BACK OFF BECAUSE YOU ARE NOT ALLOWED TO GET THAT FAR AHEAD OF ME YET.

Yes Bentley, bring me back down. I am not ready to go over the edge yet.

YOU WILL GO OVER THE EDGE WHEN I TELL YOU IT IS YOUR TIME. NOW IS NOT THE TIME.

Yes Bentley. I apologize. Please forgive me.

YOU ARE FORGIVEN MY PET. NOW IMAGINE ME LICKING YOUR BALLS WITH A LITTLE MORE ENERGY. A LITTLE MORE SPEED AND A LITTLE MORE FORCE. MY TONGUE IS GETTING ROUGHER ON YOUR BALLS. FIRST ONE THEN THE OTHER. NOW I PULL BOTH OF THEM INTO MY MOUTH AGAIN AND FLICK THEM WITH MY TONGUE.

Oh Bentley, thank you for allowing me to enjoy your warm and wet mouth. Please keep yourself busy. Pleasure me as you wish.

NOW IMAGINE YOUR COCK BEING REALLY HARD FOR ME. YOUR COCK HAS NEVER BEEN HARDER FOR ANYONE. YOUR COCK ONLY GETS HARD FOR ME MY PET.

Yes Bentley, my cock is hard, and I feel my hand stroking it whenever you remove your hand from my shaft. I feel your mouth on my balls. My cock is only hard for you my Bentley. Only for you.

MY PET, WHEN YOU ARE DEALING WITH ME, YOU WILL ALWAYS BE HARD.

Yes Bentley, as you wish.

YOU WILL ALWAYS BE HARD WHEN YOU ARE DEALING WITH ME BECAUSE I WILL ALLOW NOTHING ELSE FROM YOU. THAT IS WHAT I EXPECT FROM YOU, AND THAT IS WHAT I WILL RECEIVE.

Yes Bentley. I promise to give you what you demand.

NOW I WANT YOU TO IMAGINE WE ARE WALKING TO THE BEDROOM TOGETHER WHILE I LEAD YOU BY YOUR COCK. I USE A STRONG YET GENTLE GRIP, GRASPING YOUR ROCK-HARD COCK, WHILE I PULL AND DIRECT YOU TO WHERE I WANT YOU.

Yes Bentley, take me to the bedroom. I will go wherever you make me go. I will do whatever you want me to do. I am your pet; you are my Bentley.

NOW IMAGINE ME LAYING YOU DOWN ONTO THE BED. I AM FORCING YOU TO LAY DOWN. I AM FORCING YOU TO GET IN A POSITION TO WHERE YOU CAN START TO SERVICE ME. IT IS MY TURN TO GET TO THE EDGE. IT IS MY TURN TO GET TO AN ORGASM.

Yes Bentley, you allowed me to get to the edge, but didn't allow me to go over the edge. It is always you who should go over the edge first. I am not worthy of receiving that pleasure first. It is only for you to orgasm first.

I PUSH YOU DOWN ONTO THE EDGE OF THE BED WHERE YOU'RE SITTING AND FACING ME. YOUR LEGS ARE HANGING OVER THE EDGE OF THE BED, SPREAD SLIGHTLY OPEN SO I CAN STAND IN BETWEEN THEM.

Yes Bentley, on the edge of the bed. Exactly where you want me to be.

NOW YOUR FACE IS DIRECTLY ACROSS FROM MY NOW WET AND READY CROTCH.

Yes Bentley. You are right in front of me, I can smell your wetness.

NOW I GIVE YOU PERMISSION TO LICK MY WETNESS. YOU CAN TOUCH ME. YOU CAN PUT YOUR FINGERS INSIDE OF ME. MY PUSSY IS WET AND NEEDING YOUR FINGERS INSIDE TO ROAM AROUND.

Oh yes Bentley. Please let me be inside of you. Please let my fingers explore you deep inside. Let my fingers wander around inside you to learn the moves that make you feel good.

NOW I WANT YOU TO LICK MY PUSSY WHILE YOUR FINGERS ROAM AROUND INSIDE OF ME.

Yes Bentley, licking and lusting you. Touching you and drinking you into my mouth. Thank you for allowing me to touch you where it makes you feel so good.

NOW THAT YOU HAVE MY JUICES FLOWING, YOU MAY RUB MY THIGHS WITH YOUR TONGUE TO LICK UP THE JUICES YOU NOW HAVE FLOWING DOWN THEM.

Yes Bentley, I will clean up the mess I have made.

YOU MAY WIGGLE YOUR FINGERS INSIDE OF ME. I WANT YOU TO MAKE ME MOAN. I WANT YOU TO MAKE ME CRY OUT WHILE ONLY USING YOUR MOUTH AND YOUR FINGERS ON ME. I ALREADY NEED TO LET OUT SOME ENERGY YOU HAVE BUILT UP IN ME.

Yes Bentley, please allow me to give you a release.

YOU CAN CONTINUE TO KEEP WORKING YOUR FINGERS INSIDE OF ME. GO SLOW FOR A BIT THEN PICK UP SPEED AND MOVEMENT. GO FAST THEN SLOW DOWN. YOU HAVE THE POWER TO GIVE ME THE RELEASE I NEED. YOU HAVE THE POWER ONLY BECAUSE I ALLOW YOU TO HAVE THAT BIT OF POWER.

Yes Bentley, my fingers are roaming around inside of you. My tongue is worshiping your wetness.

WITH YOUR FREE HAND, I WANT YOU TO REACH UP AND GRAB MY BREASTS. FONDLE AND TWEAKING MY NIPPLES IS WHAT YOU NEED TO DO. MAKE MY NIPPLES HARD WITH YOUR FINGERS WHILE YOU ARE MAKING ME WETTER WITH YOUR OTHER FINGERS.

Yes Bentley, teasing them, tweaking them. I give them gentle caresses then add a sudden pinch to them to make you cry out.

RUB MY BREASTS WITH THE PALM OF YOUR HAND WHILE THE FINGERS OF YOUR OTHER HAND ARE DEEP INSIDE OF ME.

Yes Bentley, my fingers are deep inside of you, pleasing you and making you cry out with pleasure.

I WANT YOU TO WIGGLE YOUR FINGERS, TWIST YOUR FINGERS WHILE INSIDE OF ME. MOVE THEM AROUND ENOUGH TO MAKE ME CRY OUT AGAIN. MOVE YOUR FINGERS UP AND DOWN, BACK AND FORTH, IN AND OUT UNTIL I CAN'T CONTROL MY MOVEMENTS ANYMORE.

Yes Bentley. I will give you everything you must take from me.

MAKE ME CRY OUT, MAKE ME WET. I CAN FEEL THE WETNESS DOWN MY THIGHS TO MY KNEES. YOU ARE DOING VERY WELL MY LITTLE PET.

Thank you, Bentley, for allowing me to please you in this way. I will serve you if you wish. I will enjoy every moment with you. Everything I do will be how you like it Bentley. Everything just as you trained me.

THAT IS WHY I KEEP YOU FOR MY PET. YOU ALWAYS DO AS YOU ARE TOLD, AND YOU ARE SO EAGER TO DO IT JUST AS ONLY YOU CAN.

I am only for you and only how you trained me. I need you in control always. I need you to take from me what everyone else capitalizes on every day in the rest of my life.

I WILL ONLY ALLOW YOU TO EXPERIENCE PLEASURE WITH ME WHILE I AM IN CONTROL OF YOU. I AM ALWAYS IN CONTROL OF YOU AND YOU WILL ALWAYS OBEY EVERYTHING I TELL YOU.

Yes Bentley, always obey you. Always do as you wish.

NOW I WANT YOU TO TAKE YOUR FINGERS OUT OF MY HOT, WET PUSSY. I WANT YOU TO PUT YOUR WET FINGERS INTO YOUR MOUTH. I WANT YOU TO SUCK MY JUICES OFF YOUR FINGERS.

Mmmmmm, yes Bentley. You are delicious. You are my wet Goddess.

WHEN YOU FINISH LICKING MY WETNESS OFF OF YOUR FINGERS, YOU WILL LICK ALL MY JUICES FROM MY THIGHS AGAIN. YOU MUST CLEAN UP THE MESS YOU MADE AGAIN. YOU WILL CLEAN ME ALL THE WAY TO MY KNEES, FARTHER DOWN IF NEEDED.

Yes Bentley, as you desire. Always.

NOW I WANT YOU TO STAND UP IN FRONT OF ME AND PUT YOUR WET MOUTH AGAINST MINE SO I CAN TASTE THE JUICE YOU HAVE CAUSED ME TO LEAK FROM MY BODY.

Yes Bentley, licking you, cleaning you. Doing as I am told.

I WANT YOU TO LAY ME DOWN AND PUT YOUR MOUTH OVER EVERY INCH OF MY BODY. I WANT YOU TO TELL ME WHAT YOU LIKE TO DO TO ME MORE THAN ANYTHING. I WANT YOU TO TELL ME WHERE YOU WANT TO PUT YOUR MOUTH AND YOUR HANDS. WHERE DO YOU WANT TO PUT YOUR HARD COCK? DO YOU WANT TO SHOVE YOUR HARD COCK INTO MY TIGHT, WET, PUSSY?

I want to put my cock into you. Deep inside you. I want you to take my cock all the way up inside of you. I want to ram it hard inside of you.

YOU WILL IN GOOD TIME. YOU WILL FUCK ME WHEN I TELL YOU IT IS TIME TO FUCK ME. IT PLEASES ME THAT YOU WANT TO MAKE ME CUM. IMAGINE TOUCHING AND LICKING AND NIBBLING ME. IMAGINE WHAT IT WILL BE LIKE WHEN I ALLOW YOU TO TOUCH EVERY INCH OF MY BODY WITH EVERY INCH OF YOURS.

Yes Bentley. Worshiping every inch of your body as you desire. Experiencing all the joy you allow me by giving your body to me to do as only you want. I am loving the softness and smoothness of your skin under my touch.

CARESS MY BREASTS AND LICK ME CLEAN MY LOVELY PET.

Yes Bentley. The taste of you in the lingering residue of your juices is too much to handle. May I share the taste with you again?

May I caress you, tickle you, tantalize you some more with my hands and my mouth?

YES MY PET, DO TO ME WHAT YOUR HEART DESIRES. MAKE ME FEEL EVERYTHING YOU WANT TO SHARE, EVERYTHING INSIDE OF YOU. GIVE ME EVERYTHING YOU HAVE MY PET. DRENCH ME IN YOUR LUST AND PASSION UNTIL YOU MAKE ME CUM.

I will give you all that you desire.

DO WHAT YOU NEED TO DO TO MAKE MY SOFT MOANS TURN INTO ONE GIANT SCREAMING ORGASM.

Yes Bentley. I can feel myself clamping my mouth onto those pointing and thrusting hard nipples. I am sucking and suckling and slurping them all around in my mouth. Two of my fingers push their way inside of you again. They are probing inside of you, Roaming in you and dancing in you. Reaching every spot inside of you.

YES, MY PET, KEEP DOING WHAT YOU ARE DOING. YOUR ACTIONS ARE PLEASING ME. YOUR TOUCH MAKES

ME MOVE IN HARD AND DEEP LUST. MY HIPS THRUST CLOSER TO YOU. I TRY TO SLIDE DEEPER ONTO YOUR FINGERS. I TRY TO IMAGINE THE ORGASM YOU ARE CREATING WITHIN ME.

I finally find your sweet spot. My fingers are dancing there. My fingers are touching and pushing and rubbing you everywhere you like. Everywhere you desire and everywhere you have taught me to show attention to.

YES, MY PET, KEEP TELLING ME EVERYTHING. KEEP DOING WHAT YOU WANT. KEEP TELLING ME EVERYTHING YOU ARE DOING TO ME IN YOUR MIND. I TAUGHT YOU VERY WELL MY PET. YOU ARE BRINGING ME CLOSER TO THE EDGE. YOU ARE GOING TO GIVE ME THE ORGASM I WILL MAKE YOU GIVE TO ME. YOU ARE PLEASING ME VERY WELL MY PET.

My mouth is on your nipple on one side while my other hand is caressing your breast on the other side.

THANK YOU, MY PET. I WANT YOU TO LOOK INTO MY EYES AS YOU PLAY WITH MY BODY. YOU MUST LOOK AT ME ALL THE TIME WHEN I ALLOW YOU TO TOUCH MY BODY.

Yes Bentley, you are so beautiful. I never want to look away from you. I am always looking at you, always in adoration of you.

NOW STICK YOUR FINGERS DEEP INSIDE OF ME AGAIN BECAUSE I WANT YOU TO BE LICKING THEM WHEN YOU BRING YOUR ROCK-HARD COCK CLOSER TO ME.

Yes Bentley, plunging deep, long fingers all the way inside of you. I bring you to your toes as you fling your head back and let out a loud scream.

NOW TURN ME AROUND WHERE MY BUTT IS FACING YOU. I WANT YOU TO REACH AROUND AND FONDLE MY FRONT WHILE MY BACKSIDE IS IN YOUR FACE.

Mmmmmm, Yes Bentley. Thank you for blessing me with this view.

NOW STAND UP BEHIND ME AND PUT YOUR ROCK-HARD COCK BETWEEN THE SOFT SKIN OF WHERE MY THIGHS MEET MY ASS.

Yes Bentley.

NOW REACH AROUND WITH YOUR HAND AND AS YOU SLIP YOUR COCK INSIDE OF ME, I WANT YOU TO FONDLE MY SWOLLEN CLIT WITH YOUR FINGERS. NIBBLE AND BITE THE NAPE OF MY NECK WHILE YOU SHOVE YOUR COCK HARD INSIDE OF ME FROM BEHIND. I WANT YOU TO FUCK ME SO HARD WHILE YOU CUP MY BREAST IN YOUR HAND. I WANT YOU TO FUCK ME SO HARD THAT YOU MAKE YOURSELF SCREAM WITH ME.

Yes, my throbbing cock is on its way to heaven. My fingers are teasing, tweaking and fondling every part of your body that I can reach. I am shoving my hard cock inside of you. I am pushing and thrusting, biting and nipping, pushing and pumping, ramming and slamming my hard cock into your heaven. Harder and faster and deeper with every thrust.

KEEP FUCKING ME HARDER AND FASTER. FUCK ME LIKE THERE IS NO TOMORROW. JUST BEFORE YOU CUM, I WANT YOU TO PULL YOUR COCK OUT OF ME. I WANT YOU TO LAY ME DOWN AND HOLD MY LEGS UP.

Grabbing, squeezing, teasing, and pleasing. I will fuck you so hard. I am so desperate, so needy. I am about to cum. I must pull out. I must do what you desire of me. I will lay you down and raise your legs as you desire.

NOW I WANT YOU TO FUCK ME WITH MY LEGS PUSHED ALL THE WAY UP, YOU HAVE TO THRUST BACK AND FORTH GETTING AND GIVING ALL THE PLEASURE WE NEED TO BRING BOTH OF US TO THE EDGE. OVER THE EDGE. WE HAVE TO CUM TOGETHER.

Yes Bentley, I am close to the edge with you.

I WANT YOU TO START SLOWING DOWN. I NEED YOU TO GO SLOWER. I AM CLOSE TO THE EDGE. I AM

ABOUT TO BLOW. I NEED YOU TO TEASE ME. TAKE YOUR COCK OUT OF ME. RUB YOUR COCK AROUND ON MY CLIT. SPANK MY CLIT WITH YOUR HARD COCK. DRIVE ME INSANE WITH YOUR COCK. NOW SHOVE YOUR DICK INSIDE OF ME AND FUCK ME AS FAST AND HARD AS YOU CAN.

Yes, still fucking. Still more fucking please. I have to have you. I have to make you squirt your juices all over me and splash them all over this room as I slam my groin against yours. I am about to soak you with my cum.

MY APOLOGIES SIR, THE TIME YOU HAVE PRE-PAID FOR HAS RUN OUT. I HAVE TO DISCONTINUE THIS CONVERSATION UNLESS YOU CAN ADD FUNDS TO YOUR ACCOUNT. PLEASE INDICATE BY PRESSING 1 IF YOU INTEND TO ADD FUNDS TO YOUR ACCOUNT. YOU CAN EITHER PRESS 2 TO INDICATE YOU WILL NOT BE ADDING FUNDS TO YOUR ACCOUNT OR SIMPLY HANG UP THE PHONE TO DISCONNECT YOUR CALL. THANK YOU FOR YOUR TIME IN SPEAKING WITH YOUR OPERATOR,

BENTLEY. FEEL FREE TO CONTACT HER OR ANOTHER OPERATOR AGAIN AT YOUR LEISURE.

About the Author:

Bentley Williamson is the pen name of Angela Yturbe-Rozar, who has written one dystopian novel. Angie was given the opportunity to write erotica and has let her inner Bentley out just enough to test these new waters. Look for more stories from Bentley as she becomes more comfortable in her new skin and her writing only gets better.

Mask On, Thoughts Off

by Heart

Hi! You can call me Heart. Why? Because I am love, embodied and personified, silly! What, you don't believe me? Well, keep reading if you're brave enough, and by the end, you'll know that it's true.

It all started completely by accident. Well, maybe not *completely* by accident. Even as a child I noticed that when I spoke, everybody stopped what I was doing, and listened, completely absorbed in my words. Whenever I made eye contact with anybody, they froze in place and would not, could not look away until I released them from my gaze. At the time I didn't realise I was all that special, I thought this was just how people reacted to other people. But as I grew up, and began to evolve from a geeky girl into the young woman I am now, I came to realise that this was a gift I had, a gift that grew as I learned to control and harness and use more it effectively, a gift that was further amplified by people's inevitable and undeniable sexual attraction to me. A gift that I was then able to extend to the written word, a gift which is already starting to work on you. You can feel its effect, can't you? Hchc!

See? And this is only a single paragraph recap of my formative years. I haven't even got to the part where my powers really grew. What, saying 'powers' makes it sound like I'm some kind of super-hero? Or super-villain might be more accurate. But if it makes you feel better, I'll refer to them as 'skills' instead.

These skills were honed to perfection at college, studying hypnotherapy, psychology, and non-linguistic programming. I performed experiments on my friends without them realising, testing how much I could change their beliefs and behaviour through my subtle suggestions, how deeply I could program them, and have them doing whatever I wanted, while remaining convinced that they were acting of their own accord.

It led me to have a little fun with a few of my friends and classmates last October, when I sent this message out to all my contacts:

Now then, let's begin.

To start off, I just want you to relax.

Simple.

Just relax.

Let your body just flop for a second.

Like you got home from a long, long day.

A long day of either work or school and you just

Pfffft

Just like that, nice and simple.

Very good, off to a good start subject.

Now we are going to do some simple tests to start off with.

I just want you to focus on your breathing.

Focus.

I just want you to take a deep breath in through your nose.

Deep breath in now.

Hold.

Hold.

And out.

Very good, just like that once again.

Deep breath in.

Hold.

Hold.

And out.

Very good.

Just keeping that rhythm going for me.

In the back of your mind, keeping that going.

As we are going to switch that focus to your feet.

Focus.

Now, for your feet, I want you to squeeze them.

Squeeze them and tense them as hard as you can.

Squeeze squeeze squeeze.

Tighten and tense them.

Feel how tight and full tension they are.

Now i'm going to count to 3.

On 3, I want you to stop tensing, stop squeezing them and just let them relax.

And when that happens, I want you to feel that great feeling of them untensing, de-stressing and relaxing.

Good test subject, you are understanding well. Starting the countdown. Tense those feet.

1

2

3

Untense.

Untense, let the stress and tension fade as your feet relax.

Let your feet become warm, de-stressed, and relax.

That felt good, didn't it?

That feeling of destressing

Now let's do that again but this time with your legs.

Tense your legs up. Clench them together, as hard as you

can.

And again on the count of 3, relaxing them, stopping tensing

and letting them go.

1

2

3

Relax.

De-stress.

Let go.

Very good subject, you are doing so well for me.

Stomach and chest now, stomach and chest.

Tense them, tense them as hard as you can...anddd

1

2

3

Untense, relax, let go.

So very good.

Arms, hands, fingers now.

Tense.

1

2

3

And relax, untense, let go.

Now your neck and face.

Still being able to read the screen, but tense your face up, just like that.

And.

1

2

3

Relax.

Relax.

Relax.

Now then, there is one place we need to destress.

That mind of yours.

We are going to use a little bit of a different method this time.

But did you know, thoughts are stress? Even good ones?

Thinking is a cause of stress, so we need to deal with that.

So I just want you to picture your thoughts like paper.

Just like paper.

And I just want you to now,

Scrunch it up.

Scrunch it up, like you are about to throw it away.

Because that's what we are going to do.

We are going to chuck your thoughts away.

On the count of 3.

Throwing your thoughts away, so far away.

On 1

2

3

Thoughts gone.

Just relax.

Relax.

Let go and SINK.

SINK

SINK down down down down down.

SINK more and more down down into bliss

Into mindlessness

Into trace

Let your body relax and just

SINK

Every word,

Every breath,

SINK

Just a little bit more than last time

SINK

SINK

Very good subject, you have responded very well.

Let's get your mask suited on then.

This mask is a very special mask.

We made it just for you, it fits perfectly.

It's got a fuzzy material on the inside but it is quite tough

material on the outside

Let me just put it on you now as you can feel it cusp your

ears first

Feel the world drown out a little bit

Fitting on your nose now, covering it all up

Encasing it

And finally securing it on your chin

Face fully covered up with the mask

Airtight

Fully under control.

I just want you to focus on your breathing again

Deep breaths in your nose, out your mouth

The new mask makes the air around you just feel so clean

So refreshing

So pure and relaxing

It feels quite nice.

However, this mask has a little feature…

We can pump some special gas in

Special hypno-gas

Let's try it now

Feeling the gas just slowly creep in the mask

And just take a deep breath for me.

Deep breath, feel the gas go up your nose

It has a cleansing feel to it, the freshness of it all

Moving up and up

Up to your brain.

And this gas is special.

This gas makes your brain all mushy, cloudy, free of thought,

obedient

It makes the places it touches so relaxed, so warm, so

comfortable

As you take another deep breath now

And feel the sharp yet cleansing feeling

Seep down into your body

Making the places it touches into bliss

Into total relaxation

More and more deep breaths of this gas

Filling your mask

Filling your body

Filling your mind

Until it's fully captured you

The gas has filled every inch

Every corner

Every thought of your mind.

Noticing this feeling of bliss

Noticing this relaxation

Noticing this state of pure mindlessness this gas has given you.

You can stay here, in this state for as long or as little as you want.

And if you ever want to go back to this state.

With the mask on, gas filling your body and mind, no thoughts.

You can

Because whenever I or you yourself, and only us, say the words:

"Mask on thoughts off."

You can feel this mask just reapply to you

And the gas can just start sweeping in

Filling your mind and body

With bliss

You will also get this feeling

Every time you wear a mask

Any mask

Just in a moment though, I am going to bring you up and

awake

Knowing you can return to this with your new trigger

Whenever you want.

However, when you wake up, I want you to feel something

A need to email something out

You will feel a need to forward this to all your friends

"The gas has taken over"

And you will just feel a little rush of pleasure send through

you

When you send that out for me.

Very good subject

Now it's time to wake you up and out of this trance.

On the count of 5 wide awake, knowing your trigger, knowing you can activate it whenever and wherever you wish.

5

Feeling the mask slowly coming off you, getting loose.

4

Senses coming back, aware of your surroundings

3

Do a nice big stretch for me

2

Almost there, thoughts clearing up, able to think straight

1

Wide awake

Up

Up

Up and awake

*

Take a minute if you need to. You can't have been expecting to have your mind taken away when you started to read this story. And I don't expect you to remember who you even are right now, let alone the specifics of what you've just read. But there are two key points from it. One is that I instructed the reader to share the message by email (you might not know this, but you've probably already done so), and the other is that the relapse into hypnosis is triggered by wearing a mask.

This was deliberate, but all good harmless fun at first. Halloween was coming up and having half the people in costume fall into a horny trance seemed like a great way to make it the best party ever for all of us. But I underestimated the power of my own influence, and how compelling my suggestion for sharing the words would be. It went beyond the college, beyond the city, beyond the country, and worldwide. Everyone saw it, and belonged to me, just for a while. Then on Halloween, again, millions belonged to me, just for one night. But that's fine. It's nice being owned by me.

But it got *really* out of hand when the virus hit. Suddenly, everybody had to wear masks, every day, and all my control, all my influence, overcame them, overthrew them, overwhelmed them. The whole world, in thrall to me. Mine.

And the funny thing is, you always forget – oopsie, silly me! Of course, I mean *they* always forget. They pass it off as a silly, sexy dream, if they remember at all, until they put on their masks and they sink for me again. Hehe!

Now, don't you have somewhere you need to be? Of course you do, silly! And don't forget your mask! That's it. Good pet.

Mask on, thoughts off.

About the Author:

Heart is a hypno switch who has been writing erotic content for around two years, and this anthology marks her publishing debut.

Her Star Pupil

by C. Berwington

She walked around their bedroom as the storms began to roll across the skies. The lightning was putting on the best show possible as the cool breeze blew in through the French doors of her balcony. The skies showed their colors of dark pinks and blues as the shelf cloud rolled across the horizon. Her fingertips grazed the carved oak table that was now a showcase for their pictures. The curtains flapped and blew up towards the ceiling as a gust of wind made its way through. This was the best type of evening, calm and relaxing. The ocean waves could be heard crashing against the shoreline. The power seemed to flicker, but with the backup generators, she did not fear. The storm was going to descend upon the Tweed homestead soon.

Tonight was their anniversary. Two years since Candi laid her eyes on Professor Tweed. After Candi had finished her dissertation and graduated, Harris and Candi began to pursue their relationship further. Nights of board games, laying in front of the fire as Harris worked on his novels and class works. To think, a simple little board game of Scrabble and coffee had brought these two minds together.

"Harris?" Candi called out of the bedroom. There was no response. She thought he was in the shower or in the next room. But there was no response.

Candi grabbed her purple satin robe and laid it across her shoulders as she went to the balcony doors and shut them. She tied the robe and headed out of their bedroom, her feet padding the hardwood floor of the hallway. The lightning crackled and soon the thunder echoed making the windows shake. She made her way to the kitchen as the power once again flickered.

Harris was in his office at his desk working on his latest novel. He removed his glasses and set them on the desk beside his laptop, and rubbed the bridge of his nose, feeling he had been sitting there for hours. He turned in his custom-made blue leather backed chair, and looked out the window. He knew what today was, but deadlines made it almost impossible for him to admit he may not have something for her this evening.

The fireplace over in the corner flickered and cracked its burning embers as the storm became more active. The winds howled around the house making their presence known to anyone who was there. The rains hit the glass of the windows and siding like tiny daggers. The ocean also seemed to have a mind of its own. Crash after crash on the shorelines, pushing its boundaries.

"Would you like some tea Professor Harris?" a voice called to him with a slight giggle as he turned his chair and gazed upon her.

He could only smile as she made her way into his office, dressed in her purple robe with her cami and shorts peeking underneath it. He felt his heart begin pumping wildly in his chest.

He regained his posture. "Yes, sweetie come on." He took his cup and inhaled the aroma from the steam rising from the cup. "And please stop with the professor title. I've told you that there is no need for it. Besides you only do it to get a rise out of me. Don't think I haven't noticed."

Candi sat up on his desk with her cup in hand. "How far have you gotten today?"

"Not very far today," he sighed. "My brain can't seem to piece a few things and the University can't seem to get their shit together with this pandemic going on. Honestly, it's stressing me more than anything."

Candi didn't like to see him stressed out or worked up over work. This was their anniversary but with the pandemic at hand, there was very little that they could do. Or could they? She slid off the desk and into his lap as his arms embraced her. Her scent was intoxicating to him. She leaned into him and captured his lip. Kissing him softly as her hands rested against his chest.

"Do you know what today is my dear?" Her big blue eyes looked up at him as her fingers played with the hem of his sweater.

He looked down at her, his fingers gently stroking her brown hair. "Yes, I do Candi. Why would I ever forget? I've just been caught up with the University and my own writing but I would never forget our anniversary. What do you suggest we do? Game night? Readings?" He cupped her cheek and ran his thumb across her flesh. She could only blush and bite her lip.

"No Harris. I may have something else in mind. But only if you wish to." Her tone was a bit more assertive as she rose from his lap. "Give me 10 minutes and stay here." Harris watched closely as Candi got up and he felt his manhood begin to swell.

Ten minutes had passed and the storm outside was getting stronger. Harris sat there anticipating what was going to happen. Then a new sound came, one which he knew very well.

Click, Click, Click, Click

"Oh, little one," her voice sang out to him. He removed his glasses, laying them gently on the table as he made his way to the middle of the room. He focused on the doorway as it slowly opened. The lightning flashed and he saw her heels as he looked at the floor. Tonight was her night, and in some ways the way he liked it.

He kept his head low and sank to his knees, seeing only her legs. The sheer black material swayed as she walked. Her heels gave her a bit of a lift to stand over him. He swallowed hard. "How… how can I serve you Mistress?"

Candi placed a box on the side table, within his view. He knew what this box contained. But also there were other objects in her hands. He could tell by how she stood there, arranging things on the table.

She slowly opened the box as she grabbed the leather collar. Candi licked her lips, she only brought this out during *her* times.

Harris had shown his devotion to her and let her embrace her inner Domme. "Are you ready, little one?"

"Yes, Mistress."

Candi leaned down and placed the collar around his throat. Her breasts were right in his face. She felt his breath on them. "Do you see something you like or want?" She grinned as she finished buckling the collar.

He struggled to find the words that were on the tip of his tongue. He panted and nodded.

Taking a few steps back, she looked down. With her crop in hand, she tucked it under his chin and brought his face upward. "My sweet, sweet Harris. I love you and you do know this don't you?"

Harris looked up as the cool leather pressed against his chin. "Yes, Mistress. I love you too."

A devilish grin crossed her lips. "Alright then, my dearest. Remove your clothing and place it in the chair." Candi lowered her crop and allowed Harris to get up and do what she had asked.

She felt amazing in the new lingerie he had bought her. Black lace robe that was sheer, almost see through. The gown she wore was skin-tight and stopped mid-thigh, no bra or panties required. She knew that this would excite him.

He stood in the middle of the office wearing only his black collar. She walked around him, inspecting. "On your knees."

He did as he was told, hands directly at his sides.

Snap!

The sound of the crop touching the heels of his feet. "Straight" she called to him. He fixed his posture as he nodded. Candi walked over and moved his chair to in front of his desk. "Go sit." She told him.

Harris got up and headed to the chair. Candi went over to the box she had brought with her. Removing two silk ties and a blindfold, she brought them to him and placed them in his lap. His manhood stood at clear attention as clear beads of precum expelled from its tip.

Grabbing the ties, she made sure that each brushed against his cock before tying his wrists to the chair. He whimpered as his cock twitched in her direction. He wondered if she saw and bit his lip.

She looked up. "Are you alright, little one?"

He nodded as she stood up.

Darkness took over him as the thunder rattled the house. The blindfold was tight around his eyes. His hands bound to his work chair and cock eagerly desiring some kind of attention.

Tap tap tap tap

Candi had set off the Newton's cradle on the desk. Once before she had tried hypnosis on him, and it seemed to work. Tonight she figured she would try again.

"My little one. Focus on the sound before you. Allow my voice to slip into your ears and dance along the nerves of your mind, bending and controlling every reaction."

Tap, tap, tap, tap

He swallowed hard as he felt her hands over his shoulders. She moved long kisses along his neck ,her hands softly down his chest. Soft whimpers escaped his throat. She couldn't help but grin at his excitement. Her kisses trailed his torso and his thighs as she moved to her knees.

Slowly she took him between her soft lips. He whimpered "Please Goddess." She stopped. "Do not speak and do *not* cum. Do you understand?" She looked up and watched his Adam's apple move as he swallowed hard.

"Yes Goddess. I understand." He nodded as he spoke. The Newton balls still echoed in the still silence.

She took his sac between her fingers and pressed softly against its underside. Slowly her tongue worked around his hardened manhood as her lips closed around the shaft. She could smell his arousal. He craved, yearned and ached for this attention.

Harris pulled at his bindings as he panted. The way she worked his shaft he felt in heaven. Her tongue pressing against the vein, feeling his heartbeat through his cock. It raced heavy and quickened with each bob of her head.

Her hair cascaded over his lap and enticed him even more, now being tickled by each strand. How he wanted to touch her silk hair and work his cock into her mouth.

"Fuck," he whimpered as he pushed his head back into the leather of the chair. Then he felt her move.

Candi got up and shook her head. "Didn't I tell you not to speak?" He knew he had disobeyed an order. His mind raced thinking of what he had done. The lightning stuck at high velocity, cracking and rattling with thunder. She untied him in frustration.

"Grab the ties Harris, and come to me." She ordered as she took place in her game chair that sat beside the fireplace.

Harris picked up the ties and headed to the fireplace. He knelt beside her. "I will not be bringing you to pleasure tonight Harris. You disobeyed an order so you will have to handle it yourself. But you will let me watch you. Do you understand?"

"Yes Mistress." He nodded, ashamed of his actions.

She smiled and looked back into his beautiful blue eyes. "Oh, and you will be pleasing me as well. I know you can multitask. Now place those ties in each of my hands. Loop and tie me to the chair. You will remain on your knees and pleasure yourself for me."

Harris nodded and looped the silk ties around her wrists. She pulled to make sure they were tight, but she could also get out if he disobeyed her orders once again.

"You will use Plan A tonight Harris. Do you understand?" She looked down as he sat between her legs. He nodded and didn't make a sound.

He kissed up her legs and thighs as his fingers massaged her skin. Soft purrs came from her lips as slowly her legs opened. Each leg over a shoulder as his fingers kneaded her flesh. His tongue and lips found their way to her inner thigh. He inhaled her arousal.

His tongue licked up her slit and teased her clit as he fingers found their way into her core. Slowly his fingers moved and in and out of her. Caressing every inch of her insides. Her moans filled the office causing his own cock to strain and pulse against his stomach. Slower, deeper strokes caused her walls to tighten around his fingers.

She panted and looked down at him. She was in bliss. Her fingers entered his hair and pulled him closer as her legs wrapped around his head. His lips and teeth sucked and pulled at her engorged clit. "Harris," his name came off her lips as she panted. This encouraged him, working quicker as her cream coated his tongue and lips.

"Harris, now." She commanded. He lapped her cream up and removed his fingers from her as she moaned. Harris gathered Candi and moved her to the couch. She purred as his fingers worked her clit, keeping her teased and well in the mood.

"Bend and cuff," she purred.

The storm outside raged on. Thunder and lightning clashed as the tides were beginning to change. The winds pushed the rain around the house like daggers of ice against the windows, and the tree branches scraped the siding.

Harris put his mistress into position as he spread her legs slightly. He ran his hardened cock from her ass to her wet, heated core. She moaned slightly as he teased her clit with his tip. Slowly he pushed his cock into her, and gasped and moaned as her walls clasped around him. He bit his lip not to make a sound as his hands slid up her thighs and held to her hips, pushing him in deeper.

"Fuck Mistress," his words slipped his lips.

She turned her head slightly as she gripped the couch. One of his hands slid up her back and twisted into her hair as he began thrusting his cock deep inside her walls. They moaned in unison.

His thrusts became quicker and harder as the words clicked in his head. Harris moved his hand around her throat as he gripped and pulled her head back to his lips. Kissing her deeply, sensual and passionately. His mate in his arms bending and twisting as their bodies moved together.

"Harris. Pink," her breathless words slipped from her lips as she came on his cock. Her breathing became more labored as he fucked her with such passion and aggression. She knew that he was ready. She felt his cock throb inside her and the way he gripped her tightly gave everything away. "Fuck. Pink!" she cried as she felt her own cream run down her thigh.

"Ahh. Candace!" Harris clung to her as he thrusted deep into her womb.

He held tightly to her and placed his head into the crook of her neck as he released his seed deep into her. They both panted heavily and collapsed onto the couch. Candace slowly rolled to her side as his cock slipped out of her She softly moaned as she curled into his body, his hands roaming her cooling flesh.

She looked up and smiled as she traced her fingers on his chest. "Thank you, Professor."

Harris chuckled and kissed the top of her head. "Anything for my star pupil," he said softly. "But tonight, I was yours."

As the rain continued to pound against the house, the flames in the fireplace began to die. Harris grabbed the blanket off the back of the couch and covered them both, his fingers tracing over his mate's flesh, so tender and soft. As he looked down, she had fallen asleep in his arms. A smile crossed his lips as he watched her. Tonight, he had fulfilled his duties. But there was still the rest of the month for his planning.

About the Author:

C. Berwington is a young erotic author from Midwestern USA. In her spare time she likes listening to music and movies, and focusing on her family. Her writing experiences began about ten years ago, starting off with role-playing groups and evolving into more erotic story lines and other categories. This experience has left an amazing long-lasting impression and she hopes to carry on in the years coming.

Erinyes

by Selina Shaw

There is no escaping Tartarus.

The raw, jagged rock face soars into a sky the same hollow black as the base of a fire. Clouds of red ash streak across it in a perversion of eternal sunset. Harsh, hot light gushes from wells of frothing magma. The low, volcanic rumbling of stirring, captive titans is constant - a coursing, haunting noise gnawing at the back of your mind, devouring all hope and fantasy and memory of where you were before, what you were before. If Tartarus can hold the titans, it can hold you.

The Dungeon of the Damned is the deepest pit of the world. A hive of cells hacked into the vast underground mountains, trapping hordes of murderers and traitors and sinners like drops of poisoned sap crystallising to amber, then harvested and worked by the Erinyes.

The Erinyes, the Furies, the jailors of the judged.

Of course, no sinner ever thinks they will come for him.

He didn't. And now he lies naked, curled on a floor of cold embers, and he waits to be punished.

The real torture is waiting for punishment.

Megaera

Rough, strong hands steer him through the caverns, stones scratching his bare, skittering feet, the scorching air cracking his skin. He struggles against the grip, his stomach lurching, the path yawning before him. He feels like he's being pushed into an open maw. He doesn't know what waits for him at the end of this long, winding trudge, but the air is getting hotter and the stones are getting sharper. His body screams to him over and over. *Punished. You're going to be punished.*

The door to the Furies' chamber opens with a deep creak that screeches in his nerves. He is flung forward. He lands on his knees with a hard shock of pain. The door slams, ringing in his chest.

It is almost silent, except for the constant churning of magma and the shuddering of his breath. The floor under his hands and knees is smooth and warm. He looks around him. He is in a large room lined from floor to ceiling with bronze. Torchlight cascades down the rippling metal, swirling and spilling, dropping him into a cauldron of fire. Heat from the volcanic depths outside pulses from the walls. The air is dense and metallic, he can almost feel the weight of it on his back.

He glances hastily around, searching for an escape route. Nothing. As the door closed, it seemed to seal seamlessly back into the metal. He is a jewel in a trinket box.

Another sound braids into his heavy breathing, a tone higher and slicker and sharper.

Hissing.

His heart thumps. He rolls to sit and scrabble backwards, as she appears like steam in the centre of the chamber. Tall, slender, like a silver birch, the honey-red light smudging stains onto her naked, shimmering, dove grey skin. Serpents, the colour of hematite, flow from her hair, writhing down her back and arms, oozing over her breasts and wrapping her thighs. The flames from the torches slide on their satin scales. She stands still, but the slithering around her body makes her look mobile, restless. His heart bobs to his throat and blocks it. Megaera's cold, grey eyes fall to him. She regards him with a steel glare that punctures his core.

She begins to walk towards him.

His breath rasps. He scrambles back desperately, his bare ass squeaking on the metal floor. His shoulder blades bump the wall with a soft *clang*. She keeps walking, taking slow, fluid steps, like pouring mercury. His body goes concave, cramming himself into a dent in the bronze and cowering back from her. She doesn't react to his fear. Her pace cuts through it, nothing more than mist. She pauses, towering over him. He shrinks into her shadow. He hugs his body protectively and stares up at her, his wide eyes shining, as if still capped with the coins to pay the ferryman.

"W…" he stammers, "What are you going to do with me?"

Megaera tilts her head to one side, uncoiling a triskele of serpents that twist into ringlets over her shoulders. Her voice comes like the sigh of a winter breeze. "What do you deserve?"

He swallows. He fights the trembling under his skin, digging his fingernails into his palms. He frowns at the question and tries to think over the hissing and rumbling in his skull. "It's not for me to judge."

Megaera has delicate lips, like a sage leaf. They move softly, as she considers his answer. "Yet you try to hide from me."

He looks down at his crumpled form, at his knees drawn up to his torso and his tightly crossed arms. When he looks back into her eyes, their coolness is oddly soothing in the heavy heat of the room. A confession leaves him. "I'm scared."

"Of what?"

"You."

"Of justice?"

"Punishment."

"But you deserve punishment." She says it simply. A snake slips down her forearm. She breaks her stripping stare to look down at it, twisting her hand to pet its head.

His cheek twitches. "That doesn't mean I want it."

Megaera shrugs, unspooling another cluster of snakes that trickle down her long, supple arms. "You'll learn."

The snakes stream over her hands and begin to leave her body, spiralling like ribbon to the floor, sliding silently over the bronze towards him. His muscles turn to stone. He pushes his spine against the wall, flooding his back with heat. The snakes move with

313

Megaera's harmonious slowness, with complete confidence that he cannot run. One brushes his foot. He shivers.

Megaera moves her eyes around his hunched body. He feels his nakedness intensely, the horrible, thrilling vulnerability of it, as if he's been peeled. Her gaze is so thorough, so penetrating. Somewhere behind the terror, he is charmed.

"Please," he whispers, "Mercy."

Megaera's eyes continue to rove over him. She shakes her head. It rattles a hiss through the serpents that ricochets off the walls. She flexes her fingers. The snakes enclose him, circling him against the wall. The circle closes. His breath comes short and stabbing, as they lift their arrow-point heads, all fixing him with the same sharp glare, then slither onto his skin.

He clenches against them, waiting for something clammy and greasy. But it's velvet. The snakes creep over him and their scales have the same gentle drag of fabric, warmed by the air, a humming friction flickering to life in his flesh. He tenses and holds his breath, going as still as possible, eyeing their long, forked tongues and their needle fangs. He pleads with himself not to disturb them. He shuts down every movement of his body, even his pulse, to keep them from striking him. Their bodies are thick and weighty, they pin him to the floor, force his legs down and his body open. Megaera rotates her hand.

They bind him.

He gulps teaspoon-shallow breaths, as the serpents slither round and round his body, wrapping his arms into his sides, lashing his thighs together and his ankles crossed. They loop and knot and interlace. He feels like a papyrus being inked and rolled, like silk being stitched. More snakes run off her, like oil. They compress his ribs, tighten around his shoulders. They link and wrench, like chains.

His lungs shrink, he gasps. He looks back up to Megaera. Her eyes dance over him, tracing the interlocking bodies of the serpents, as he submerges beneath them. Strings of onyx light wind around her body and strike flint flares in her eyes. The snakes are sparse on her now, writhing around her face, but leaving her body exposed in dripping light. Her nipples are hard pebbles. Her clit gleams red, like magma showing through cleaved stone. His mouth goes dry.

The heat of the room intensifies brutally under the layers of snakes, twisting closer together, chafing his skin. He burns. He breaks into a slick sweat, making the snakes slide smoother. They stroke his flesh deeply. Tingling erupts over his body. He twists too, wild sensitivity leaping in his skin. He writhes inside the bondage, dragging the bodies of the serpents over him. Their stroke both quells the sudden need he feels for their touch, and stokes it.

Need? It can't be… I can't…

A long, velvet stroke over his cock. A serpent's movement clamps it against his abs and rubs in a soft, slow rhythm. He shudders. The snakes grip tighter. They coil around his arms and legs, but loosen a fraction over his middle and begin to slink and slither. His cock is trapped between them and his smouldering flesh. It heats. It hardens. He grits his teeth. His gut jolts. He locks all of his joints and ploughs his focus into dousing the flame growing in his core. He can't be responding to this. Can't be enjoying it. Tartarus is the den of eternal torment for the basest of mankind. What does it make him if he wants *more*?

His eyes fly to Megaera. She is smiling. The upturned corner of her mouth twitches in amusement, as she watches him brace himself against this new sensation.

"What do you want, Sinner?" she whispers, the echo of it threading into the chorus of hisses singing on the bronze. She is framed by the restless glow of the chamber.

He can't answer. He doesn't dare admit it to himself. He is a sinner. He has never felt so sure of that in his existence. His eyes fall from her hypnotic stare to the wet swell of her clit. He licks his lips. His cock pulses. He sucks in hard through his teeth, hissing like his bonds. He tries to shake the feelings away, but the snakes wrap him tighter, mummifying him in his shame. Megaera's eyes snare his and he watches the red light pirouette in her slit pupils. His whirring mind dulls a little. The writhing on his cock presses harder. His spine arches. He rides the spike of pleasure back down into the nest of snakes. Their bodies are supple, cradling. He nestles into them. As his muscles unravel, the ache of his tension pours into his cock. The snakes twist again, this time he feels it like thunder in his core. His eyes roll back into his head, Megaera hurtling out of view.

Her voice drifts to him through the sludge of air, flowing on the current of lapping hisses. "We claim you for punishment. The Erinyes, keepers of the damned, daughters of darkness. You are our prisoner. We bind you. You cannot escape. Freedom is death for you. Choice is death. Thought is death. There is only your body and our will."

The silken stroking on his cock drowns his struggles, pulls him from his fear and his disgust. He sinks, he sighs. "There is only my body and your will."

"There are no princes in Tartarus. No man rules here. There is only chaos and the Erinyes."

"Only you." The words are teased from him, like fraying threads from weaving.　　　　Pleasure surges in his blood. He moans thickly, but the sound is strangled, as a fine body coils around his throat. Stars burst in his eyes, oxygen flees him. He goes dizzy. The room spins, a tumult of flame and shadow.

Tightness. Whether from the grip of snakes or the winding need in his centre, he cannot tell. The idea of release torments him. He wants to be let go. He wants the rush of it. But the binding is safe, close. He feels like he is returning to the womb, ready to be reborn. Another twist. Another penetrating ache.

"Release me," he wheezes.

"In what sense?"

His tongue tangles around the answer.

Megaera closes the inches between them with a single, silent step. She raises her delicate foot and presses it to his chest, pushing him into the firm cushion of bodies, making him wriggle for deeper friction. Her foot floats to his mouth. He catches the scent of charcoal on her skin. He is suddenly wildly hungry. He plunges forward, loosing a cacophonous hiss, and takes her toes into his mouth. He licks around them, sucks greedily, kisses her worshipfully over and over, gazing dreamily up the long, graceful curve of her leg to her stretched, shining seam. Hunger rolls. Pleasure rolls. The bonds constrict. He chokes. He sucks. He forces himself back from the brink, as the need in his cock surges.

Megaera looks down at him with stoic command. Her mesmerising eyes sap the will from him. He can't breathe. His larynx is crushed. His chest is pinned. His limbs are corpse heavy.

He kisses her foot and surrenders to darkness.

*

Ash and dirt streak in the gum of sweat on his skin, as he is thrown back into his cell, cold and empty and alone. His doll-like body hits the stone floor and the pain shocks into his still hard cock. He curls on his side and groans.

How could he feel like this? What's wrong with him? The Erinyes are monsters, tormenters, more spiteful than gorgons, more vicious than harpies, stronger than centaurs, and older than gods. They exist only to carve the hope and the joy and the pleasure out of shades, to make them hollow, to make them pay.

He swallows, it throbs against the bruise on his throat.

He closes his hand on his cock and buries his face in his forearm, trying desperately to block out the invasive light and the humiliating, devastating want.

Tisiphone

The brutish hands steer him all the way into the chamber this time. They force him to kneel, his knees banging against the bronze floor and kicking a bark out of him. His ankles and wrists are shackled to hoops in the floor, their loud, heavy clink stinging his ear canal.

He is left alone.

The chains rattle shrilly, as he struggles uselessly in them, more testing how badly they bite than expecting any give. They graze his wrists raw. He grunts in frustration and slumps. He feels a prickle between his spread thighs. His stomach squirms, as he looks down and sees his rising cock. He grinds his teeth, the blood shooting to his cheeks. This is madness, perverse. His mind snarls into itself, commands him to be afraid, to fight, to weep, to do anything other than stay on his knees and ache. The snarl wisps into nothingness. His cock thickens.

The sound of hard boots thunking on the bronze floor thrums through him. Someone is approaching him from behind, their gait purposeful and steady, the metal under his knees vibrating, like a struck gong. He begins to turn to see, but as his head tilts, a large, powerful hand grasps the roots of his hair. It fills him with an enlivening sting. The grip forces his eyes forward. The sting on his scalp trickles through his nerves. It converges on his cock. He shifts uncomfortably. He tries to cover his shame with his hands, but the chains restrain them at his hips. The cuffs run sandpaper tongues over him, as he wrestles with them. The grasp on his hair tightens, fizzing in his body, extinguishing his struggle utterly. He hangs from

321

the prickling pain, like a pheasant being hauled off the field for dinner. His heart pounds hard, hammering in his pulse points.

His head is pushed forward.

A cold blade scrapes down the back of his neck.

He starts, almost jumping, but reining himself in fiercely, with a blade so close to cutting him. The blade glides across the smooth line of his shoulders, leaving a hot tension in its wake. It slides down his bicep and skims the hair on his forearm. Someone leans close behind him, reaching over him. Warm breath brushes the tender trail of the knife. He smells charred meat and something caramelised. A soft hiss sneaks into his senses. His abdomen knots and tingles.

The presence at his back withdraws and the blade lifts from his arm. The hum of footsteps invades him again. She prowls around him and comes to stand at his front, a fearsome woman that takes his breath away. While Megaera ensnared his eyes, Tisiphone assaults them. She is so tall, he has to crane his neck, broad and thickset, with strong, angular shoulders. Her skin is deep, blood red, as if she has bathed in gore, staining her. The flickering light glimmers on the mounds of her muscle and the pillow of her full lower lip. Her eyes are empty and scarlet, pools of blood with an eerie glow that spills over the jut of her proud cheekbones. Three copper pythons wrap her skull and braid down her tapering back. She is dressed in hunting clothes, her muscular thighs emerging from the short hem of her dress, her sculpted torso encased in bronze armour that melts into the wall behind her. Her fingers curl around a long, elegant hunting knife, blade the shape of a lily petal, catching the firelight, so it looks like she's holding a lick of flame.

His lips part, jaw slack. He tries not to lean forward, to resist the magnetic pull of the keen, flashing metal.

Tisiphone raises the knife and draws her finger along the flat edge. It whispers under his skin.

"Megaera said you were afraid." Her voice is like the tumble of boulders. It harmonises low with the rumble of magma through the walls.

He opens his mouth to reply. No sound comes out. He doesn't know how to answer. He was afraid. Is he still afraid? Or is there another feeling drowning it out?

"You should be afraid." Tisiphone says, with a venomous lilt.

"I…" He gulps, a sweet tension squeezing through his thighs and the small of his back. "I am."

Her finger sings along the blade. "I don't believe you."

His stomach flips. His fingers splay on the hot floor. His admission comes hoarse. "I want to be."

Tisiphone's austere pout tugs into an intrigued smile, haunting beneath her swirling, empty eyes. Her arm extends, she runs the tip of the knife lightly around his jaw. He holds in a shiver. She takes a step to him and cocks her knee. His eyes flick to the hem of her skirt and the wisp of shadow that hides the most intimate part of her body. His cock rises towards it, pointing like a compass.

The knife skims his cheek. He hisses. The pythons echo him, beady eyes peeking around her hip.

"I'll make you afraid, Sinner," she says, "Kiss the knife."

His heart bucks. He looks into her eyes, sinks into them. He presses his lips to the blade. It's cool. In this furnace of a room, of a realm, in this endless, unrelenting, clawing heat, the blade is cool. He pulls back, seeing a mist of his breath on the polished bronze.

She hooks the blade under his chin and raises his eyes to hers again. "Don't move, or I'll cut you."

His gut twists. His cock pulses. His cheeks flare. He can't see her pupil-less vision move, but she must be able to see his arousal. The chains prevent him from concealing it, he is open and exposed.

Her lips twitch. She bends and drags the point of the blade from the hollow of his throat down the furrow in his chest and abs to poke his belly button. His back goes rigid. She seems to sense it. She steps around him, boots tapping. The point of the blade trails over his arm and across his shoulder blades, as she returns to his back. He flexes, his muscles gripping the shudders that threaten his body in waves. The knife lays with the keen edge flat along his smooth skin and moves down the plain of his shoulder blade, like she's spreading butter on bread. A sharp pleasure flows down his spine under the blade. He groans.

"Ssh!" she hisses, the knife flashing to his throat.

The sharpness digs into his jugular. He gulps, to keep from choking, to keep from whining like a sow. She rocks the blade, drawing his blood to the surface. If she presses just another pound, she'll slice him open. He'll bleed to death. Can a shade bleed? He can certainly feel blood coursing through him, too close to the surface, too easy to draw and drain. It boils in his wrists and the insides of his thighs, thumps in his fingers and lips and the tip of his cock. He is so full of blood and he knows she can smell it, that she's thirsty for it. He wants to shiver. He earths himself in the weight of the cuffs on his wrists and ankles.

She bends over him from behind. The knife slides from his throat down to his chest, her skirt fluttering on the back of his neck. Her glimmering skin heats the side of his face, as her arm passes. He feels a sudden urge to lean into her, to rest his cheek on her forearm. To kiss it. The point of the knife skewers his nipple. He winces and yelps. Her fingers comb into his hair and grip. He fails to contain a burst of trembling and his nipple sparks under the point. The knife continues its dance. He is held still by his hair, as the light scoring and cool snick of bronze laces him in a web of furious sensation. His skin pulls taut, brutally inflamed. He is sure that he'll split before he's cut.

Cut me. Please, don't cut me. Please, cut me. Don't cut me. Please…

His heart thrums so fast it goes into one continuous note, as if it's stopped. His skin is flushed and marred with the trails of the knife, a mess of berry red almost-wounds, turning him into a patch of earth scattered with rose petals and smeared with nightshade. He stings all over, aches between his thighs. The effort of keeping from shaking and writhing cracks his spine and his pelvis like lightning-struck oak. He breathes rasping and shallow, hot air pricking his lungs, warring with the icy lick of the knife. Tisiphone moves around him, like cloud around a mountain. His vision is shrouded with her; the way her muscles roll under her dark skin, the way the pythons slink with her spine, her dexterity and precision and monstrous thirst. He wants to quench her. He wants to be drained. He's terrified of it. He wants to survive. He doesn't know if he will. Can the dead survive? Can the dead perish? She presses the blade over his kidneys. Pleasure and terror shock up his core.

Please, don't cut me. Please, cut me.

The knife rests on the back of his neck. "Are you afraid?"

He catches his breath. He rocks back infinitesimally, pressing his skin to the blade. "Yes," he whispers.

"Not enough."

"I am." He coughs. His plea jets out of him unbidden, he isn't even sure if it's sincere. "Release me."

Tisiphone's deep, cold laughter resounds in the metal space, like a striker spinning around the inside of a great bell. "You don't mean that."

She picks up her pace. She begins to move like a war dancer. She spins and steps and strides around him, buffeting him with her charred meat scent, kicking up hisses from the pythons, the hum of her boots on the bronze vibrating his bones. She glides the knife down his back, up his arms, over his thighs, around his jaw, across his throat. She nicks his ear, ices his cock, clips his nipple, flashes over his abs, as if filleting him. She never draws blood. He wants to bleed for her. He wants to be drunk from. He wants to be wine. His skin bursts into song. His cock swells. Bronze rains cold onto him and he casts his head back, eyes staring up to the swarm of flame and shadow on the ceiling.

He is afraid. But not of the knife. He's afraid of it lifting from him, of freedom. He's afraid of the moment he's alone again and has to face how intense the pleasure of brutality has become. His throat closes. His heart drums.

Her voice fills him like smoke, searing him under the freezing scratches. "Fear the Erinyes, Sinner. We will end you, we will reforge you. Feed us with your terror."

He swims in her eyes, her gaping, bloodpool eyes. "Yes."

"All your desire will be tainted by fear. All your pleasure will be ruled by it. You will never feel again, unless it is for the Erinyes."

He can feel her inside him. He cannot tell if the knife still touches him, but he can feel it everywhere across his body. He feels torn, raw, skinned. His cock strains. He moves to grasp it and the chains bite. He heaves in trembling breaths and stares up at the monstrous beauty glowering down at him, all intent and ravenousness.

"I feel for you," he murmurs.

The knife flashes across his heart.

He rolls on the floor of his cell, caking his blazing skin in ash, patting out the needy, maddening stinging. It only crushes the sensation deeper into his flesh. He claws at his hair, running his fingers in the tracks of Tisiphone's. He runs his hands around his body, painting himself in filth. He rolls onto all fours and begs himself not to touch his weeping cock. He fails. He's a sinner already, he's dirt already, why strive for virtue? He pumps himself, chasing relief until he's ragged.

His moans of longing echo through the cavernous wastes of Tartarus.

Alecto

His hands are braced against the bronze wall of the chamber. His body aligns into restraint, his waning strength holding him up and ready and taut. The churning of magma buzzes in his fingertips, heat surging through the wall and braising his body. He swallows rapidly, his throat drying, while his mouth waters.

Where is she?

The third.

The Unrelenting.

Adrenaline whisks through his veins, making him itchy and fidgety. His fingers flex, his feet shuffle, his shoulder blades fold like wings. The stroke of serpents, the slice of blades, his skin feels tattooed with echoes of sensation. He exhales sharply, but expels nothing.

A door slams.

It shivers around the walls and up his arms. He shimmies his shoulders. His breath halts. His cock jabs.

Sharp, metal-capped heels clack along the hard floor behind him, growing louder, encroaching as if stepping up his spine.

"How do you feel?" A voice like a hearth roaring to life fills the room.

He closes his eyes and registers the myriad of need and terror and self-pity battling in his system. "Afraid," he husks.

"Who do you belong to?"

"The Erinyes."

She draws closer. The hairs on the back of his neck stand up. Under the constant low din of the Underworld, he discerns the creak of braided leather. He stiffens.

"My sisters seem to have prepared you well for punishment."

"P-prepared?"

"Of course." Disdain leaks into the voice at his back and spills across the floor to chill him. "You didn't think that was the infamous retribution of the Furies? Soft caresses?"

He squirms, pressing his palms into the wall, as they prickle anxiously. "I…"

"Fool." It cuts through him. His shoulders drop. He feels himself shrink under her gaze on his back. Her voice is stern. "You're here for pain." The crack of a bullwhip a few paces away rips through him. "Real pain."

His blood careens around his arteries, his heart galloping, pummelling his stomach. He presses hard to the wall, steeling himself. "Do it." He doesn't know if he's braving it, or begging.

Clack, creak. Alecto positions herself. He hears the whisper of her thighs brushing together, as she moves. Sweat breaks between his legs and down his flanks. He grits his teeth.

The dense, baking air is rent by the whip. It flails overhead and strikes his upper back. Pain tears him, like wasps bursting from a nest. He cries out coarsely. He almost buckles, but claws at the wall to stay standing. He can feel his ankles and wrists affixed to bronze, burning and twisting. She doesn't wait to strike again. The whip is tipped with knots, it bites him deep. It leaves him trembling. He thought he'd grown used to his nakedness, but now his exposure cascades around him, saps his will and his strength, reduces him to fallen fruit to be devoured, to be crushed underfoot.

The crack of the whip booms around the enclosed room, shooting pain into his skull, as it lances his back again. He howls. The pain wrenches the air from his lungs, the thoughts from his mind. Another strike. He is slammed against the wall. He presses his brow to it and whimpers like a pup. The next hit slashes across the backs of his thighs. The impact thuds into his cock. He moans roughly and presses his mouth to the wall, his panting misting the bronze. A trickle of saliva escapes his lips and drizzles down the shining metal. She flays him, raining sharp, dragging, biting blows down on his back and shoulders and ass and legs. He feels like a strimmed tree, left bare, skeletal, everything of him stripped away, save for pain and longing. Longing for what? To be free? To never be free again.

The snapping, sawing agony shreds him. The whip carves highways of delicious pain into his flesh, criss-crossing asteroid trails of delight and horror. Each impact throws him forward, spurring on his pulse and jarring in his cock, forcing him harder, more desperate, more confused. Alecto snarls like a wolf, as she beats him. Her hungry rage is palpable in the sweltering air between them. She lashes him with passion. This is her purpose, her only joy, her only love - bringing a man to his knees. Snakes hiss, her voice growls beneath them, surrounding him with the sounds of predators. A hard crack on his ass hurls his arousal to the edge. His fingernails screech down the wall. His knees almost give out. He groans thickly. Fresh sweat erupts across his body, droplets pour into the gashes, coating him in a burning sting. The sharp salt of his blood and sweat and arousal infuses with the metallic air.

He feels ready to fall apart, shivering and caged in sensation. He can't stay standing, his muscles have turned to oil.

"Release me," he sighs, twisting in his bonds.

"You aren't restrained."

He stills. "W-what?"

The hush of leather being drawn through clever fingers. Alecto's honey and gravel voice tinges with something like amusement. "You aren't restrained, Sinner. You can walk away at any moment."

Stars sprinkle behind his eyes. Cold seeps down his spine. He looks down to his feet, then snaps his head up to gape at his hands on

334

the wall. They are bare. No chains, no cuffs, no rope. He blinks. He fights to recall being brought to the chamber. He doesn't remember hands. He doesn't remember being collected from his cell. He remembers stumbling, blind and yearning. He remembers falling against a door in the rockface. He remembers clinging to the bronze wall and a deep, gnawing ache at his core dimming for the first time in hours, in days. He starts to shake.

He looks down at his cock. It is thick and dark, the dancing light rippling on the hard ridges of protruding veins. A diamond droplet gleams on the tip, the torchlight turning it amber. Something inside him solidifies. He raises his head and glares into the liquid, red-gold glimmer on the wall.

A single word sighs out of him. "More."

Alecto shifts her weight with a soft hiss. Her command laces his skin, like venom. "Beg."

The venom sinks in, it rushes in his blood. He doesn't even think to resist, to question. He drops his brow to the hot bronze, his face flushing, and lets loose a knotted string of breathless murmurs. "Please. Please, oh, please. I'm yours, Erinyes. I fear you, I worship you, I love you. Punish me. Please. Punish me."

Alecto doesn't answer. The whip does. He roars and arches his back, as a gale of pain whirls around him. She flings him into sweet agony. Welts and weals bloom over his body, a flourishing garden of bloodied pleasure, fed by the downpour of strikes, slits, slashes. He flings through moans and cries, half scrabbling at the wall and yelping for relief, half thrusting his body backwards to summon the whip again. The white heat of pain and the red heat of lust collide in his core.

Maybe he was always meant for this. Maybe he sinned to bring this on himself. Maybe there is no damned and blessed, only those who belong in the river, and those who belong in the fire. Belong in Tartarus. Belong to the Erinyes.

The darling agony weaves a thread between him and Alecto. Her unceasing strikes spin a powerful, humming cord between them. They bond him to the chamber, suspend him in the firelight. He feels himself forging into the mountain, his blood turns to molten ore, his bones to granite, his nerves to tracks of singing silver. He surrenders to the pain, it avalanches into pleasure. The whip sends zaps through his cock, falling into the rhythm of his heartbeat. Every lash is soothed by a wave of want. The chorus of cracks and moans and snarls echo in the chamber, flurrying the shadows. He is high. He is helpless. He forgets his own name and his past and his hopeless eternity.

There is only the Erinyes. There is only his body and their will.

With a slither and snap, the whip withdraws. His body is left wreathed in smouldering embers. He groans, his tension unfurling, and slumps against the wall. He heaves in his breath and unravels into the heat radiating from the bronze.

"You're the first to take so much from me without pleading for release throughout." Alecto's voice is imperious, but there's a golden vein of warmth in it.

He gasps for breath, his reply shudders out of him. "Oh, I want release."

Alecto chuckles, it ripples up his spine. "So do we."

Sinner

"So do we."

He hears the clack of heels behind him again. Then the thud of boots. Then the whisper of serpents slithering. He freezes. He soars. He is thrilled by fear. Exhilarated.

Hands grasp his arms and peel him from the wall. He tumbles backwards, crashing with a cry to the bronze floor. He stares up. He sees Alecto for the first time. His heart stops. She is proud, statuesque, sculpted in flowing curves draped in sheer black, the details of her body murmuring through the thin veil. Her hair writhes, thick with golden serpents. More of them coil in gold on her round arms and thighs. Her skin and eyes are obsidian black with the same cruel sheen, as if she is moulded from volcanic glass. She brandishes the black whip, streaked with his blood. At one side of her, Tisiphone glares down at him with her entrancing, horrifying, bloodpool eyes. At the other, Megaera, wreathed in snakes, regards him with smoky curiosity, her fingers idly tracing the body of the serpent concealing her clit.

For one long moment, there is silence in the chamber. Even the churning of magma hushes.

"Who do you belong to?" Alecto repeats.

He gazes up at his three torturers, his heart pounding, thudding in the gashes on his back. His lip trembles around his reply. "The Erinyes."

And then everything is darkness and sensation and obliterating bliss.

Alecto smothers his face, her smoky, gushing vulva filling his mouth and her scalding flesh pillowing his cheeks and eyes. Her humid heat roars around him. Megaera's bare cunt drags over his cock. He moans desperately into Alecto, as his cock is submerged in Megaera's steamy body. Her strong core seizes him brutally. Tisiphone's boot compresses his chest. He flails underneath their combined, crushing weight, buried under an avalanche of rock and lava. His motion only tempts them. Megaera hisses sharply, leans hard on his abs, and thrusts and twists on his cock, her wetness slipping and sticking on his shaft. Alecto shivers, jostling her flesh stormily around him, and grinds into his mouth. Her juices spill over his tongue, her pungency consuming him. He laps gluttonously, slurping her wetness, gorging on her folds. He bucks his hips and swirls his tongue and gives himself over to pleasure. To being used for it. To having it torn and hewn out of him. In the embrace of

Alecto's swell, the din of Tartarus is finally silenced. All his hideous reality whirls away from him.

There is only the Erinyes.

Tisiphone kicks his flank. He rolls onto his side, taking her sisters with him with an explosion of hissing that shivers through him. He nestles into the cushion of Alecto's thigh, her other clamping around his face, as she settles on her side, scoops her hips, and forces her clit along his tongue. Her fingers wind into his hair and twist. Megaera presses to his torso, hooks her leg over his hip, clutches his nipples, and ups her vigorous thrusting, their entwined flesh clapping and screeching on the metal floor. He feels Tisiphone's hard body line his back.

He is pierced.

She slides into him like a knife into a sheath, her metal cock striking his prostate and sending resounding soreness and pleasure through him. She thrusts too, grasping his shoulder blades with sharp fingernails.

The three of them overwhelm him. Megaera's core sucks his cock, the hisses rising riotous as he swells and pumps inside her. Tisiphone fucks him like he's nothing but meat, ramming him hard and fast, coring him like an apple. Alecto steals his breath, his senses, force feeding him her lust, drowning him in a bath of wine and sweat. He reels. He flies between elation and agony. His arms wrap Megaera, velvet serpents dragging on his skin. Snakes slink down her spine and bind his wrists behind her. Her body grazes him, scales sliding on his torso and tormenting his screaming sensitivity. Tisiphone grates on the welts on his back, pouring sweet pain into the rough, manic pleasure that she pounds rhythmically into the deepest part of him. She tenderises him.

He puddles on his side, running liquid into the tight casing of their bodies, letting them mould and consume him. The scrape of the hot metal floor against his flank, the aches in his muscles, the dire need in his cock, they all rage beneath the enveloping indulgence of Alecto's powerful, peppery taste. He plunges into her flesh, lets it muffle his wails and squeals. His tongue strains to reach all of her, lick and suck and scour all of her. He heats like he's in a cauldron. Tears splash from his eyes and mingle with her juices, soaking him with steam and salt. Her weight is oppressive and anchoring.

The drowning delight of Alecto plummets into the piercing, drumming, violating pleasure of Tisiphone, which punches into the wild, bestial hunger of Megaera. Megaera moves ruinously on his cock, her cunt swallowing him. He pistons into her in Tisiphone's thuggish, rapid rhythm, his hips almost splitting from the strain. He surges. His body fills with pulses. He fights them back. He ploughs his face into Alecto, feasts on her, his first meal in weeks. He tenses himself to a bowstring, letting Tisiphone and Megaera strum him, saw him between them. He surges again. He whimpers for release, but it is lost in the maze of Alecto's flesh. The blood roars in his ears. He can hear no commands. He can only let them hack the pleasure out of him like a felled tree. Constellations wheel in his eyes. His flesh blazes. His sweat sizzles. His bones and muscles groan. His core burns and beats. They tangle and thrust and flail on the floor, moans and rasps and snarls filling the chamber.

Erupting hisses shred the dampening of noise through Alecto's thighs, as she comes in a series of powerful quakes into his mouth, shaking him to his bone marrow, unmaking him. Her juices cascade over his tongue. He slurps them down desperately, quenching weeks of parchedness. His saliva sloshes over his chin, as she slows her rocking and draws her climax out along his lashing tongue. Her thighs relax around him, like warm honey being poured over his face.

Tisiphone barrels into him. Hisses rise again with her violent climax. His core is shocked with intense, gripping pleasure, as she rams him hard, the other end of the metal cock inserted into her, thrusting hard. Her fingernails gouge the wounds on his back. He yelps into Alecto, his voice gurgling with her wetness. Tisiphone slows and huffs. She unhooks from her metal cock and peels from him, leaving it in his core. He clenches around it fiercely, as Megaera's cunt squeezes his cock hard.

Megaera spasms in his arms, snakes rippling over his body and channelling her orgasm through his nerves. The hissing is ear-splitting. She twists his nipples and grinds on his body, friction flowing into every furrow of his muscle. He senses her across his flesh. He feels like stone overgrown with ivy, wrapped and clasped and breaking apart. Her moan sneaks to him through Alecto's thighs and drugs him.

His cock pounds. He is a split second from coming in Megaera's heat, when she and Alecto roll from him, his serpent binding slipping away. He floods cold. He writhes delirious and bereft on the floor, his hair drenched with sweat, his body streaked with blushes and bruises, his mouth hanging open and his tongue moving needily. His blurring eyes skitter between them, lounging around him, draped in drooping snakes, bodies glowing with undulating, dark light, as they catch their breath. Their proud, imposing faces smear with satisfied, scheming smiles. His hips keep bucking, racing to throw himself over the edge of pleasure, wild want puppeting his body.

Alecto grabs his shoulders and rolls him onto his back. The scalding floor cauterises his back. She pins him there, her tantalising scent drifting to him and making him moan pitifully. Megaera prowls over him, snares his wrists and covers his mouth. Tisiphone seizes his cock and pumps him, like she's squeezing the seeds from a pomegranate. He pants and cries into Megaera's palm. His vision bursts white. The rough, brutal pounding on his cock savages him. Pleasure rockets in sparkling fireworks up and down his body. He thrusts and shudders on the floor like he's being electrocuted.

Release lacerates him. It riots in his body, draining him, shattering him. He screams into Megaera's hand. His spine arches and cracks. His blood boils. Silver shoots across his torso, scattering heat across his skin that congeals sticky, clinging, anointing him in this demonic temple. It marks him as a sinner and a slut.

He falls into a tumult of torchlight.

*

The stirring of titans rumbles through the jagged walls of his cell. He lies sprawled and wrung out in the dust, dirty and broken, smiling and floating. He closes his eyes and swims in remembered rippling bronze and smothering flesh, slicing blades, wicked whips, and encapsulating bonds. He sucks on his tongue. He runs a limp hand up his torso and the encrusted gems of his bliss.

The real torture is waiting for punishment.

About the Author:

Selina Shaw is an erotica writer, particularly of femdom, fantasy and queer stories. She hails from the rural North of England, and is still totally in love with the countryside and folklore she grew up with. Alongside writing, she loves other geeky stuff, like historic sites, comic books, role-playing games, and anything with witches in it. This is her first published story and she's really excited to be part of a project with so many awesome contributors.

Christmas DeLights

by Lindsay Crook

It's Christmas Eve and a text message on my phone wakes me up. I fumble around my bedside table, knocking over anything in my way until my hand lands on the beeping gadget. Typing in my passcode and tapping the message app I see what or who has woken me up.

The message is from her, my mistress, my domme, my angel. It instructs me to be ready at 4 o'clock, showered and clean. It says tonight is special. That we are going to get a tree, and that the tree is going to be me? I flush at the humiliation, and the vision has me reaching under the covers squeezing my cock just once just to relieve some pressure. The message says to be waiting in nothing but … oh god crotchless knickers! I gulp and take a deep breath. I can do this, I want to do this

I'm hot and turned on and I've still got hours before she arrives home. I spend the day in a daze, the time ticking by slowly, making me anxious and excited. I try to watch TV but I can't concentrate, so I opt for Christmas music before finally deciding to get ready for the festivities.

I take my time in the shower. I shave and wash my hair, and scrub myself with my favourite body wash until my skin is shiny and clean. Stepping out of the bathroom, I hear the front door slam shut and my excited nerves became electrified. I breathe deeply, in and out before drying myself off. Then I slip into the garment I'm instructed to wear and make my way downstairs.

I look at the clock from where I'm stood – I'm in the corner, just like I've been told, counting down the seconds till 4 o'clock. Hands behind my back, head up and back straight, wearing nothing but red crotchless knickers. The feel of the silk against my skin makes my cock twitch and my cheeks flush with heat. I don't know what she has planned. I just know I'm eager and ready. I'm so excited my hands tremble.

She walks into the room, so fucking sexy in tight blue jeans and a white vest of mine tied in a knot at the front, showcasing her slender hips and perfect bellybutton. Her feet are bare toes painted a deep dark red, sending a shiver down my spine. Looking me over humming in approval, she puts the box she was carrying just out of sight.

She stands in front of me and pulls out a red Santa hat with a giant gold bell right on the pointy end. Smiling, she runs her hands over my shoulders and down my arms, her nails lightly scratching, leaving goose bumps everywhere she touches. Then she turns back to the box, pulling out a string of Christmas lights, and tells me I'm about to become her living Christmas tree.

I huff out a laugh but her beautiful face tells me she's serious, her chocolate brown eyes sparkle with mischief, and I know I'm in for a world of trouble. She starts at my ankles, kissing each one before wrapping the string around them, then up my calf where she licks the behinds of my knees, making them wobble and weak. She carries on around my thighs, kissing and biting my hip, causing me to moan deep in my chest. She moves higher with the lights around my stomach and I try not to clench my muscles. Further up my chest she stops, sucking a nipple hard enough to pull a whimper from me.

God, we've only just started and I'm ready to explode. Over my shoulders and down my arms till my wrists are tied together. The feeling of being restrained always turns me on, and she know it. She stands back to admire what she's done, dipping her hand in the box and pulling out baubles, each one attached to a clip. She smirks as she looks at me, her glossy plump lips tipping up at the corners, and before I can work out what she's planning with that mischievous look, she leans forward she bites my nipple.

I yell and squirm, but she doesn't stop, she sucks and nibbles more, doing the same to the other side, making my nipples so tight they ache and tingle. Just when I think I can't take anymore she clamps a gold shiny bauble to my right nipple, a glittery red one gets clipped on to my left, and I moan out loud making her giggle. She loves hearing my pleasure, so I don't hide how I feel.

I love the sharp pinch, the hint of pain as she kisses down my chest, around to armpit, and to my shock starts clipping shinny baubles down my sides. The sting making my erection throb even more.

Next from the box comes red and white striped candy canes, and a filthy smile passes her lips as she drops down to her knees. I squeeze my eyes tightly shut, breathing deep, hoping for her mouth. But instead she runs a candy cane around the head of my cock through the pre-cum beading there, circling the head, a hint of peppermint causing a slight burn that makes me shudder and shake as she dips the cane under my foreskin. Teasing me with the confectionery makes me sticky and so fucking needy, much to her own evident amusement and arousal.

She removes the treat and holds it in front of my mouth, so I open up and suck, tasting myself as well as the peppermint. Taking it back, she runs it down the crack of my ass and pushes it into my hole, pulling a shocked curse from my lips. I gasp when she takes another, sucking it before returning to my cock, sliding her candy cane filled mouth down my shaft. The simultaneous pleasure from both sides has me seeing stars as she continues with the candy canes, waiting till I'm on edge, needing to cum, when she stands up and steps back.

I nearly cry at the loss of tight wet heat and the tingling fresh zing of the peppermint. She flips the switch of the plug socket and the string of lights turn on, lighting me up as the human Christmas tree she had planned. Looking so pleased at her handy work she takes one more thing out of the box, an old-fashioned Polaroid camera, and starts snapping picture after picture of her living Christmas tree.

Photos fall, littering the floor, and I'm so mesmerised by them that I almost miss her seductively removing her clothes. First her jeans, which she shimmies down her long legs until she's flicking them somewhere behind her.

The faint sound of Silent Night is playing somewhere in the house, making her strip tease even more heavenly. Her vest is next, balled up and tossed aside. She's not wearing a bra, and I wish to a hundred different deities that my hands weren't tied up so I could worship all that creamy smooth flesh. She stands before me in just a pure as snow, white lace thong, and my mouth waters. I know she tastes sweeter than the red and white peppermint treats she teased me with, but I wait, eager to see what happens next.

She stands on her tiptoes and places a sinful kiss on my lips, licking and nipping. She flicks the baubles on my sore nipples, making me cringe and grunt, and she does it again, my pain turning her on so much that the damp patch on the front of her underwear gives her away.

My fingers twitch. I want to touch her so bad, but she shakes her head. She knows what I want and instead takes hold of my still hard cock, stroking her fist up and down my length. I groan in pleasure, loving her hands on me, making me impossibly harder. I grit my teeth, teetering on the edge and once again she backs away, leaving me frustrated and tense.

In front of me is my Christmas miracle, a real live angel bent at the waist, her thong pulled to the side, her folds dripping wet and shiny. Looking over her shoulder she tells me to be still: after all Christmas trees don't move.

She backs up on to my cock and both of us groan in pleasure. Her tight wet heat is my every wish come true. She rolls her hips, taking what she wants, moaning when I hit her g-spot, sending her wild. She uses me like one her toys, fucking me hard, her ass bouncing off my groin, the slapping of our flesh drowning out the haunting sounds of hymns playing through the hidden speakers. And just as the choir hits their crescendo, she hits hers too and she screams out my name. I'm seconds behind her, no longer able to hold it back, and I let it all go, let everything go.

She stands on shaking legs with a huge smile on her face, her blonde hair a sweaty mess like a halo atop her head. She gathers up the photographs and her fallen clothes, and says with a satisfied sigh:

"Good boy … and Merry Christmas."

About the Author:

Lindsay Crook, or Linz to her friends, is a 37-year-old brightly coloured hair unicorn enthusiast. She has always been an avid reader and loves everything from fairy tales to horror. Lindsay loves words and if she hasn't got her nose in a book you can usually find her in the kitchen cooking up a storm.

BONUS EXTRA STORY!

Villain's Submission

by Nessa Sparks

"Not the face! I need to look good for the cameras after this fight is over!" the Villain exclaimed.

I ducked to avoid a wave of shadows my opponent sent my way after I tried to clock him in the face.

"You need to look good for your mugshot, Shade?" I taunted.

"Aw, Moonstar, you know me better than that! I wouldn't be caught dead with a mugshot. Those things are dreary. No; I have a photoshoot for a magazine."

He smirked at me as we danced around each other trying to get a hit in. He used his shadows to pin me for a moment and took advantage of the situation by leaning close to whisper in my ear:

"I will be naked in those photos."

I flushed and used our proximity to strike hard at his chest, pushing him away. His shadows dampened the hit, but he ended up winded anyway.

I fumed at the shameless man, but the truth was: I was no match for Shade. I could hold out long enough for the other Heroes to get on the scene, or to flee, but I had no chance of defeating him and his powers. Why a Supervillain took interest in a predominantly support Hero like myself was a mystery, but the fact remained that he pestered me constantly. On one hand the time he spent bantering with me was time he didn't spend inventing death rays or scheming how to take over the world... but on the other hand this whole situation was annoying as fuck.

I just wanted to do my job, but nowadays minor Villains just fled on sight. Apparently, I had a reputation now.

It made me want to hurt Shade at least a little bit.

I activated my light to get a few precious seconds without his shadows and attacked him.

Only, instead of doing it with my fists I did it with my mouth.

I sucked a deep hickey on his neck and left an imprint of my teeth on one of his pecs. The ridiculous boob window in his costume was finally useful for something.

I pulled back to look smugly at his frozen form.

"I hope you have a hell of a time trying to cover those marks for your photoshoot," I said with vindictive glee.

He finally unfroze and his hand flied to cover his neck.

"So *mean*," he said with something like awe in his voice.

Why did he have a smile on his stupid face? I wanted to inconvenience him, not make him happy!

"Do you want to put more marks on me?" he purred. "I would let you."

He tilted his head to show the other side of his neck. The one that was completely unblemished, untouched, unmarked... and I had to fight an urge to leave my imprint on it.

But really, why shouldn't I? Having sex, or even a whole relationship with a Villain, was more of a rule than an exception in the Superhero industry. But this felt like he had too much of an upper hand...

I leaned forward to brush my lips against the pale column of his neck and placed a kiss on his racing pulse before I pulled back with a smirk.

"Maybe I will give you more if you are a good boy. Refrain from causing any trouble for a week and we will see," I tempted with a voice full of heat.

I shattered into thousands of stars before he could reply, as I teleported away.

*

A week later I was on a patrol when Shade found me. I was *this* close to bagging the small-time Villain I was chasing when he showed up and ruined my day.

"That. Was. Not. Being. Good," I said through gritted teeth after he used his shadows to devour the poor guy I was after.

"Oh? He would end up like that sooner or later," he waved his hand in an uncaring manner. "He didn't have permission to work on my territory. And as for being a good boy…"

He advanced upon me and I took an involuntary step back.

"The deal was I would be good and not cause problems for a *week*," he grinned toothily at me. "And the week is over. I can be as bad as I like. In fact, there is so much mayhem I could be causing…"

He went silent for a moment, but his dreamy expression told me he was imagining exactly what kind of trouble he could inflict on the city. Fire, blood, and screams flashed in front of my eyes. I shivered.

"Unless."

My attention snapped to him at the word. I knew what he was capable of and I really didn't want to see the devastation he could leave behind. I needed to put out the flame of murderous glee I could see growing in his eyes.

"Unless I can find something better to occupy my time."

I swallowed and stared at him. The look of anticipation on his face morphed into disappointment as I stayed silent.

He huffed and ran a hand through his hair before he turned away. He didn't look as feral anymore, just dejected, so the city was probably safe… but I found myself bristling at him looking away from me.

Teleportation and shining like a star weren't my only abilities. The moon in Moonstar referred to an ability opposite to my light. I could create darkness. Darkness darker than any night.

My power of absolute blackness unfolded around me and swallowed Shade. I heard him gasp as his shadows come to life, like dying plants that were granted water. I knew he was at his mightiest on the darkest of nights and with this darkness blacker than the void surrounding him now… I could see his hands shake at the amount of energy that was within his reach. At this moment he was not a Supervillain. He was something more.

I made him as powerful as a god.

"Kneel," I said.

He fell on his knees with a joyous laugh.

When the darkness faded he stayed kneeling in front of me.

I came to him and put one finger under his chin, tilting his head towards me.

"You wanted me to put a mark on you. And I did, didn't I?" I asked. "You will never forget this, will you?"

"Never," he nodded with reverence.

"Be a good boy. A truly good boy, and maybe I will give you what you want," I said as I walked away from the Supervillain, not bothering to use my teleport.

He stayed kneeling.

Good boy.

*

A few days later I woke up in the middle of the night to horrible things happening in my city. I geared up and went to do my duty, as the call for action reached every Hero in the area. This wasn't one Villain on a rampage; no, the situation was more dire. All the people under my protection were in danger as The Darkest Villains - a group of truly fucked up superpowered people – were seeking to destroy my city.

They attacked in multiple key points and soon a skyscraper was just a pile of rubble, a bridge fell with cars still on it, and there were many fires spreading and devouring homes.

Class A Superheroes were taking care of the attacking Villains, but the collateral damage from those fights only added to the destruction. I convened with the search-and-rescue group and used whatever abilities I could to save as many people as possible.

As another building collapsed in front of me, burying people inside, I knew that my efforts were not enough.

I had to do *better*.

I turned to Mindflare, a support Hero I have worked with multiple times in the past. She was brilliant at coordinating rescue efforts due to her ability to send messages straight to someone's mind.

"Mindflare, I need you to send a message for me," I said seriously.

"What is it?" she asked distractedly, occupied with sending forth alerts about people in need to the closest Heroes who could help.

"I need you to contact Shade for me."

She blinked a few times. Her gaze focused on me as she scowled.

"Now is not the time for your personal-"

I gripped her shoulders hard.

"I promise you; this will save lives."

She scrutinized me in silence for what felt like minutes, but finally said:

"You serious? Fuck, you are. OK, I will trust you, Moonstar."

I took a deep breath in and told her the message.

*

When Shade arrived, it was to not much of a fanfare. Everybody was just too busy and a local Villain - even a Supervillain - was a preferable sight to an unknown Villain who wanted to destroy your city. He looked tired and I could see a line of blood streaking down his cheek from under his mask.

"Moonstar. Sorry to keep you waiting. I had to get rid of a pest that encroached on my territory," his smile looked predatory and I was pretty sure one of the invading Villains was dead. "What is it that you want from me?"

"What I always want. I want you to be good for me. You have so much potential to do the right thing today. You could save so many lives if you let me…" I cupped his cheeks between my hands and I saw understanding down in his eyes. A shudder went through his body, like a junkie who was just offered the drug he was addicted to.

"Yes," he said earnestly, breathlessly. "*Yes*, do it, please. I will do whatever you say."

"Perfect," I murmured as I hid our first kiss in the preternatural darkness that surrounded me at my call.

He gasped and then moaned into the kiss as the energy around him skyrocketed, flooding him with unbelievable power just waiting to be unleashed.

I reluctantly pulled back from his lips. We had a job to do.

Shade was the stuff of legend, really. Well, the whole battle for the city was epic, but it said something that Shade started to top the charts of favorite *Heroes* in every pool that had the option to suggest your own candidate. A mere thing like Shade being a Supervillain and not a Hero couldn't stop his fans. And the amount of those was rising everyday as he worked tirelessly, helping thousands of people. He used his shadows to get into the places where nobody else could reach and dangerous spaces, like basements of collapsed buildings or houses on fire. The energy that he shaped into his shadowy puppets could take any form and get into even the smallest cracks to search for survivors. At the same time, it was tangible enough to carry a child out of a flame-filled room or to help rescue a man drowning in his car.

Without my help Shade was able to keep a few shadows out for a few hours. With my help he produced hundreds of them and went for two days with almost no breaks. I could keep the magical darkness around him for only a few minutes before I got dizzy from expending too much of my own power, but I repeated this action as many times as I was able, and his body stored the additional energy, consuming it steadily over time. Between augmenting Shade's powers, I worked with Mindflare to coordinate the rescues of people my Supervillain located but couldn't help on his own and I made sure to direct medical teams to all those he managed to save from danger.

It took only an hour for the news crews to arrive to capture a Villain's change of heart. I didn't have time to really pay attention to them, but even then I knew the story would be a hit.

After two days Shade collapsed. I rushed to him and I decided we both helped enough. I was pretty sure there were no people left under the rubble, all the fires were already put out, and the offending Villains either killed or captured. I could leave the rest to the next shift of Heroes.

I teleported us both with the last spark of my power, letting a Supervillain enter my home.

*

When I woke up - still clothed in my Hero costume and snuggled up to a sleeping Shade - I decided to take the best care of my Villain I possibly could. I always showed my love for my friends and family through cooking so, once I cleaned myself up and changed into civilian clothes, I strode into the kitchen, ready to prepare an amazing meal.

Shade woke up an hour later with a groan. I started a bath and then went to him. He looked at me pitifully. The strain of two days of being overpowered had caught up to him.

"Welcome to the land of living!" I said cheerfully, though I tried to keep my voice down, not wanting to exaggerate the headache he must have been dealing with if his scrunched up eyebrows were any indication. "Let's get you cleaned up and then we can eat."

"I could eat a horse," he said hoarsely. Between the two of us, we managed to get him into the bathroom and into the tub I started filling with water.

He looked at me askance when I perched on the edge of the tub and added scented bath oil to his bath.

"Ugh, Moonstar. Why do you want me to smell like…" he considered, taking a good whiff of the familiar scent and titled his head like a puppy. "Like… you?"

"Just marking my territory."

"Oh."

He blushed so prettily. I only wished he didn't have the mask half-covering his face. His still dirty face. Either the mask or I had to go, so that he could finish cleaning up. I reached tentatively for the last bastion of his anonymity and asked softly:

"Can I?"

He hesitated and my heart clenched.

"I don't know, Moonstar…"

"You don't have to call me that. My name is Jane."

"I… know," he admitted sheepishly.

I sent him an exasperated look, but honestly, I would be more surprised if he didn't already know my identity. He was, after all, leagues above me and had many grunts to gather information for him.

"I will leave you to it then…" I sighed and started standing up.

"Wait!" his hand shot out to clench around mine. "Don't… don't go."

His fingers shook slightly as he reached for his mask. He turned his face away as he slowly took it off. He let it drop to float on the water and when he looked at me again his eyes looked lost, as if he forgot how to live without his mask.

That may very well be the truth. Small fries could keep two separate identities but when you reached the big leagues having a private life became incredibly hard, often impossible. From what I heard Shade stayed in costume almost all the time and on his own territory you could catch him doing mundane things, like shopping or eating at a restaurant, in his full Villain attire.

I cleaned his face gently with a damp towel. The half-mask he wore didn't really obscure that much; I already knew those vibrant blue eyes and those sharp cheekbones. But at the same time, I could see him fully, without any barriers, for the first time. It bared more than just his face to me.

"You were so good for me," I whispered, and he whimpered at my soft words and gentle touches.

I could see the tension in his body. I wanted to make him relax, to go boneless under my hands, to let himself just sink into the warm bath and drift.

I abandoned the towel and put my hands on him.

"Do you want your reward now?"

He made a high pitched sound, neither agreement, nor protest.

"I don't know if I have enough energy for this…"

"Just relax and let me," I said and trailed my hands down, leaving one to gently circle his nipple, while the other drifted even lower, dipping under the surface of the water. "Let me?" I asked when I made my intentions clear.

He nodded and pushed a bit into my hands. A delightfully needy creature I was going to spoil horribly.

I started with petting him all over. My hands slid against his wet skin in a deliberate caress, as I found all the spots that made him feel good.

"You have done so much. You have given it your all, hadn't you? I'm proud of you," I kept a steady stream of praise as I circled his nipples with the tips of my fingers, gently coaxing them to harden. Once he was panting softly, I moved my hand to the place I promised to touch at the beginning of this game.

He bit his lip and arched his back as I closed my fingers around his cock. He was half-hard, but it took no time to bring him to fullness. I delighted in him growing in my hand as he let himself go and threw his head back, surrendering to the pleasure I was giving him.

"Beautiful," I continued my litany. "So strong. So brave."

He closed his eyes as if the words I was gifting him were too much. As if they were flying him raw, leaving him open. He often boasted about being the best as Shade, but this wasn't Shade, the Supervillain, anymore, was it? I didn't know his name yet and I wasn't planning to push him to share when he has already given me so much trust, but I was certain that the man painting and shuddering beneath my hands was the man under the mask.

The water splashed around my moving hand as I picked the pace and he gasped, teetering on the edge, looking for that last push to set him free.

"Good boy," I whispered in his ear and it was all it took.

He gasped sharply and I felt him come against my hand.

"Nnngh," he made an incoherent noise as I pulled the last drops of his orgasm from him.

I had to keep him from sliding under the water, he was so boneless. Bliss and extreme tiredness combined to make him as weak as a kitten. We stayed like this for a few minutes - one of my hands carding through his hair, while I pressed the other to his chest to keep him propped up - before his stomach made a loud rumble. I hurried to get him to the dining table after that.

Clean and adorably sleepy, Shade was properly fed, and a spark of energy finally returned to him.

"Hey, Jane, was that *all* of my reward for being good?"

I snorted.

"Can you even take more right now?"

He shifted in his seat a bit.

"I... could. If you used your power on me once more."

"Huh. Doesn't it only augment your powers? How will that help?"

"It actually feels like downing a few energy drinks as well. And..." he blushed and didn't continue.

"Hey! that's not fair!" I poked him in the ribs. "Finish what you started, or I will die from a fatal case of curiosity. What else does it feel like?"

"It makes me…" he mumbled something under his breath that I couldn't hear, and I poked him harder. "It makes me aroused, alright!" he exclaimed.

Was it my birthday? Why was life giving me so many presents today?

"My power makes you hot?" I purred and unceremoniously abandoned my chair for his lap, straddling him, letting him feel my hot breath against his ear as I spoke. "Or is it just the fact that I can give you something that nobody else can that gets to you?"

"Both!" the word rushed out from his mouth as if it couldn't be kept inside for even one second longer. "Do you know how much power over me you hold? You can make me better. You can make me more. But the one thing I want above all else is that… you can make me yours."

"That's fortunate," I whispered as I touched my forehead to his. "Because I do want to make you mine."

The darkness that curled around us at my behest hid my giddy smile.

I felt Shade spasm as if he was struck by lightning and his dick twitched under me. He groaned as he absorbed the rising power, and I kissed the noises from his lips. I kept the magical darkness around us for less than half a minute, still not at my best, but it was enough to make Shade look devastated.

"Oh, sweetheart, how hard was it to keep yourself from making all those delightful sounds when I did it to you repeatedly in front of all those Heroes?"

"Very hard. Incredibly hard. Extremely hard."

"It's okay now, you can make all the sounds you want now. I want everybody to hear you. For my neighbors to wonder what kind of wild creature I brought home." I rocked against his erection and I was rewarded with a strangled gasp. "You can use your words now and ask for what you want."

Was I cruel demanding that of him? Maybe a bit. I expected a blush. A plea to get more pleasure. But what I got outshined my expectations.

"Let me pleasure you. My mouth, my fingers, my cock… I am at your service. Jane, let me touch you."

Each time my name passed through his lips he delivered it with reverence, like being allowed to call me that was the greatest gift. And this silly Supervillain didn't want his own pleasure; he wanted to please me. How could I resist such sincere dedication, such devoutness?

I stood up and pulled him towards the bedroom. By the time we reached it we were both devoid of clothing.

I sprawled on the bed, amused to be the pillow princess for once.

"Show me how you can service me," I commanded, and he obliged wonderfully.

He started with my neck. A good choice as I was really sensitive there. As he kissed the pale column of my throat and sucked a mark into the skin, I realized it mirrored the place where I marked him first in my moment of pettiness. I smirked to myself thinking about the lasting impression I left with that prank.

His hands travelled over my body, taking sensual trips from my feet to the end of my fingers which he kissed gently. I was like a putty hardened over time, coaxed into softness by his warm hands, made amenable to the idea of pleasure. His lips on my nipple were the last straw and I demanded hoarsely:

"Give me your fingers!"

He did.

I was so wet his one finger slid inside with no problem. He immediately followed it with a second one. That was more like it! The motion of his fingers stimulated all the right places inside of me and I wondered, a bit deliriously, how it would feel like if he wore the leather gloves that were a part of his costume. Those slender fingers already felt so good inside of me even without the black leather. I moaned as Shade lavished attention on my breasts while his hand was working me towards a spectacular end.

"Harder," I instructed, and he slammed into me so hard I whimpered. It took only a moment of this brutal pace before I came.

"Can I?" Shade asked as I was still panting from the bliss of my orgasm.

I blinked at him and only after a moment I realized what he was asking for.

"Yes. Fuck. Clean it up," I said, entranced by the way he started lapping at the fingers dripping with my juices with his tongue.

He really was perfect, wasn't he?

I was pretty sure of my opinion when, after he finished cleaning up his fingers, he dived in to lick my inner thighs and the lips of my pussy as well.

I took a sharp breath and pressed his face closer to where I wanted him, curling my hand into a fist in his hair and guiding his movements. Directing him to abandon the pretense of cleaning and instead get on with making me even more of a mess.

He ate me out eagerly, drinking me in as if I was ambrosia stolen from the gods. All that talking he did as his Supervillain persona paid dividends; he was absurdly good with his tongue.

"Yes. Just like that," I praised him. "You are so talented with your mouth. Ah, give me more of that tongue—"

I rolled my head from side to side, my breath shaky, getting steadily closer to another slice of heaven despite (or maybe because of) the sensitivity brought on by my first climax.

I looked down at the man between my legs and saw he was reaching for his own erection.

"That's for me!" I ordered darkly and he stilled his movement, caught. "Now, keep your hands where I can see them. I know you want to come, honey, but you do want to wait for me, don't you, hmm? I want to ride that beautiful dick, to clench around you like a vice-"

He worked on my clit with the hand that couldn't be on his own cock, channeling all his desperation to come through it, and I couldn't last long under the mind-blowing assault of this magnitude.

I came so hard my legs started shaking and he gentled me through the throes of my orgasm. When I laid on the bed boneless with the afterglow, he peppered sweet kisses all over my abdomen.

He was so patient waiting for me. He deserved a reward.

I tried to get up and do a cool move, like pushing him onto his back and climbing on top of him, but my limbs didn't really want to cooperate.

"Ugh, I didn't think this riding thing through, did I?" I complained at my stupid body.

"Give yourself a minute. And, ah, I would prefer a minute too. Jane, you looked so magnificent right now… and the sounds… I don't think I could last more than a few seconds if we did it now."

That was quite a compliment. I gathered him to myself and we spent some time exchanging kisses, enjoying the feel of our bodies against each other. Soon we were both ready to go again.

I pushed him onto his back, and he went willingly, with a look of anticipation in his eyes.

"Tell me what to do," he begged shamelessly.

I grinned at him as I took my place atop his hips. I gathered his hands in mine and placed them above his head.

"Keep them here. Maybe I should tie you up…?" I mused.

"A-allow me," he said, and I watched in surprise as a thin line made out of his own shadows coiled around his wrists binding them together.

Oh, that was an even sweeter victory than tying him myself. Having him to do this to himself willingly, without any prompting…

I savored his submission and I had to kiss him hard. I left him with a hard bite to his lips and positioned myself over his straining cock.

I looked him straight in the eye as I took him inch by inch. His dick was as big as his Supervillain ego and I was filled to the brim, full with his heavy manhood carving a space for itself in my insides. My mind was steadily overtaken by explosive pleasure as I rocked my hips to feel him even deeper.

"Jane," Shade groaned under me, his face a spectacle of open-mouthed delight. I could see his hands clenching hard where they were bound, but the magical binding stayed tight, held in place by the power of Shade's mind. Seeing his magic used like this made me wonder how else it could be utilized in bed.

I was curious how it would feel against my fingers when we weren't fighting. I reached out and put my hand over the binds, holding him down at the place where his wrists crossed, making him moan under me. The shadowy rope pulsed slightly, swirling like a never-ending current of captured power. I liked how it felt. I liked so many things about Shade. So, I told him that. I told him how pleased

I was, how he exceeded my expectations, how I couldn't look away from him. I filled him with million shreds of praise, and each pierced him like daggers until he finally accepted them, let them build a mirror showing how I perceived him. He went under so beautifully, floating in the subspace as I made him fly with my words, and later, when words no longer reached his dazed mind, I coaxed him with my gentle tone full of heat and tenderness.

"Good boy. Nnn! Shade, you are such a good b-boy. Ah, *ah*!" I shouted as I came, and Shade cried out as well as I clenched around him. His hips flied of the bed, desperately seeking completion in my wet heat as he rutted into me almost mindlessly, but I noted that his hands stayed obediently in place.

"Come for me. Give it to me. You are mine," I managed to pant out and he exploded in me as I claimed him. The tortured sound he made fell somewhere between a shout and a sob, and he whimpered as the waves of his orgasm rolled through him. I wished to keep this expression on his face forever. I wished to see the thousands other expressions he could make. I wished to own him fully.

"My name…" he whispered after the long minutes where I smothered him with affection so that he could resurface from the bliss of subspace slowly. "My name… it's Cayden."

He whispered his secret just for me.

And in that moment I realized…

I already did own him fully.

About the Author:

Nessa Sparks writes short erotica stories and is often inspired by fantasy, sci-fi, and paranormal themes. She is a crafter who is totally not learning how to make a crochet dick at the moment. You can find many of her steamy stories at http://nessasparks.medium.com

Printed in Great Britain
by Amazon

24130563R00215